Silence in the Tortured Soul

Anne Louise Bannon

HH
Healcroft House, Publishers
Altadena, California

Satellite photo courtesy of Smithsonian Open Media Access

ISBN: 978-1-948616-38-6

Library of Congress Control Number: 2024903934

Contents

Acknowledgements

There is never enough space to thank everyone who has ever helped me do anything related to my writing. There are the tangible, visible helps, like my father, David Bannon, Sr., answering my questions about satellite technology in the 1980s (some of which he helped develop). And my husband, Michael Holland patiently listening to endless variations on plots that he has already heard too many times.

Then there is the less tangible, obvious kind of help that comes from the people I am blessed to call friends. If I am hesitant to put your names here, it's because I know darned well that someone will slip through the cracks. And that's the other half of the blessing – that there are enough of you out there, that slipping through the cracks is a real possibility.

So thank you, all. I remain profoundly grateful that I do not have to do this writing thing without you.

Dedication

To David Bannon, Sr., my father.

Dad, I have learned so much from you. But most important of all, you taught me to think logically and that learning never stops. Because you do, I will hopefully continue to.

My grief lies all within;
And these external manners of laments
Are merely shadows to the unseen grief
That swells with silence in the tortured soul;

From Act IV, Richard II, William Shakespeare

July 2 – 4, 1986

"**N**icholas Flaherty!" I snapped.

"Mom!"

I wasn't angry enough to use all four of his names, but I was getting close, and my thirteen-year-old son knew it.

"I told you yesterday. Your father and I are going out to dinner tonight, so no friends over."

"But where else are we gonna go?" Nick's brilliant blue eyes began to fill behind his glasses.

He's also got dark wavy hair and a dimple in his chin. Normally, he's happy and energetic. And, I had to admit, I sympathized with his plight. His buddy Rob's mom thought the girls chasing her son, mine, and Lety Sandoval's were simply hilarious and cute. Lety was praying that her son Josh would show more interest in girls, period, which is why she wasn't going to do anything to stop the little tarts. Our place was the only safe house the boys had.

"I understand." I sighed. "But I know darned well Josh's mom will not let you three stay here by yourselves and I'm pretty sure Rob's mom won't, either."

In truth, I was pretty sure Rob's mom, Clarissa, would. Clarissa Lopresti was convinced that her darling boy could do no wrong, never mind that I'd seen him do plenty. Rob Tolmann wasn't a bad kid, just not very disciplined. Lety, on the other hand, was a lot more realistic about Josh and his younger brothers, and agreed with me that judgment was not Josh's strong suit yet. Nor was it Nick's. Nick was (and is) bright and capable, which meant he often overestimated his ability to handle things. Come to think of it, that was the same problem Josh had. Between them and Rob, they were not a good combination for extended time without some sort of supervision.

"What are we gonna do?" Nick wailed. "Those girls won't let up."

"I know," I said with my teeth gritted. "But your father and I cannot re-arrange our entire lives just so you and your friends don't have to deal with an annoyance. And, yes, I agree those girls are annoying. But they're not trying to shoot you, Nick."

Nick's groan was both defeated and defiant. There was that other perspective that Nick's father and I could put on things that made things like persistent pre-teen girls seem trivial.

Within the structures of the FBI and the CIA are several shadow organizations so secret that mostly only their members know they exist. Nick's father, Sid, and I work for one called Operation Quickline, which is under the FBI. Our primary mission is to pass information around, but we also do investigations and other chores that come up. Sid and I had also recently been promoted to a supervisory position as a floater team. Nick knew his dad and I were spies, but not much more than that even though we were training him. Nick had seen some of how dangerous things could get for us. So, when I pointed out that the girls that he and his buddies were so desperate to avoid were not shooting at him, he knew I was not exaggerating.

"Look," I said. "We'll find some other time to do a sleep-over or two. But at some point, Nick, you guys are going to have to learn how to deal with girls, including annoying persistent ones."

"Even Dad says they're worse than the ones he used to know."

"I know and I understand, but you are still going to have to learn how to deal with it."

Another defeated and defiant groan escaped my son and he slumped off to his room, presumably to call his friends and commiserate.

I went back to my desk. As aggravating as Nick's problem was, it was the least of my worries at that moment. Sid and I were also freelance writers for magazines, which was our cover career. Sid, until the year before, had been doing a column reviewing various singles' hot spots for a magazine aimed at swinging adults. The owner and editor, Hattie Mitchell, had given Sid the column as a way of keeping in touch with Sid and with her brother, who was in hiding.

However, almost eighteen months before, Sid had given up sleeping around and hanging around singles' hot spots and surrendered the column. Hattie was not about to let Sid or me go that easily, at least not as writers. Being the dilettante she was, she'd also bought another more mainstream women's magazine and had asked us to be the news and lifestyle editors. I suspected that Hattie, who was also up to her backside in various classified activities thanks to the defense plant that she also owned, and who was one of our liaisons, may have been persuaded to keep Sid and me on. But that was one of those things that you just didn't do in the spy business. You didn't ask without a good reason, and I didn't have one yet.

The editor position meant that Sid and I could give up much of the freelancing, which made life easier in that we had a more predictable schedule to work around and didn't have to worry about writing work suddenly getting hot when our spy business was. That we also had relentlessly regular deadlines made life a touch more difficult. It was also early July and time to plan for the magazine's Christmas issue. So, not only did I have the October issue to worry about, I had to find and assign two articles for the holidays. The queries (or letters offering articles) that I'd received had not been very promising.

I went back to sulking over queries. I must have gotten more absorbed than I would have thought, because some time later, I looked up and there was Sid, my darling and relatively new spouse, leaning in the doorway. He's not a large man, just three inches taller than me, and I'm average. Sid is how Nick got his bright blue eyes, dark, wavy hair, and cleft chin, although I would put good money up that Nick is going to be taller than his father.

Sid smiled softly at me, obviously thinking about something romantic and sexy. I kind of felt bad that I was in such a lousy mood.

"So, did the drop get off okay?" I asked.

"Naturally." He straightened, then walked over and leaned his backside against my desk next to me. "I take it the offerings on Christmas articles have been a little demoralizing."

I rolled my eyes. "What hasn't been today? Christmas queries, pre-teen angst..."

"What's got Nick upset now?"

Long John Silver, a gray one-eyed cat with a mangled ear, silently jumped to the top of my desk and began rubbing up against Sid. She's very partial to him. She's also the mother of our other two cats.

"It's the same thing. The girls. He, Rob, and Josh want to spend the night here and I had to say no. We're going out to dinner tonight."

Sid chuckled as he petted Long John. "Speaking of demoralizing."

I sighed. It wasn't going out to dinner. It was that we were meeting yet another total stranger to create a visible reason we knew this person, as opposed to the secret reason we did. The secret reason was Quickline and the total stranger was Desmond Moore. He was the last operative on our line that we hadn't met. Most of the others had been very nice, so I wasn't entirely dreading dinner. I just wasn't looking forward to it. Fortunately, Sid understood.

Then Sid's smile got that cute, but really hot bent.

I had to smile. "You're not thinking about dinner, are you?"

His grin got even hotter. "How about a nice little afternoon break? Might cheer you up some."

"It would." I bit my lip. "But Nick's home."

"We go to our room, then."

"And we have work to do."

"We can't do anything about those queries until Monday at the soonest."

I felt myself weakening. "What about not developing bad habits?"

"We are, essentially, working tonight, so a longer afternoon break is in order."

He knew I'd say yes. Neither of us can say no to the other, at least not where making love is concerned.

I briefly debated letting Nick know that his dad and I were about to get otherwise occupied, but Nick usually figured that out. One of the many crosses he had to bear was that his parents were, um, active that way. [What's the big deal? We love sex. That it occasionally caused the kid embarrassment, well, hey, as crosses go, that one was pretty lightweight. - SEH]

"So?" I asked as we mounted the stairs to our bedroom. "What brought this little mood on?"

Sid squeezed my shoulders. "Admittedly, it doesn't take much when it comes to you. But I was thinking about the potential damper on activities this weekend and am hoping that if we get a little overactive now, it will be easier to deal with later."

I winced. The next day, Sid, Nick, and I were headed up to South Lake Tahoe to spend the Fourth of July weekend with my parents. That my maternal grandmother, Grandma Caulfield, had moved in with them was the complicating factor.

Okay. I understand. However happy some people are that your sex life is going well, almost all those same people do not want actual, audial evidence. Even Sid doesn't want to listen to other people having sex, although it does not embarrass him. The problem is, Sid and I get, well, noisy. We really do try to keep it down, but we don't always succeed. If we were not going to worry my parents or offend Grandma Caulfield (who takes a very dim view of sex), there was either not going to be any sex at all (not likely, nor welcome from Sid's and my perspective) or we were going to have to find some way to keep the noise level down. That was not going to be easy.

I wasn't going to tell Sid that his idea of getting us fully satiated didn't stand a chance in Hades of working. And, I suppose, there was always the chance it would work. In any case, the interlude did a lot to improve my mood.

Afterward, Sid did his second shave of the day. He usually shaves twice because his beard comes in fast and dark. It was also late enough that I got out a nice dress made from a cotton lawn print from Liberty of London and Sid put on a lovely Italian cut light gray suit with a snowy-white shirt and a tie made from yet another Liberty print. The dress I wore featured a dark green print with gray and pink. The tie happened because I'd made a blouse from the other print and there was still extra fabric, but not enough to make anything else with it.

I called Clarissa Lopresti to tell her how sorry I was that Rob couldn't come over. It was a defensive maneuver, since Rob had been known to tell his mom that Sid or I had said something was okay when we hadn't, and Clarissa would not believe us that it was Rob who had fibbed. Lety already knew to verify anything the boys said. It's not that Nick or Josh were prone to lying, but they could come up with some elegant twists on the truth.

Nick got the usual lecture about no friends over (and thanks to the house's security, no way was he going to be able to hide any), no leaving, any long-distance phone calls came out of his allowance, and only page us in an emergency. Technically, the pagers Sid and I had were only for Quickline business. Everybody used them for personal purposes as well.

We got to the restaurant in Westwood in plenty of time. Better yet, Desmond Moore was there waiting for us. I was happy that we'd already met some years before. Desmond was a youngish Black man, about medium height with dark-colored skin and well-built shoulders. We'd met on a case in Tahoe. He'd been a bartender in one of the casinos.

"I'm writing software now," he told us after we'd ordered. "I mean, I always had, but now it's a visible job."

"So, how did you get transferred to us?" Sid asked. "Weren't you with Eleven-B or something?"

Desmond snorted. "Yeah, that was a kind of scut-work division the Company wasn't too excited about. They folded it right after I transferred out to work for Congressman O'Connor directly. When this position opened up about eight months ago, I jumped at it."

"To a lowly courier position?" Sid asked.

"To part-time." Desmond laughed. "Guess who my primary client is for my software business?"

I made a face. "The Company?"

The Company was what we called the CIA when we weren't using ruder terms. We paused as the waiter brought our food.

"Yep. The Company." Desmond shook his head and dug in. "They can't keep me busy enough for full-time. But even with a full-time gig, they still expect me to write software for them on demand. Not enough people are cleared on our level who can do what I do." He shrugged. "That's where most of the work's going to be in a few years. Given what spy satellites can do these days, they won't need nearly as many folks on the ground."

"They'll need some folks," said Sid.

"Yeah. But which is easier? Send in a team to scour the countryside for whatever nuclear arms plant there might be? Or just fly over and take a picture? The hard part is getting the pictures back to earth, but they may have gotten that one beat." Desmond grinned. "There just may happen to be a new bird going up this summer that I have a little payload on."

I frowned and looked at Sid. "We had heard there was one they were trying to keep extra quiet."

In fact, we'd been hearing about it for much of that spring. We had reason to believe that the Cat's Paw project was one our good friend Esther Nguyen was working on. Esther's an engineer for a defense plant in the South Bay. She'd never let on. However, since Sid and I had gotten promoted, we'd been getting a lot more information about who was doing what top secret work. Not only did we know that Esther's company was coordinating all the other companies working on the satellite, Sid and I had figured out from Esther's work ID that she was in the division doing the coordinating.

Sid's eyes narrowed as he looked at Desmond. "And why are you sharing your involvement with it?"

Desmond shifted. "That. I was in DC the other day and met up with Congressman O'Connor."

"Who knows that you're on our line." I nodded. "What does he want?"

"Apparently, there's a leak on the project." Desmond held up his hands as Sid and I groaned. "You won't be going undercover. But our buddy Dale wanted me to give you a heads-up that I'm involved on the project. He said that probably all three of us will get pulled in on the case, but wasn't sure how yet."

I glanced at Sid, who shrugged.

"It would make sense," Sid said. "We're the closest people they've got. But that will have to wait until next week."

"We're going up to Tahoe for the weekend," I told Desmond with a slight sigh of disgust.

"That's right. Your folks are up there." Desmond looked at me. "Bad blood?"

"No." I smiled and sighed. "My folks are fine. It's just that visiting them is not the only item on the agenda, so to speak."

Sid chuckled. "Lisa's got her high school reunion."

"It's the Fourth of July." Desmond looked puzzled for a moment, then nodded. "So, which hotel wants to make the locals happy and shore up its catering business?"

I'm from South Lake Tahoe, which is on the California side of the border with Nevada. But it's a major tourist area and Fourth of July weekend is one of the biggest tourist weekends of the year.

Now, you might wonder why anybody from our area would schedule an event on one of the biggest tourist weekends of the year. The reality was that there was no good weekend. Tahoe is one of those rare areas where the tourist season is year-round. Fall tends to be slower, but most people can't travel after school starts and a lot of my class had left the area. And, not surprisingly, there are very few conventions and other large parties requiring big spaces and catering on holiday weekends. So, the hotels are more willing to do something like a reunion than you might think. Add that many of us had family who could put us up, no matter how booked up all the local places were, and Fourth of July wasn't such a bad option after all.

"Anyway," I continued. "I'm not really looking forward to it, but I told a friend of mine that I'd go. And I have a couple friends I'd like to see again."

Desmond grinned. "Yeah. I know how that goes."

Dinner went on pleasantly. We stayed somewhat later than we'd planned. But eventually, we sent Desmond on his way and went back to the house. Nick was still up. Well, it wasn't that late. We sent him to bed and went upstairs, ourselves.

The next morning, we got up around seven-thirty to go running at eight. That was one of several blessings that being married seemed to have brought. It would probably be more interesting if the later running time had been the result of a knock-down, drag it all out fight. But it wasn't. Nick and I had merely asked Sid shortly after school had let out why it was so important to run at six a.m. rather than later? Sid had conceded that the early hour was his preference but pointed out that he didn't want to be waiting too long for breakfast (he didn't want to run after eating), which was fair. So, Nick and I agreed to get up at seven-thirty, which was a heck of a lot better than five-thirty.

Nick and I had also convinced Sid that he'd better have a really, really good reason before scheduling a flight that would require us to get up before the crack of dawn. Sid had agreed it would be appropriate to check with me, specifically, before making the reservation. Sid is a morning person. Neither Nick nor I are. We're working on the compromises.

We got into Tahoe in mid-afternoon. Sid rented a car, and we got to my parents' place, at the back of their resort there, before three o'clock. Daddy was helping the desk clerk down at the main lodge get folks checked in. I offered to lend a hand, but Mama refused to let me.

She's a small woman, as pert and lively as a bird. Crossing her was not usually in one's best interest, however. Grandma Caulfield was in the living room. She was about as tall as my mother, with considerably more rolls about her waist.

Sid and I are well off. Sid had gotten an inheritance some years before and had bettered it several times over. A year and a half before, we had formed a business partnership and mingled our assets. That last part meant nothing to my grandmother. That Sid had money did.

You see, I had done what any right-thinking young woman would do. I had held out for the guy with the cash. That Sid and I happened to be crazy in love with each other went right past Grandma. Marriage was about bettering yourself economically and I had done that with a hey nonny. Which meant I was Grandma's golden girl.

So, Grandma was particularly happy to see me. My parents were, too, but they're always happy to see me. We had a lovely evening, with Sid playing the piano, then all of us playing cutthroat Monopoly. Nick won that one.

The only problem was the next afternoon, I got the feeling there was some dross getting in the way of me as Grandma's golden girl.

"What's going on with Grandma?" I asked Mama as we gathered flatware and the tablecloth for the picnic table out back next to the barbecue where Daddy had some pork shoulder cooking very, very slowly.

Mama sighed. "Do you really want to know?"

Her eyes flitted down to my tummy and suddenly I knew.

I sighed. "She does know that Sid and I can't get pregnant, right?"

Mama winced. "I tried to tell her. It's not the sort of thing that makes sense to her, though."

"Well, it's got to be obvious that we're making an effort."

"Good lord, Lisle! I asked you to keep it down."

Lisle is my other grandmother's name. She's German, and I was given the American version. But my parents frequently used the German version when they talked to me.

"We did." I flushed a little. "We just may have made a little noise, and that's all to the better. She can't fault us, or you, if a baby doesn't happen."

Mama sighed. "You know how she feels about sex."

"I know. But it's going to be hard to make a baby if we aren't having any. Even she knows that."

"There is that." Mama sighed. "Just don't go too crazy tonight, will you?"

"I'll do my best."

Later, we went down to the lakefront to watch fireworks. Nick had a blast and talked my parents and Grandma into buying him every snack we came across, and some of them twice. We had one awkward moment when the D .J. playing the music for the fireworks display asked all the veterans in the audience to stand and be acknowledged.

"Sid," Mama asked. "You're a veteran. You can stand."

"And I will not," Sid replied.

Grandma looked at him. "Why, on earth, not? You oughta be proud of your service."

"I am not proud of the two worst years of my life," Sid said quietly.

Mama nodded and sighed, but Grandma clearly did not understand.

"Sid—" Grandma began.

"Mama," my mother cut in. "Let him alone. He's entitled to feel however he does."

Grandma snorted but let it go, and I was profoundly grateful.

Later, Sid and I did our best not to get too noisy. However, Grandma got the message that we were trying to procreate, which did better her mood a little. At least, she had Nick to cheer her up.

July 5 - 6, 1986

I honestly have no idea why I was so nervous about that reunion. Admittedly, large parties are not my favorite thing in the world. I'll also admit that if I don't know the larger part of the people there, it will scare me. But I knew pretty much everybody who would be at this shindig and didn't really care about most of them. Or maybe it was that I only thought I didn't care.

Either way, that afternoon before the reunion, I was a nervous wreck. Sid did what he could. He helped me do my nails. He did my hair, softly curling it with my curling iron, then feathering back my bangs. Sid knows how to do hair professionally because of an undercover assignment as a hairdresser some years before I knew him. We'd spent the week before going over which dress I'd wear, a blue silk noil sleeveless sheath with a trumpet skirt, so that was already set. He made sure I had my aquamarine necklace and earrings on. He had on another perfectly tailored Italian-cut suit, this time in dark, charcoal gray, a pink silk broadcloth shirt and colorful tie.

When we walked up to the sign-in table at the hotel, Sid and I oozed the understated elegance of the truly affluent. In fact, that's what I was humming.

"What?" Sid asked.

"'We got elegance. If you ain't got elegance, you can never, ever carry it off.'" I swallowed, quoting a tune from the musical we did my junior year.

Sid chuckled as I gave my name to the woman behind the table. She looked vaguely familiar. Her name badge said Veronica Small Evans, but that didn't entirely register with me.

"Oh, here's your badge." She looked at it, puzzled. "Lisa Wycherly, with Sid Hackbirn, right?"

"Yes."

"Your form said you got married."

"I did," I said. "This is my spouse."

I was still having some trouble calling Sid my husband for some reason.

"Oh. Do you want us to re-do your name badge with your married name?"

"I don't have a married name. I'm keeping the name I was born with."

"Oh."

"Thanks, Veronica." I picked up the badges. At least, they were the pin-on kind rather than the sticky ones, and the silk of my dress was the nubby kind that wouldn't show the pinhole.

I handed Sid his. "This is going great already."

"It'll be fine, honey." Sid smiled. "Bucking the expectations, right?"

"Right." I swallowed.

We stood in line for the bar. Sid got a bourbon and water. I got a glass of white wine. I said hello politely to several people that I hadn't come to see. Lynn Fremont came up and said hi with an odd smirk as she ogled Sid. Rhonda Jefferson saw Sid and pulled him aside in a panic.

I rolled my eyes and looked for Pete Jefferson and didn't find him. I did find Jimmy and Terry Roth. They were two of the people I was hoping would be there.

They came over and I kissed Jimmy's cheek.

"It's good to see you two," I said, finally feeling the warmth I was expressing.

"You look good," Jimmy said. "I heard you got married."

"Yeah, just this past spring."

Jimmy looked just past me, and his jaw dropped. "Him?"

You must understand, the last time Jimmy and I had seen each other, Sid was still sleeping around. Sid and I had been in Tahoe on a case, unfortunately, as ourselves, and Sid had gained some notoriety thanks to quite a company of women throwing themselves at him. Which is why my stomach clenched at that moment and I realized what I had not been looking forward to.

"He's reformed," I said, smiling tightly.

Sid walked up to me. "Hey, lover."

"Hey, sweetie. Did you get a chance to meet my old friend Jimmy Roth and his wife, Terry?"

"I don't think I did." Sid smiled and held out his hand to shake theirs. "Good to meet you."

"Uh, Lisa," Jimmy said, still a little shaken. "There's a table with some of the other drama club crowd. We saved a place for you and your husband."

The drama club crowd was hardly a crowd. There were about six of us that had hung out together. I was glad to see Leslie Bowman there. She'd made it to the wedding, and we'd kept in touch, so she already knew Sid and about his randy past. And I knew all about her work as a radio reporter in Denver. Leslie was still single, as was Mary

Faber. Gabriel Ordonez was there with his wife, Maria. Andrew Englander wasn't there, nor was Michael Tipton.

I asked Mary, a medium-sized woman who had gained a few over the years, about Michael. The two had been really close friends in high school, although Michael had taken me to the senior prom because Mary had a boyfriend at the time. She made a face.

"I'm so sorry, Lisa. He died a year or so ago."

"Oh, no. What happened?"

She winced. "He told me you knew about him."

"About being gay?" I sighed and shut my eyes. "Oh, crap. Was it AIDS?"

"Yeah." Mary shrugged. "I'm not saying that, though. Not here."

"No. Better not."

That was when they announced that dinner was served. It was a buffet with two identical service stations, and Sid got ahead of me in line.

"Oh, man!" groaned Tim Dulles. "I had to get behind Wycherly. Leave some for the rest of us, will you? Man, some things never change."

He was right. He was still a jerk. I left plenty behind, but it was true that my plate was decidedly full.

At the table, Leslie sat next to me, with Sid on my other side. Sid chatted pleasantly with Jimmy and Terry. Leslie leaned over to me, mischief in her eyes.

"You've been getting the looks, kiddo," she said.

"I know." I sighed.

"I hear he cut quite the swathe through here a few years ago."

"As in, years ago," I snarled.

Leslie laughed. "I know. You two are obviously besotted with each other. And it's like you told me last year. It's all past tense." She looked at me for a moment. "I thought his former girlfriends didn't bother you."

"Oh, they don't. It's the having to explain why I married him that's getting to me."

Sid laughed loudly at something Jimmy said.

A tall redhead with a hatchet face walked up. "Leslie, it's good to see you again."

"Charlene." Leslie's smile got tight.

Charlene Dempsey glanced my way, then ignored me. Sid's back was turned to her.

"So, what have you been up to?" Leslie asked Charlene.

Charlene shrugged. "Still living here. I'm a manager at Harrah's."

"That's moving up in the world. Your hubby around?"

"I divorced him years ago." Charlene's eyes rolled. "And husband number two."

Sid turned to me. "Hey, honey—" He saw Charlene and put on an absolutely gorgeous smile. "Charlene, isn't it?"

"Good of you to remember." Charlene did not seem happy to see him. "Last time I saw you, you were a busy boy."

"I was, wasn't I?" Sid laughed, but it was just a touch unfriendly. "Now, I am a reformed man and happily married. You know Lisa, don't you?"

"Of course. Good to see you again, dear."

"Good to see you, Charlene." I smiled.

Charlene grinned nastily. "So, Sid, just how many of the women in this room have you slept with?"

"I'll never tell."

"I'm not asking for names. Just numbers."

Sid shrugged. "Honestly, I don't remember." He squeezed my shoulders. "And couldn't care less, even about the ones I do remember."

Charlene looked at me, trying to look superior. I suddenly realized what she was up to and that I really didn't care what she thought or was trying to do.

I shook my head. "Charlene, if you think you're going to upset me by throwing Sid's past in my face, don't waste your time. All that is past tense, and it really doesn't bother me. So, go be petty someplace else."

Charlene sauntered off.

"Good one, Lisa," Leslie said, turning back to her dinner. "I can't believe she's still such a witch."

I shrugged. "It's her problem, not mine."

We had just finished eating when Mindy Deeter and Shawna Larson got up and took the microphone. It was time for speeches and prizes for who came the furthest, who had the most receded hairline, who had been married the longest.

"We've got a double prize for the next one." Mindy giggled. "It turns out that the classmate of ours who has been married for the shortest amount of time also has the oldest kid. Lisa Wycherly, can you come up here and explain how you have a thirteen-year-old son? I mean, I don't remember seeing you pregnant."

Rolling my eyes, I stood. "I adopted my spouse's son. Not hard to figure out at all."

I sat back down. Mindy seemed a little flustered that I didn't pick up my prize, but Shawna hurried down to the table with it. It was a gift certificate to a restaurant on the California side that I didn't really like. I stuffed it in my purse. There were a couple more speeches, which

I ignored, then they turned on some music for dancing. I chatted with Jimmy and Terry and was glad to find out that Jimmy had gotten into law school after all, and the two were living in Sacramento. Mary Faber and Gabriel and Maria moved off someplace else. Sid and I would have danced, but whoever had picked the music seemed to favor tunes from our freshman year, and I'm sorry you can't really dance to Bad Moon on the Right, Smoke on the Water, Nights in White Satin, and Stairway to Heaven.

The Roths said good night because they wanted to get back to Sacramento and had a good two hours' drive. Sid, Leslie, and I decided to go across the street to one of the other casinos.

"Actually, I wanted to talk to you two privately," she said, as we dodged a couple late firecrackers in the street. "Maybe we can help each other out on this one."

"What do you mean?" I asked.

Leslie waved me off until we landed at a bar, comfortably far enough away from the live act at the other end of the lounge so that we could talk. We ordered white wine all around.

"So, what's up?" I asked Leslie when the waitress had brought the wine.

"You have a friend named Esther, right? Esther Nguyen?"

Sid and I looked at each other.

"Yes," I said slowly.

Leslie leaned into us. "You two being freelancers, you probably haven't gotten anything on this yet, but it's gone out to a lot of different news agencies this past week that there's a nuclear-armed satellite being launched later this summer, and the anti-nuke group protesting it put out a list of the engineers on the project. One of the names is Esther Nguyen. I met an Esther at the wedding last spring. Could this be the same person?"

My mouth had gone dry.

"Could be," said Sid. "I mean Esther's an engineer, but she doesn't talk about her work."

"Do you think she'd be willing to talk to us about it?" Leslie asked. "See, the thing is, everyone's trying to get confirmation on this one, but the project is top secret, so the people on that end aren't saying anything. They won't even say if there is a satellite, let alone if any of those names on the list are legit."

I sighed. "If it's top secret, I can imagine they wouldn't."

"What makes you think the information is legit?" Sid asked.

Leslie shrugged. "There are just enough details. Like your friend Esther. If we could get her to talk on deep background, maybe we can blow this story wide open."

Exactly what Sid and I did not want. I looked at Sid again.

"Okay," said Sid. "I can see how this benefits you, but how does this help us?"

"You're long lead. You can do the deep background on the story, maybe get it in Vanity Fair or one of the other big magazines. Me, I'm broadcast, so it's no competition." Leslie grinned. "If I can pull this one off, it will really make me look good to my new bosses."

"You're leaving Denver?" I asked. "You just got that on-camera gig last fall."

Leslie laughed. "I start Monday at a network owned and operated affiliate, and it's on camera. The hours are going to bite, but it's L.A."

I yelped happily. "You got it! Oh, my god, Leslie, that's wonderful!"

"Yeah. Next stop, anchorwoman." Leslie shuddered with joy. "Well, that's probably going to take a few years. But believe me, getting into the Los Angeles market is everything. Only thing better would be New York, and I do not want to go anywhere it snows anymore." She giggled. "Tahoe is bad enough. Denver is just as bad, and I've been there four years."

I sighed. "The only problem is I can't help you with Esther. She's not going to talk about her work. I'm as close as anyone is, and she tells me things she doesn't even tell her family. But she does not talk about what she's working on."

Leslie shrugged. "I kinda figured. Those folks don't get their kind of clearances if they get chatty about their work."

"Do you have a place to stay yet?" I asked.

"Corporate housing near the station for at least a month." Leslie shrugged. "They don't pay much, so I'll have to look around a lot."

"Probably the Valley," I said, glancing over at Sid.

"One of the producers was saying she could use a room-mate," Leslie said. "We'll see."

The conversation meandered elsewhere from there. Sid did offer to introduce Leslie to our friend Henry James, who was in the process of retiring, but was the public information officer for the Los Angeles office of the FBI. It was quite late when Sid and I started back to my parents' place.

"You okay?" I asked Sid as we pulled out of the parking lot.

He shrugged. "Well, it must be that leak we heard about. Kind of a strange way to go about it."

"You mean releasing it to the press?"

"No. That they released the names of those engineers. And that Esther's on the list is going to make things really interesting for us."

"Oh, boy, will it." I frowned. "Leslie said that it was an anti-nuke group protesting it."

"That's also an interesting twist. Is it even possible to arm a satellite?"

"I have no idea."

Sid sighed. "I guess we're going to find out soon enough."

The next morning, Nick was bouncing off the walls from three days of being spoiled rotten by my parents and grandmother. He was also eating an unusually large amount, finishing a second box of cereal.

"I'm hungry," he said when Sid asked him.

"He's a growing boy," Grandma said. "I remember when Steven and Leonard turned thirteen. Both of them ate me out of house and home, they did."

Given that both my uncles were portly men, I doubt that made Sid feel any better. At the same time, I had a feeling that Grandma was right. My sister Mae had complained to me the week before that her son Darby's appetite had gotten exceptionally heavy, which she said was a sure sign of a growth spurt. Given that Darby was just a couple months younger than Nick, the odds were looking good that Nick was about to shoot up a little. The top of his head was already even with Sid's shoulder.

Sid pulled his son into the back of the house to finish packing for the flight home that afternoon. Grandma followed me into the living room, then held me back.

She looked at me critically. "How is it you're not pregnant yet?"

"One of those things, I guess." I smiled weakly. "I'm not doing anything to prevent it."

"Well, I certainly hope not!" She looked me over again.

"You know, Grandma. We've barely been married four months. The doctors say that it can take up to six months to a year to get pregnant. In fact, I read somewhere they won't even talk to you about it unless it's been a year."

"Hm. Maybe I better mix something up for you."

My heart stopped, but I smiled anyway. "Can we see what happens in the next few months first? After all, the problem could be on Sid's end and until we know that for sure, we don't want to hurt his feelings, do we?"

"No. I suppose we don't. But I'm not getting any younger, and I want to see your children. They're gonna be so pretty and you deserve that."

I bent over and kissed her cheek. "Thank you, Grandma."

What Grandma didn't know, or maybe she did and didn't understand, was that the problem was on Sid's end. He'd gotten a vasectomy when he was in his early twenties. Between how long it had been and a few different bouts with social diseases, the doctors had said a reversal would be impossible.

I was still a little shaky by the time I got back to my old bedroom, where Sid and I had been staying. Nick had already bounded off somewhere else. I'd seen him run past.

Sid took one look at me and sighed.

"Did your grandmother give you trouble about no babies?"

I sat down on the bed. "Worse. She's thinking about mixing something up for me."

"Any harm in that?"

My face went pale. "What if it works?"

Sid looked at me, grinning. "Are you trying to tell me you're sleeping with somebody else?"

"No way!" I laughed. "I'm tired enough."

He laughed, too. "Well, that's one more good thing about all our activity. So, how is one of your grandma's elixirs going to reverse a vasectomy?"

"I have no idea. But it's my grandma. She's really good that way, as you well know."

"True." Sid looked at me again. "And you're worried that it will work."

"So?" I got up and started checking our bags and the rest of the room.

"What happened to wanting a baby?"

I stopped. "You're right."

I frowned, trying to parse out my feelings. I had been having a tough time when someone around me got pregnant, feeling a deep ache that I would never be able to get pregnant myself. Suddenly, though, the mere thought that getting pregnant might be possible after all, that had terrified me.

"I don't get it." I sniffed. "It's both. I want your baby, but I don't want to have a baby. What's wrong with me?"

"Nothing." Sid pulled me into his arms. "Maybe it's wanting what you can't have even if you really don't want it that much."

"How capricious." I made a face.

"And adorable, if occasionally inconvenient."

"Maybe it is both, though, wanting a baby and not wanting one." I shrugged.

"Sweetie, it's been barely four months. We've got plenty of time to figure this one out. And apart from your grandmother, no one is going to question us waiting until we've been married a year, at least."

Which was true. And not only that, it wasn't anybody's business, including my grandmother's. I snuggled into Sid's embrace. It wasn't easy bucking expectations, but it was easier from his arms.

July 7, 1986

You know how it goes. Life goes along on a perfectly even keel and then everything decides to go to hell on the same day. That was that Monday. It started early.

I will spot some points to the little tarts who had been stalking Nick and his buddies. They showed up on the end of our driveway at the ungodly hour of eight-something-or other, because they were there when Sid, Nick, and I finished our morning run, accompanied by my liver-colored springer spaniel Motley. There were four of them and if I only remember one of their names, well, that had to do with what happened later.

"Hi, Nick," giggled one of them, a little redhead, as I recall.

Nick ignored her, part of the advice his father and I had given him, and hurried for the front door. The girls called after him.

Sid rolled his eyes and faced the girls. "Ladies, at what point has Nick shown the least interest in any of you?"

The girls looked at Sid, startled.

"Well?"

They all started sniffing and blinking.

Sid shook his head. "Please, ladies, I say this as much for your sakes as my son's. Chasing boys like this will not get them to like you. Develop some respect for yourselves. Nick and his buddies are not the only boys out there. They're not even the only cute boys out there. If one boy doesn't like you, there are other boys who will and you don't have to chase them, and you don't have to put out to attract them. For crying out loud, you're not even through middle school yet. You've got all of eighth grade, then four years of high school, even four years of college to find a boy or two who will treat you with respect and like you for it. But you've got to respect yourselves first. Think about it."

He stalked off into the house. Okay, I may have given them the stink eye before I followed Sid. I was pretty sure that at least three of them were blubbering, but I didn't care. And I was also proud of Sid. It wasn't just protecting Nick. He cared enough to tell the girls what they really needed to hear. [Oh, for crying out loud. Why weren't those parents teaching their girls to respect themselves? With all the schmucks and assholes out there, you would think lesson number one would be, "You're better than that." Kinda like your parents taught you. Best protection those girls could have gotten. - SEH]

Sid was still in a bit of a state as we got showered and dressed for the day. I put on a flowered skirt and knit top and sandals. Another blessing of the marriage thing. I had pointed out to Sid that what I wore had no bearing on how much work I got done. If he was more comfortable in business-wear, that was fine. I wasn't. Oddly enough, he'd been dressing down a little, too, choosing a sport coat and slacks that morning instead of a full three-piece suit. [Three-piece suits were starting to go out of style. - SEH]

"Those girls really got to you," I said, as we headed downstairs to breakfast.

"Sort of." He frowned. "I'm just questioning a few things I used to take for granted."

"I don't understand."

He sighed, then looked to see if Nick was within earshot, which he wasn't.

"I know I was sexually active at thirteen." Sid winced. "At the time, it didn't seem like it was that young, especially since I knew younger kids who were active. But then, I look at those little ding-a-lings chasing Nick, and thirteen is starting to seem really, really young. I like to think I wasn't quite that stupid when I was a kid, but now I have to wonder."

I patted his arm. The reason Sid had lost his virginity so early was that he'd been raised among a group of communists, beatniks, and (later) hippies who all believed in free love and that sex was just something you did.

"The good news is, I don't think Nick is going to be quite that stupid," I said.

"That can change pretty quickly."

I looked over at the breakfast room. Nick was probably in the kitchen, or possibly still in his bedroom.

"It may yet. But it's the way he talks about the girls. It's not that they're gross or icky. It's that they're stupid." I chuckled. "It would appear that our son wants some substance from his female companions. Which, by the way, is not that much unlike his dear old dad."

"I'm not that old."

I kissed him. "But you are that dear."

"Mom! Dad!" Nick came out of the kitchen with a huge bowl of fruit salad and what looked like half a loaf's worth of toast.

Sid's jaw dropped. "Who's going to eat all that?"

"I'll put a good dent in it." I grinned.

"Besides you." Sid turned to his son. "Nicholas, what in the world…?"

"I'm hungry, Dad." Nick put the bowl on the table, then dished out half of it onto his plate. "Besides, Grandma Wycherly says the amount you eat wouldn't feed a baby bird, let alone a growing boy."

Sid looked at me and sighed deeply. He'd put on a few pounds during our honeymoon, and they weren't coming off that easily. The weight didn't show, but Sid felt it and had really re-committed to healthy eating, apart from one rather spectacular fall off the wagon earlier that June. Shaking his head, he went into the kitchen to fetch the coffee. Nick had gotten the water boiling in the kettle, so all Sid had to do was put the filter in the cone, grind the beans, then pour the water over it all so that it dripped into the coffee pot we'd bought in Italy.

Nick had already brought the mugs to the table, along with the milk and sugar for me. That was another thing that had changed since the wedding. Sid had formerly banned caffeine, and it was understandable. He used to be hooked on the stuff, coffee especially, and would get terrible headaches if he didn't get more. However, he had discovered that he could drink a cup or two a day and it wouldn't upset his stomach or give him a headache if he skipped it the next day. Which was great because he really loves good coffee. Nick wasn't sure if he liked it that much but refused to doctor his with milk and sugar like I did. I had never really liked coffee until the honeymoon, but I was getting to like it.

I waited for Sid to take however much of the toast and fruit that he wanted and tried not to wilt under his annoyed glare as I piled the rest on my plate. The reality is that I can (and often do) eat like a horse and never gain an ounce. I gained a pound or two on the honeymoon, but not quite as much as he had. One thing I didn't tell him was that I'd already lost the gain and a couple more pounds.

Things didn't get any better in the office. Sid slid out of his sport coat and put it over the back of his chair while I laid out the queries we'd gotten on his desk. Long John Silver leaped into his lap, her preferred napping place. Her offspring (now full-grown) were in various places. Fritz was probably outside hunting lizards and mice. I wasn't sure where Blueberry was, but she usually liked to sleep on the library fireplace mantle. We'd lost a vase or two that way.

"These three are the best ones," I told Sid, putting that pile of queries next to his left hand. "Then this pile is the idea's good, but the idiot can't write. This pile is workable, but with some significant massaging. And this pile is why did the main office send it?"

Someone at the magazine's main office had weeded out the worst of the queries and sent on the queries we had.

Sid flipped through the three I'd liked and shook his head. "These are the best, huh? Did any of these idiots even read the magazine?"

I shrugged and picked up the messages on the answering machine because it was my turn that morning. Leslie had called the night before to let me know she'd made it to Los Angeles okay and to invite me to lunch sometime that week.

"Oh, that's right," I groaned. "We've got to call Henry about what Leslie said about that leak on the satellite."

"Your day for the phone." Sid didn't even look up from the piles.

"You sure it won't disturb you?"

Sid sighed. "If it does, I can move."

Henry was in and picked up right away. He knew about the leak on the satellite and that the names of the engineers had been released to the press.

"My last week on the job and this has to happen," Henry grumbled. "Every network and newspaper has been trying to get us to confirm that the satellite exists and that it's nuclear-armed."

"Well, if you don't mind too much, could you add one more? My girlfriend, Leslie Bowman, just got on with one of the local TV stations. You may have met her at the wedding."

"Was she your friend from high school?"

"Yeah, that's her."

"Have her call me and give her my direct number," Henry growled again. "I'll have to introduce her to my replacement, Fred Merryweather, but she will not be happy to hear from him."

"What do you mean?"

"He's an idiot!" Henry barked so loudly Sid looked up from the queries. "Gives me and the rest of the press this big song and dance about transparency and good communication, then lied about the freaking satellite. Said it didn't exist."

"Does he know that it does?"

"Probably not, and he doesn't need to. He neither confirms nor denies." The reason Henry knew the satellite existed was because he knew a good many other secrets, too. Besides being a public information officer, Henry had also been Sid's and my supervisor for Quickline. "If you don't know what it is, you neither confirm nor deny. That way, if whatever damned thing does exist, you've got an out because it's top secret. And if it doesn't exist, nobody cares."

I had a bad feeling that it wasn't just the satellite and his replacement making Henry angry. He's usually pretty easy going. Worse yet, I didn't really want to ask, but I had to.

"How's Lydia doing?"

Lydia was Henry's wife. She was dealing with cancer. Her prognosis had been fair to good earlier that spring. As soon as I mentioned her name, Sid looked up from the queries.

Henry sighed deeply. "The cancer's metastasized. It was looking good after that last round of chemo in April. But it's not only back, it's all over. Mostly in her bones. We could have weeks. We could have months. There's no way of knowing. That's why I want out of here so badly. Except for that idiot."

Well, he didn't say idiot. The term he used for Fred Merryweather was exceptionally obscene.

Henry sighed again. "Listen, Lisa. Don't let me get you down. There is some good news. Angelique is in her new position and even in her new office. I know she'd love to show off her new digs. Why don't you set up a lunch date with her?"

"I'll do that. And I can swing by and say hi to Lydia, too. Is she at home?"

"Yeah. She'd like that. Why don't you and Sid come by after the retirement party on Thursday. You're coming to the party, aren't you?"

"We wouldn't miss it, Henry."

"Good." He cursed again. "Another call. I'll see you two Thursday."

We hung up. Sid's eyebrow was raised, so I told him what Henry had said. I choked a little when I got to Lydia's cancer.

Sid sighed as well. "There's nothing we can do about it, Lisa."

I shook my head. "I can pray."

"Then do that." Sid smiled warmly. He's an atheist, so my praying doesn't entirely make sense to him, but he sees it as the glue that holds me together.

I also called Leslie at the number she'd left. It was her new office number. I told her to talk to Henry and about the problem that the new guy was going to be. Leslie was less than enthused but appreciated the direct number for Henry. We didn't quite get around to scheduling lunch, though.

Then Sid and I made our decisions on which two articles we could assign. Sid printed out the rejection letters, based on the different queries, and then the acceptance letters. We were assembling all the different letters when the phone rang.

After a quick glance and nod from Sid, I put it on the speakerphone so that I could keep working.

"Hello?" I asked.

"Is Mr. or Mrs. Flaherty there?" asked a woman's voice.

Sid stopped tearing tractor paper off the return letters and looked at me. After all, Flaherty was Nick's last name, not Sid's or mine.

"May I ask who's calling?" I said.

"This is Josie Prosser's mother. I need to speak with Nick Flaherty's parents."

"This is Lisa Wycherly," I said. "I'm Nick's mother. And your name is...?"

"Madeleine Prosser."

"Good to meet you, Ms. Prosser. How can I help you?"

"It's about Nick's father."

"That would be Sid Hackbirn, yes."

"I thought you two were married."

I sighed. "We are."

I could almost hear her biting her tongue. Okay, it was a little odd that Sid, Nick, and I all had different last names, but we did for reasons that were important to us. Why that upset people, I do not understand.

"You need to speak to your husband. He brought my poor daughter to tears this morning."

"By suggesting that she needed to feel more respect for herself?"

"My daughter has plenty of respect for herself."

"Then why is she chasing my son and two other boys who have no interest in her?"

Ms. Prosser coughed. "It's harmless nonsense. And if your son and those other two boys have no interest, you might have something to worry about."

I took a deep breath. "I have nothing to worry about. There are lots of reasons why Nick and his friends are not interested in her or her friends, and being followed around might just be one of them. If my husband suggested to them that their behavior was less than attractive and showed poor self-esteem, he had a good point."

"And what gives him the right to decide that?"

"Excuse me," Sid cut in. "This is Sid Hackbirn. I'm Nick's father. I also have a past and let me tell you something else you don't want to hear, but you really might want to think about. Girls like your daughter were who I preyed on when I was in high school. Because they needed a male to make them feel good about themselves, I got a lot of fast, easy lays without having to deal with going steady or any of that other crap. A lot of those girls got married too young. Some even got abortions as soon as it was legal. Now, if that's the future you want for your daughter, that's up to you. Me? I don't want that for my son. I want him to respect the word no and to spend his time with girls who respect it when he says no. So, I do think your daughter could do with a lot more self-respect. Because what she and her friends are doing is not harmless. It won't hurt my kid because he has his head on his shoulders. But it will hurt yours. Think about it."

Sid reached over and slapped the phone off. I sighed.

"What?" Sid glared at me.

"Yes, you were right." I bit my lip. "But you were pretty hard on her."

"You were trying to be nice, and it didn't do a thing." Sid looked away. "She didn't understand. How else to get through to her?"

"You're probably right. We just have enough trouble with the other parents at Nick's school."

Sid shrugged. "Maybe it will get us off volunteer service."

He fervently hoped so. We'd already had one dust up over the parents' newsletter, which had resulted in being shifted to another committee. [And a really crappy newsletter. - SEH]

The phone rang again, also on the personal line. I popped it onto the speakerphone.

"Hello?"

"Hello, Lisa," said Stella, Sid's aunt who raised him. "Is Sid there? I've got some news for the two of you."

"I'm right here, Stella," said Sid. "What's up?"

"Well, all the pieces have finally fallen into place. I've sold my music school. I'm moving to Los Angeles this week."

"What?" Sid gaped.

Stella had been living in South Florida, where she was originally from. It was a long story, but she didn't particularly like being there.

"I have considerable incentive to be in the Los Angeles area, namely a grandson." She paused. Since she hadn't given birth to any children of her own, she meant Nick. "And a son." Which meant Sid. "Sy and I are flying in on Friday to finalize the location for my new school and to find a place to live."

Sy was Stella's lover. Their relationship was another long story.

"Why aren't you going to New York?" I asked. That was where Sy lived and worked as the head of the strings department at Juilliard.

"For a lot of reasons. Sy wants to retire someplace warm. He's got a year or two, but he likes Los Angeles. He likes being a grandpa. And he is fed up to his back teeth with administration. He's going to spend the rest of the summer out here with me to see if we can make it work. He's also got a couple guest lecturer jobs around town for the fall. If he can keep that up, it will be easier to leave Juilliard sooner rather than later. In the meantime, I've been meeting with several Los Angeles school district officials, so there may be something we can do on that level."

"Do you want to stay here at the house until you get your place?" Sid asked, swallowing. "You're more than welcome."

"That will do for the time being." That was, actually, high praise on Stella's part. "Sy and I are going to rent a car, so you won't need to pick us up at the airport. The plane lands at one. We should be there sometime after two."

"We'll make a point of being home," said Sid.

"Good. I'll see you Friday."

I looked at Sid, who looked a little flummoxed.

"It's not even lunchtime yet, is it?" he said.

"I'm afraid not."

The phone rang again. This time, it was our good friend Jesse White. He and his wife, Kathy Deiner, wanted to meet us for lunch. Jesse and Kathy had been recruited into our side business the previous fall, and Jesse said he had a pickup for us. Sid and I agreed to meet them at one of our preferred Mexican restaurants in Westwood. We went over the rules again with Nick regarding staying alone, let our housekeeper, Conchetta, know that she only had to feed Nick, and hurried out.

Jesse and Kathy were waiting for us in the restaurant's foyer when we arrived. Jesse is a little taller than average, with his black hair cut round, and skin the color of cocoa. Kathy's skin is more dark chocolate, and she's almost as tall as Jesse and has her hair clipped close to her head. The four of us were shown to a booth at the back almost immediately and the waitress brought us a basket of chips and two bowls of salsa, even before she brought us glasses of water. Sid glared longingly at the chips, then took one and dipped it in the extra spicy salsa. We chit-chatted until the waitress had taken our order, then brought the food.

Sid spooned as much spicy salsa as he could over his tostada salad.

"So, what's going on?" Sid asked.

"Besides the usual nonsense at church?" Kathy asked, mischief in her dark eyes.

Church is where I'd met Kathy and Jesse. Sid got to know them as he got more involved in my life.

Jesse handed Sid a manila envelope. "Had to run to Vegas yesterday for this. It's addressed to you two."

"Goody," I said. Information addressed to us usually meant more work.

Sid opened the envelope, read the letter inside, hmm'd a couple times, then cursed.

"What?" I asked.

He handed me the sheet and whispered the keyword in my ear. It took me several minutes longer to decipher the code, but when I did, I almost cursed.

"They've got to be kidding," I said.

Jesse and Kathy were both concentrating on their food in a way that strongly suggested they were dying to know. But, hey, it's the spy biz. They understood they didn't necessarily have Need to Know. Sid looked at me. I shrugged.

"They're going to find out," I said.

"True." Sid sighed and looked at Kathy and Jesse. "Alright, for once, you're going to be on the ground floor on something."

"It's about time," said Kathy, slapping the table with an eager grin.

"You know we can't help it," I told her.

"So, what's up?" Jesse asked.

"Our current assignment," said Sid. "There's a spy satellite due to go up later this summer. The problem is, there's been a leak on the project and the anti-nuke group protesting the launch has not only released some of the information to the press, they've released a list of the engineers that they believe are on the project."

Kathy's eyes narrowed. "Esther is an engineer doing top secret stuff. I mean, no reason to assume she's involved."

"But she is." I crossed myself. "She's one of the engineers on the list. And since Sid and I first heard about the satellite, we noticed that the division at her company working on it is on her work badge. Our orders are to protect her and Frank, and when Frank's security clearance comes through, start training them as couriers."

Kathy gaped. "What?"

"They're being adopted?" Jesse swallowed. "What did they do to get signed on?"

"Know us, apparently." Disgusted, Sid folded the sheet of paper and slid it into his sport coat's inside pocket. "Our group likes to recruit friends. It would seem that friends of good spies tend to have the same qualities that make them good spies, too."

"Esther does have an advanced clearance," I said. "She has to, so that she can do what she does. Frank's too close to her not to be involved, and he has a lot of freedom to move around."

"But is he going to be responsible enough?" Kathy asked.

She had a point. As much as I loved Frank, he could be pretty wild.

Sid smiled. "Frank? No problem. He's where he needs to be when he needs to be there. He can be a little crazy, but never at the expense of anything important."

"Oh, I don't know," I grumbled. "What about our wedding pictures?"

Jesse and Kathy started breaking up. Jesse had gotten the close-up, so there was no doubt. But, yeah, Frank had pulled one of his more infamous stunts for our wedding. We still had no idea how he'd managed it, but he'd somehow painted "HI" on the soles of Sid's shoes, so that when Sid and I kneeled at the kneeler in front of the altar, that's what everyone saw. That didn't even count the games he'd played with the wedding music. [The shoes weren't Frank. I know that's what we thought then. But it was Mae and Neil who pulled that one off, although we didn't find that out until, what, our fifth anniversary? – SEH]

"I will get him back for that," said Sid. He shook his head. "In the meantime, we need to do some reconnaissance on their place, plus set up monitoring shifts, get the surveillance cameras and mikes in place. All that fun stuff. There's some sort of hold up going on, so who knows how long we'll be monitoring them."

I looked at Sid. "I'll take care of the recon vehicle tomorrow. I have a meeting anyway."

Sid nodded. We finished lunch going over a few more details, then went our separate ways for the time being.

July 8, 1986

"**M**om!" Nick called just before lunch that next morning. His holler came from the direction of his bedroom, but he quickly appeared in the office. "Josh, Rob, and I want to go skateboarding at Coldwater Park. Can we? And can I bring Motley?"

Motley's stub of a tail thumped excitedly at the mention of his name. He usually slept in the office during the day, although he loved running around wherever Nick went.

I looked at Sid, who nodded.

"Sure, Nick." I looked severely at him. "Just make sure you walk on Sunset. No skateboarding there."

I was terrified that Nick would fall off his skateboard right into oncoming traffic on the famous boulevard. However, as Sid pointed out, it was more likely that Nick would get hurt by some of the dangerous things we had him doing for the business.

"It's safe," Nick groaned.

"Not for anyone else on the sidewalk," said Sid. "And you need to be home in time for dinner. I've got a job tonight and your mom has Bible Study."

"Job?" Nick frowned.

"It's an easy, safe one." Sid smiled.

Well, as safe as anything we did was, which meant Nick would worry. Nick knew that the side business existed, and we'd been training him because it was the safest thing for him and also because he'd probably end up doing similar work. Once Nick had found out about the work we did, he'd been locked in, too, and there wasn't much we could do about it.

"When are you going?" I asked Nick as I checked my watch.

"Right after lunch."

"Okay. I'll see you at dinner then." I got up. "I'd better head out if I'm going to get to lunch with Angelique on time."

I kissed Sid, then Nick, then hurried out to the garage and my truck.

Between getting into the parking lot at the Federal Building in Westwood, then getting past the reception desk to the FBI offices there, then finding Angelique's new office, I was a little late.

"What do you think?" Ange said as she ushered me into the room.

It was pretty much like any other office I'd seen at the FBI headquarters. Gray-green file cabinets with security bars on them lined one wall. The desk was metal, but good-sized, and had a computer on top. A black metal credenza behind the desk held a printer, a fax machine, and a couple standing file racks, and there was a window above it. The walls were a little bare yet. However, Ange had put a vase filled with mixed flowers on top of one of the cabinets.

"You rated a window," I gasped. "And a door that clos-es."

"Yeah. Isn't it awesome?" Ange laughed. She's tall and model thin with full brown hair and high cheekbones. "Are you ready to go?"

"Uh, I need to do some business first." I shut the door and locked it.

Ange sank into her desk chair with a puzzled look on her face. I flopped into one of the two chairs in front of the desk and grinned.

"I need to requisition a recon van for Division Fifty-Three-Q, code eight-six-four-one-seven."

Ange's jaw dropped. "Fifty-Three-Q. That's Quickline."

"Yeah, it is. Call me Little Red."

"You mean Sid's Big Red?" Angelique's gape only grew. "Oh, my god. You're Henry's replacements!"

"Yeah." I chuckled. "When did you get to find all this out?"

Ange blinked and shrugged. "Well, I always knew that Henry was doing other things than public information. It's one of those jobs they give to guys who should be put out to pasture, but they don't want to hang it up yet."

"Like Fred Merryweather?"

Ange shuddered. "Exactly. But Henry had never been that kind of person. So, I asked him about it a few months after I'd started with him. He admitted he had a few top-secret projects going on and said he couldn't tell me about them. Then about three and a half years ago... Come to think of it, you'd been working for Sid for maybe six months by that point. Anyway, Henry says he's going to train me on some of this stuff. It was mostly about processing paperwork, but I had to learn a lot of the codes to do it."

"That makes sense." I nodded. "Apparently, Henry's been working on his retirement for a while. That's why I was recruited."

"Really?"

I shrugged. "Sid needed a partner."

"I would have loved to have done that."

I flushed. "I know. But think about how Sid was back then. No one lasted more than two weeks, not even you. The only reason I lasted was that there was no sex."

"You're right." Angelique smiled and shook her head. She used to be in love with Sid and they were good friends as well. Sid had slept with her more often than any other woman I'd known. Then she realized she didn't want to sleep around anymore, and nine months after that, Sid stopped sleeping around. We'd all remained friends throughout and now Sid and Ange were better friends than they'd been. Ange nodded at the vase of flowers on the file cabinets. "And it's just as well. I'm happier now than I ever was with Sid."

My eyebrows rose, and I grinned. "That's good to hear."

"Yeah." Ange cocked her head and looked at me. "You know, I used to wonder a little bit about Sid, but when I realized he couldn't keep his pants zipped, I figured no way."

"That threw off a lot of people." I rolled my eyes.

"Then you showed up, and you were way too nice to be in that racket."

"Again, throwing people off." I shrugged. "So, how come Henry told you about Quickline?"

"He had to. He told me about the shadow agencies a couple of weeks ago. He's been doing favors for a lot of folks, let me tell you."

"And perhaps you shouldn't."

Ange laughed. "Maybe. But Quickline is the one group he actually worked for, and I have to be on top of that to get you what you need and to be sure the paperwork goes to the right person."

"Always the paperwork." I rolled my eyes.

"But he didn't tell me about you guys." Ange rolled her eyes.

"It's how we work." I sighed. "We don't get to know anything until we absolutely must. Anyway, about that van?"

"Oh. Right." Angelique pulled a multi-copy form out of the standing file on her desk. "I'm going to need a case number. Wait. You gave me a code. Was it five digits?"

"Yeah. Eight-six-four-one-seven."

"We'll use that. Whose name goes on the form? Yours or Sid's?"

"Neither." I pulled an ID case from my purse and slapped it in front of her. "How about Special Agent Linda Devereaux?"

"I've seen that name before." Ange looked up from the form. "And Charles Devereaux?"

"Guess who."

Ange shook her head. "This is going to take some getting used to. When do you need the van?"

"Tonight."

"What?"

"Hey, we only found out yesterday that we needed it. That's when I called you and we had to set up lunch."

Ange's face grew pained. "There's somebody I'm supposed to call if I need something right away." She sighed deeply. "I'm going to have to call Henry. Do you mind?"

"No. Go ahead."

Angelique picked up her phone and dialed. Henry must have picked up right away because she explained that she needed a recon van for that night, and, yeah, it was 53-Q. Then she held out the receiver to me.

"He wants to talk to you."

I took the phone and pulled it as far away from the desk as I could. "Yes, Henry."

"Was Ange surprised?"

"Shocked to her core. Are you happy?"

He laughed. "Thrilled." His tone shifted to more serious. "I got a call this morning from your friend Esther."

"Oh?"

"She told me a week or so ago about the list she's on that some anti-nuke folks released."

I sighed. "I heard about it over the weekend."

"Well, apparently, she and her colleagues have all been getting threats, nothing that worrisome, but still, we have to take it seriously. She wanted some protection for herself and her crew."

I thought. "Do we have enough personnel? Or should I call in some folks from elsewhere?"

"I'm going to let regular channels handle her friends. Her and Frank, though, we've got to handle them differently."

"Uh-huh." I glanced at Angelique. "Wouldn't happen to have anything to do with a certain letter we got yesterday?"

"So, you know about them being adopted. Good."

"How did this person get through to you directly?"

Henry cleared his throat. "I gave her my card at the wedding last spring. Why not? Things were already in the works by that point. And, uh, we may have talked a couple other times."

"No kidding. It would have been nice to know."

Henry chuckled. "That wasn't going to happen."

"I hear there's a hold up."

"Yeah. Believe it or not, it's Frank's clearance. His father was born at home, so there's a problem with the birth certificate."

"He was clearly alive." I knew Frank's father had been killed some years before.

"But was he who he said he was?" Henry growled. "It's just the usual bureaucratic nonsense. It'll be fine. Just keep them under surveillance and make sure those anti-nuke idiots don't hurt them."

"Shouldn't we be investigating the idiots, too?"

"Nah. The investigation is already in progress through normal channels."

"Okay. But we'll need the recon van. Can you make that happen by tonight?"

"No problem. Let me talk to Ange."

I gave the phone back to her and tried not to fume. Angelique talked for a few more minutes, filled out more of the form, then hung up.

"I've got to make one more call, then drop this off, and then we can go to lunch."

"I'm looking forward to it." I forced a smile onto my face.

Ange laughed. She made the call, talked for a couple minutes, then had me follow her to another office upstairs. I waited outside the office while she dealt with copies and picked up some keys.

As we left the building, I asked her where the van would be. Ange pointed.

"It's the far end of the lot. It'll be there by five or so." She handed me the keys.

"Thanks." I slid the keys into my purse.

She sighed. "Can we go to lunch now and gossip about our personal lives?"

I laughed. She drove us to a restaurant in Brentwood.

After we'd ordered, I leaned over the table.

"How much of the request for personal gossip has to do with that vase of flowers I saw on your file cabinets earlier?" I asked.

Ange tossed her head back, laughing happily. "Everything. Oh, my god."

I couldn't help laughing, too. Ange and Sid's best friend from high school, Tom Freeman, had met at the rehearsal dinner for our wedding.

"So, I'm guessing Tom sent the flowers." I smiled.

"Yeah." Ange took a deep breath and closed her eyes. "You know we've been trying not to rush things. We've been working on keeping things cool, taking our time. Except that Tom went and got a job at a high school here in Los Angeles. He starts in September."

I watched her. "Is this good news?"

"It is." Ange shivered a little. "I mean, it's pretty scary. We haven't even had sex yet. Can you believe it? We've been together almost every weekend since your wedding, and we haven't done it. I don't know why, but I told Tom he can stay with me when he moves. The only thing is..." She sighed. "You know Tom's in recovery."

"Yeah."

"Well, there's my wine collection." Angelique looked at me. "I need to get rid of it before Sunday. That's when he's coming in. Tom says he's okay with it and I believe him. It's just that I have been drinking a lot by myself and I really don't need it. I'm bringing some to Henry's retirement party. But I do have some really good bottles and I'd rather they went to people who'd really appreciate them. And I do owe you and Sid."

"For what?"

"For Tom. If he hadn't been at the rehearsal dinner, we wouldn't have met."

I laughed. "I'm so glad you two did. Henry asked us to go over to his place after the party. We could pick up the bottles then."

"Thank you." Ange sighed with intense relief.

Our food arrived and the two of us continued talking about Tom and Sid and being happily in love, oh, and life in general. It was a perfectly lovely lunch.

Sid laughed when I told him about Ange's reaction to us being in the spy biz. He was also excited about taking over her wine collection. I'd had some of her bottles. They were amazing.

Nick showed up in plenty of time for dinner. Motley looked happy, but exhausted. Conchetta Ramirez, our housekeeper and cook, had cooked a wonderful dinner of beautifully grilled chicken breasts, salad, and green beans. There was just a lot more food than she usually cooked.

"What is going on here?" Sid asked.

Conchetta is a medium-sized woman with a few rolls around her waist and black hair threaded with silver that she almost always wears in a braid down her back. The t-shirt over her jeans that day featured the Twisted Sister tour from the year before.

Conchetta rolled her eyes. "Nick is growing, Sid. He told me at lunch how hungry he was. I made some extra for him."

Sid sighed. He ate one of the half breasts, a decent serving of salad and a few green beans. Nick wolfed down three half breasts, half a plate of salad, and another half plate of green beans. I got the rest.

"I never ate like that," Sid grumbled later as Nick went to watch TV.

"Do you want me to ask Stella that?" I couldn't help it. My smile was just a touch smug.

Sid winced. "Mae said Darby is doing the same thing?"

"She did."

"Okay."

I had to leave for Bible Study after that. Kathy arrived almost at the same time I did. Frank and Esther were already there. Once I saw that, I went back to my truck and used the recently installed car phone to let Sid know. He and Jesse were going to install surveillance electronics on Esther's duplex. As Sid had told Nick earlier that day, it was an easy and safe job. Sort of.

Esther and her father had bought both units of a duplex on the eastern edge of West Hollywood a couple years before. When Frank's latest attempt at making a living as a musician had crashed and burned, Esther had him move in with her and her cousin Thu. Esther's father and her two brothers lived in one side of the duplex. Esther, Frank, and her cousin Thu lived in the other. Except that the previous fall, Esther and Frank had moved well past just good friends.

Then one of Esther's brothers moved to New York. Given Esther's general disdain for whatever her brothers did, I have no idea if this was a good idea or not. However, Thu decided she was in the way in Esther's side of the duplex and had moved to the other unit sometime in April.

So, with both Frank and Esther at Bible Study, Sid and Jesse should have had an easy time of it. There were only two small problems. Frank's dogs. They were two little mixed breeds, each about the size of a large Chihuahua. One looked vaguely like a Yorkie (Reilly) and the other was white but with the same rough coat (Coco). I once joked about them being snacks for larger dogs, and Frank immediately set me straight on how not funny that was since Esther's father had no problem with eating dogs. Esther, fortunately, had been in the U.S. long enough to know that one didn't do that. However, Esther's father was having some significant trouble getting used to the fact that his daughter wanted to be with a foreigner. That said foreigner had dogs didn't help.

Both Coco and Reilly knew Sid and Jesse fairly well. But the two were prone to yapping extensively at anything and everything. Which turned out to be the saving grace. When the dogs started up as Sid and Jesse entered the duplex, everyone in the other duplex tuned the little nuisances out. At least, that's what Sid and Jesse told us later.

After bible study, Kathy followed me to our house, where I put my truck in the garage. She then drove me over to Frank and Esther's, parking her car right behind a dark van sitting at the curb across the street from the duplex. We could see Henry James' car in the driveway to Frank and Esther's side of the duplex.

An L.A. County Sheriff's car sat double parked next to the van. Sid stood outside on the sidewalk talking to the deputy. He looked up as Kathy and I walked up.

"Here's Agent Devereaux now." Sid pointed at me.

I got out my FBI case. "Can I help you, Deputy?"

"Sorry, Agent." The deputy in the tan shirt was fairly large and dark-haired. His nameplate read Zemby. He took the ID case and flashed his light on it. "We have to be pretty careful. As I was telling your partner here, one of the neighbors called us."

"Nice to know we have alert citizens." My smile got tight.

The deputy laughed. "Even when you'd rather they weren't. I get so many calls on dogs barking and cats in trash cans."

"We're going to be here for several days," I told him. "Protection recon. I can't say who. We'll try to move the van during the day, but we'll be here most nights."

"Protection?" Zemby's eyes rose. "That's different. I hope nobody gets hurt."

"That's the idea, Deputy." I held out my hand, and he gave me my ID case back.

Kathy, Sid, and I waited while the deputy got in his car and took off. Inside the van, Jesse and Nick watched a bank of monitors along one side of the van. In the back of the van was a bed. I could faintly hear Henry James talking to Frank and Esther.

The duplex had been built sometime in the 1920s or '30s, and not unlike many of that type of house, had a plastered off-white exterior and red tile roof. The two front doors were squeezed together, with bay windows on either side. Like the others on the block, the lot was fairly narrow, but a two-car garage for each side of the duplex had been added on in the '60s or '70s sometime, with the drive-in door facing the side yard and driveway.

"And how was your evening?" Sid asked as we squeezed into the van.

"Good enough." I looked at the monitors. "Looks like you got everything set up."

"In spite of canine interference." Sid shook his head. "I do not understand what Frank sees in those two little terrorists."

"They're not bad dogs," Jesse said. "They're just small."

"Whatever," Sid said, then cursed. "We're going to have to be extra careful. Henry just pointed out the van to Frank and Esther."

"She's pretty upset." Jesse shook his head.

"I'll say," muttered Nick. "I think she just called Henry a bleeping horse."

I sighed. It figured Esther would be teaching Nick how to curse in Vietnamese.

"When did Henry get here?" I asked.

"Just before the deputy did." Jesse looked at the monitors. "And Henry's leaving."

A minute later, the van filled with angry voices and yapping dogs. It was a good thing we were only trying to protect Frank and Esther because none of us could understand a word. It was surprising how fast Frank had become fluent in Vietnamese, but I suspect that was because that's the language Esther and her family usually spoke at home. Finally, Esther broke down in tears and we could hear Frank's voice get soothing and soft. Her sobs slowly let up and his voice teased a little, then... Well, Sid plugged in an earphone. They had moved into their bedroom, but the cameras in there were aimed at the window and the door.

Some minutes later, Sid pulled the earphone from his ear and sighed.

"Didn't think you guys wanted to hear that," he said, glancing at Nick. "Jesse, do you have any plans for Saturday night?"

"That's our Ladies' Night Out." Kathy pointed to the duplex. "Lisa and I will be in there."

Sid nodded. "Jesse, why don't we take Frank out for a little night on the town?"

"Not if it's going to be anything like your bachelor party." Jesse laughed.

Sid rolled his eyes. Neither he nor Frank were going to live that one down any too soon.

"I'll make a point of driving," Sid said. He glanced at the monitors. "We need to have a little talk with Frank, though."

Jesse's and Kathy's eyebrows both rose. I looked over at Nick, who moaned softly. Nick didn't have any problem with talking about sex as long as it was in the general sense. But as soon as an adult he knew became part of the conversation, that's when he got grossed out. [He was very good about coming to me with his questions, as long as it was just the two of us. - SEH]

After making sure that Frank and Esther were both in bed and the lights were out in both parts of the duplex, Kathy and Jesse took off. Sid took his contacts out - he's very near-sighted - and slid onto the bed to get some sleep while Nick and I took first watch. We couldn't exactly read because we had to keep an eye on the monitors for signs of intruders. So, Nick and I knitted. I had taught Nick that first spring we'd known him, and my mother had only added to his interest. Nick really liked relaxing in front of the TV or listening to music with a pair of needles and some yarn in his hands.

"I kinda wish I could do this at school," he told me that night in a hushed voice.

"Why?" I was making a pair of socks out of some yarn leftover from several other projects, working the first one on a set of five double-point needles.

"Well, you know how school gets boring sometimes, and it's really hard just sitting there. Drawing sometimes helps, but I can't usually think of anything to draw and I'm really bad at it, anyway." Nick paused and counted the stitches from the marker on the circular needle. He was making his first sweater and had just gotten past the ribbing. "Is this right?"

"Yeah. Add another marker, then do your purls."

He nodded and on we went. Nick went to sleep after another hour, then Sid got up and I went to sleep, and the next thing I knew, it was morning.

D oing the surveillance on Esther and Frank wasn't that big a deal in that they weren't likely to start shooting at Kathy, Jesse, Nick, Sid, and me. We were more worried that they'd spot one or more of us following them around and realize that something was up.

Quickline is made up of four different routes across the country named by color. Each route has eight different cities, called stops, and no stop is more than a two-hour flight away from one of the other stops, no matter which color it is. Each line is supervised by a floater team, which is the position Sid and I had recently been promoted to.

Sid and I had called in reinforcements from some of the members on our line, which is the Red line, then also called the other three floater teams and got about six other people to take shifts, as well. Which helped a lot with the being spotted problem. And Sid and I had other things to do besides watch Frank and Esther, such as celebrating Henry James' retirement that Thursday.

Lety Sandoval offered to take her son Josh, Nick, and Rob to the beach that day, then let the three boys sleep over, and Sid and I accepted with pleasure.

The retirement party started as an early luncheon at a restaurant in Westwood, with boatloads of cronies and members of the press telling impossibly wild (but probably at least partly true) tales, and the usual speeches. The real shock was in the middle of the afternoon when we got to Henry's house in Encino. Lydia hadn't been at the other party, and Sid and I could see why when we saw her. Her face was pale and drawn and she sat in a wheelchair. Her two daughters-in-law scurried about, keeping the buffet table full and making sure there were enough plates and silverware, even though it was a relatively small party. Angelique sat with Lydia, introducing people where necessary. Lydia, however, knew Sid and me and was thrilled to see us.

The only thing marring the event was Henry's younger son, Colton. He sneered at everyone, was out and out mean to Angelique, and especially angry at his father.

"He thinks his dad should have retired when I got cancer the first time," Lydia explained to Sid and me. "He doesn't understand that his dad couldn't."

We spent as much time as we could at the house, then promised Lydia we'd come by to visit the next week. Ange walked us out and gave us the wine bottles she'd saved for us. We had to leave early because Frank and Esther had asked us and Kathy and Jesse to meet them for dinner.

The six of us all arrived at roughly the same time at the restaurant on Santa Monica Boulevard, which meant Sid could wave off the team tailing Esther and Frank for the time being.

There are lots of reasons why the six of us have become close friends, but that restaurant kind of exemplified those reasons. For one thing, it was on the eastern, less trendy end of Santa Monica Boulevard. For another, the food was Thai. Sid and I had never eaten Thai food before.

Now, among the six of us, Sid, Esther, and I are the ones who really love the kind of spicy experience that sears our sinuses. Kathy and Jesse don't mind spicy food, although they don't like it that spicy. Frank is learning to like it. All of us love trying new things.

The final thing that cemented this place as a new favorite was that it was one of those small, slightly ratty joints where the emphasis was on the food and not so much on the atmosphere. This was our kind of place and then some.

We went to town. Do I remember all the dishes we ordered? I'm afraid not. We drank cold Thai beer and sniffed and burped and had a wonderful time. As we finished, Frank looked at Esther.

"We've got to tell them," he said. Frank has dark hair and is fairly tall.

Esther, who had cut her black hair short again, sighed, her round face creased in a frown. She's closer to me in size, although her figure is rounder.

"I don't know," she grumbled.

"Aw, come on, sweetie pie." Frank's voice was cajoling and almost irresistible. "John said we should."

She sighed. "Frank and I are getting married."

The rest of us cheered, albeit quietly.

"It's about time!" Kathy chortled.

"I know." Esther sort of glared at her. "It's just that we're getting married at camp this year."

Camp is a week-long retreat for our teen group that our church puts on at a Christian camp on Catalina Island.

"What?" I gasped. "How did you set that up?"

Frank laughed. "We told Father John that we wanted to elope. Esther does not want a big wedding and I wouldn't mind skipping the mess my family would want to get going."

Esther cursed. "It's about my father. He is not happy that I am marrying Frank. He wants me to marry Vietnamese. I would, but I fell in love with Frank. So, what do I do? Besides, weddings are stupid."

Sid laughed. "We've had a good time at a few."

Everyone at the table except Sid and Esther rolled their eyes.

"Yours was a bore," Esther snapped. "Then I realized it was the first time in a couple years that I went to a wedding without us sitting together and making dirty jokes at the reception."

Sid laughed even harder. He and Esther had quite the reputation for turning the air blue around them.

"Most people would not be proud of that," Kathy said.

"Who cares?" Esther said, adding yet another foul epithet.

Frank laughed and slung his arm across Esther's shoulders. "Look. Esther and I are not your conventional couple. Why should we have a conventional wedding? John loves the idea. We're going to do it after the big commitment ceremony on Wednesday. My sister will already be there." Frank's sister, Doreen, usually volunteered as our camp nurse. [That's right. She didn't marry Pete until the next year. - SEH] "My mom and my brother are coming in from Chicago. Mom and James will stay at the duplex and watch my dogs, then she and James and, hopefully, some of Esther's family are going to meet us in Avalon when the group goes into town that day. It'll be great."

"Besides, Janet Weinstock and Sylvia Perez will never know until after it's happened." Esther managed a grin for that.

I looked at Sid. "I wish we'd thought of that."

"And you were going to tell your mother?" Sid grinned at me, knowing darned well that my mother would not have settled for anything less than a full matrimonial blow out.

Janet and Sylvia were an ongoing problem in the Single (but most of us were married) Adults Bible Study on Tuesday nights. Frank and Esther were the last couple who weren't married in that group, so Janet and Sylvia had taken over the baby showers for everyone else, whether or not the shower was wanted. Kind of like they had for those of us who'd gotten married over the past couple years.

"Alright," Kathy said slowly. "What about flowers and things? Esther, have you even thought about a dress?"

"Why?" Esther asked. "Yeah. I know I worked in a bridal salon, but that's the biggest reason why I don't care. Who would want to be in that kind of mess?"

I sighed. "We've got a little over a week. I suppose I could put something together."

Esther groaned. "You are not making me a wedding dress. I'll wear whatever. It doesn't matter."

"You will not!" Kathy snapped. She looked at me, then Esther. "We will find a nice dress for you. We just have to find a time to go shopping, that's all."

"And Jesse and I will see to it that Frank looks good," said Sid.

There might have been an undercurrent of mischief there.

"Look," said Frank. "We want all of you guys to stand up with us. I'm not having a best man, so it doesn't matter if Jesse or Sid is next to me. But, Sid, do you mind coming in with our families on Wednesday?"

Sid grinned. "For you, Frank, I'll do it."

Sid, being an atheist, does not come to camp with me.

"The same goes for me," Esther said emphatically. "I don't care if Kathy or Lisa is next to me. We just want you part of our wedding. That's all."

"We'll be there," I said. "And it will be a nice, simple wedding."

"With some flowers and a nice dress," said Kathy.

The hard part was finding time to go shopping for that dress since Esther worked weekdays. Kathy and I got her to agree to go on Sunday afternoon, which would give us a couple of extra evenings the following week if we didn't find anything. Kathy also agreed to find a florist in Avalon and order a few flowers. We left the restaurant soon after that.

Sid and I took a different route, but we ended up near Frank and Esther's duplex. The recon van was back in place with the Los Angeles hub team for the yellow line inside. Sid and I checked in. Yellow Knife and Dark Yellow were Hispanic and another husband-and-wife team. They were average-sized, with dark, graying hair, solemn brown eyes, and looked almost alike.

Dark Yellow looked at the monitors, then at his wife, and laughed. "I hear you know these folks."

"Yeah. So?" Sid asked.

"Good thing you brought in some help." Yellow Knife giggled. "Your target can make a tail like nobody I've seen and get away from it."

She meant Frank, who was technically our secondary target.

"He made Red Light in less than three minutes this morning," Dark Yellow said. "You should have heard Red Light curse."

Red Light was not one of Sid's favorite people for a lot of reasons. But even Sid admitted he was darned good at tailing targets and staying unseen.

"So, our secondary has been taking our primary target to work and back?" I asked.

"Yeah. Every day," said Yellow Knife. "That's the only reason Red Light was able to pick him up again this morning, for all the good it did."

"Huh." Sid looked at the monitors and mused. "Good to know."

We headed back to our car. Sid's mind was focused on Frank's ability to make and evade a tail. Then he looked at me.

"I wonder how long it would take Frank to make Nick." Sid turned his attention back to the traffic.

Nick is an extraordinarily good tail. In fact, he could give Red Light a run for his money.

"Well, Nick is familiar to him. Still..." I suddenly thought of something else and sent my hand running along Sid's thigh. "You know, Nick is not at home, either."

Sid's chuckle filled with lechery. We got inside before the clothing went flying and landed in the library.

The next morning, we were back at our desks. Sid was preoccupied.

"What's going on?" I asked him as he got up and paced for the third time that morning.

"I'm just thinking. You know, our condo?"

We owned a small condo across from the one where Kathy and Jesse live on Wilshire Boulevard. We'd bought it the year before when we'd needed a place to stay while our house was being remodeled.

"What about it?" I asked.

"It's been sitting empty since last December."

That was when we'd moved back into our house.

"I know," I said.

"What if we let Stella have it?"

"I suppose." I thought it over. "We can't have her living with us."

"Not with our side business." Sid shook his head. "She doesn't want to, anyway. At least, that's what she said when I talked to her on Wednesday. You okay with not selling it?"

I shrugged. "I'm not worried about it. Having the condo sitting empty might be more of a problem."

"Good. We'll talk about it when they get here."

The sound of a skateboard clattering on the front porch announced Nick's arrival home.

"Mom!" he hollered as he came into the house. "Mom, can I have Josh over to watch the baseball game tonight?"

Sid looked at me. "Why does he always ask you these things?"

"I have no idea." I looked up as the boy came running into the office. "We'll see. Stella and Sy are coming in this afternoon. If they want to go out to dinner, then no."

Nick's eyes widened. "Hey, think we can get them to go to a game this weekend? I mean, it's just the Cubs."

"We'll see," said Sid. "There's a lot going on right now, like keeping an eye on Frank and Esther. On the other hand, a game might be a good diversion for Sy and Stella."

"And they like Josh, too," Nick said.

With that settled for the time being, Nick went to go read in his bedroom. Sid, however, was still pacing, which I pointed out.

He made a face. "I'm also trying to figure out how we're going to keep Frank and Esther under surveillance while you're at camp."

"Kathy, Jesse, and I will be there."

"What if Nick and I were, too?" Sid did not look happy.

There were two reasons he did not want to go with me. One was that he'd seen the camp and how rustic it was. Not his cup of tea at all. The other was more to the point - it was a retreat, meaning religious event, and he did not care for that either, never mind how much he was already doing at my church. [No little thanks to Frank. And John Reynolds. And you. – SEH]

I bit my lip. "That would help, to be sure. And Dan has been fussing that I was going alone. I need to be with my spouse and son, you know."

Sid tried not to roll his eyes and utterly failed. "Even money he was hoping you wouldn't go if I refused to."

"Oh, please. He's not that bad." I looked at Sid. "Are you sure you want to? I mean, you were pretty adamant when you saw the place."

Sid's sigh was truly profound. "I never said I wanted to, but I have to admit, it's possibly the safest place for Frank and Esther. Given where the camp is, it's going to be really hard to sneak up on us. And there are lots of places where we can begin training if we need to. Besides, I agreed to be there Wednesday night, at the very least."

"One final potential problem. Can you keep Nick busy and out of trouble during the seminars and reflection times?"

Sid shrugged. "I should."

"Then I'd better call Dan."

I was a little surprised when Dan was perfectly happy to have Sid and Nick along. He even suggested that Nick participate like a regular camper.

"We've got incoming freshmen who are more squirrely than he is," Dan said when I'd gotten him on the phone. "He'll be fine."

"What about Sid?"

"He won't be part of the leadership, but he'll be okay."

[Even odds Williams was hoping to convert me. - SEH]

"Okay. Thanks, Dan. I'll get the check for them to you on Monday."

We ate lunch just after noon, per usual, only again there was extra because of Nick. The boy wolfed down the larger part of the chicken salad Conchetta had made. Even Sid was a little hungry after the fact.

Stella and Sy did not show until well after two that afternoon. Stella was out of sorts about the terrible traffic on the freeways, but Sy took it all in stride. She's somewhat shorter than Sid and has dark gray hair, but she has the same bright blue eyes and dimpled chin that Sid and Nick both have. Sy is significantly taller, with a rounded belly and dark gray hair and beard.

"I've got an appointment Monday morning to sign the papers on the building for the school," Stella told us. "And the movers are going to come, I hope, later next week. That's assuming I have someplace to move into by then."

"We might have something for you," Sid told her.

We took Nick with us to see the condo. Sy thought it was quite charming. Stella said it would do. That was high praise for Stella. To be honest, I do not know what terms Sid and Stella worked out. I'd already told Sid that I didn't really care and that I trusted him. He'd rolled his eyes since the condo was very much a part of our joint holdings. I would have let Stella and Sy live there for free. Sid would have, too, but didn't think Stella would go for that. He was right. He made that offer and she didn't accept. I think they worked out some terms on renting it for the time being. [And, of course, she eventually bought it, maybe a year or so later. – SEH]

Nick did not get to have Josh over to watch the ball game on TV that night because Sy wanted to take us all to dinner. But Sy and Stella happily agreed to take both boys to the stadium the next night and supervise the resulting sleep over so that Sid and I could have a nice night out together. Okay. Sy and Stella did count as adult supervision. The problem was that they also loved indulging Nick. My guess was that they'd keep the boys from burning the house down, but little more.

The restaurant Sy chose was some older steak house he'd read about. Sid wasn't thrilled but went along with it. Nick ordered one of the larger steaks, maybe a full pound of meat.

"Can you eat all that?" I asked when our plates arrived. I would have been challenged and I can eat a lot at one sitting.

Nick shrugged. "I'm hungry, Mom. If I can't, we can take it home in a doggie bag, right?"

"Right."

Stella laughed. "I thought he'd gotten a bit taller than when we saw him last month."

"He's growing," I sighed.

"With an appetite like that, I would think so." Stella chuckled and looked at Sid. "Right on time, too, I might add."

Sid sighed. "Did I?"

"Oh, my goodness!" Stella flat out laughed. "I thought it was the sex, at first, because you'd just lost your virginity. But no. You were growing. You'd go through two or three cans of Spaghetti Os at one sitting."

"Ugh!" Sid was clearly trying not to wretch. "I'll never eat that crap again."

"You liked it back then." Stella looked puzzled.

"No!" Sid glared at her. "Those cans were the only edible food in the apartment."

"I could have cooked you something."

"You would have burned me something." Sid shuddered. "Please excuse me, but I did not like subsisting on carbon."

Stella shrugged and shook her head. Sy laughed softly.

"My darling," he said, somewhat ponderously. "The boy has a point. Cooking has never been your strong suit." Sy looked at the rest of us. "I do the cooking when necessary."

"I like my food well-cooked," Stella said.

"Then why did you order a rare steak?" Sid glared at her.

Stella sighed. "There may be some exceptions."

I didn't say anything and shot Nick a solid glare meant to tell him not to say anything, either. The boy didn't. Sadly, Sid had grown up not entirely sure Stella had wanted him, never mind that she'd wanted him a lot. In fact, Sid had suggested at one point or another that he was certain Stella was trying to poison him, the food was so bad. As we were coming to see the reality, it was that Stella had no interest in cooking and even less skill. Sid had come to accept that Stella had wanted him. There were still issues with the food. [Stella scarred me for life with her cooking. - SEH]

We got through dinner okay. However, there was an urgent message from Kathy on the answering machine. It was just late enough that I hesitated, but I called anyway. We were in the office because that's where the answering machine is. Sid shut the door and locked it.

"What's going on?" I asked when I got her.

"It's Esther," Kathy said. "She's thinking about canceling the wedding and not going to Catalina this year."

"Cold feet?"

"I don't think so. I heard Frank in the background saying that Henry thought she'd be safer at camp."

I sighed. "She must have gotten another threat."

"Lisa." Kathy swallowed. "Maybe she would be better off not going. What about the kids?"

Sid waved at me and pointed to the speaker.

"Kathy, Sid's here. I'm going to put you on the speaker."

"Okay."

"Esther told Kathy she's thinking about canceling," I told Sid as I put the speaker on. "And Kathy's worried about the kids getting hurt."

"Kathy," said Sid. "That camp is exactly where Esther needs to be. Hell, if I could arrange it, I'd have her there now."

"But why, Sid?"

"Because there's no way for anybody to approach that place without being seen. You can't drive in. You can walk above it, but you'll probably be seen, and if you try to fire from the ridge above, there are several good spots where a sniper can return fire. If you come in by boat, you'll be seen and, again, lots of good spots a sniper can go after you from."

"How do you know?"

"I've seen the place. Don't ask how."

"But what happens after dark?" Kathy was not ready to give up. "There is no light there."

"Which means anybody coming in can't see, either. And we'll have military grade night vision goggles."

Kathy fired her last salvo. "What about the kids? That's what's really worrying her, I'll bet."

"If we can keep Esther safe, the kids will be, too."

I sighed. "Do we have any idea what the actual threat is?"

"We're not going to get it out of her," Kathy grumbled. "She won't even say that it's happened."

I frowned. "Henry said that they weren't that worrisome. You know what? I'll make a call on Monday, see if we can get some background on the group that sent out the list. What is it?"

"Stop Nukes Now," said Kathy.

"I'll touch base with the recon team," Sid said. "If they contacted her at her place, decent odds they'll have picked up whatever threat she got."

We hung up and Sid opened a cabinet on the far end of the office. It held a radio and monitors and other bits of weaponry and equipment that most people would have been shocked to find out that we had. He radioed the recon team, runners from two different stops on our line, and they had figured out that Esther had gotten some sort of threat in the mail but didn't know what it was because she told Frank about it in Vietnamese. Sid signed off and groaned.

"It would be really nice if we knew what we were up against." He shook his head.

"It would." I shrugged. "But it wouldn't be the first time we've had no idea."

He sighed. "Nope. We've just got to make sure she goes to camp."

July 12 – 17, 1986

Ladies Night Out has become a regular thing. There are eight of us, including myself, who like to get together once a month and play penny-ante poker at Esther's duplex. We bring snacks and drinks and talk about everything. It's an interesting group, too, in that we're all pretty different. In fact, the only common denominator is that they all know me. That's because the evening started out as a bachelorette party for me right before my wedding earlier that spring.

We'd added Lety Sandoval to the mix in April, after the fact. But Lety, full of energy with dark hair and eyes, fit right in with Kathy, Esther, and the others.

That night, Angelique Carter was bouncing with excitement as she placed her last few bottles of wine on the counter between the kitchen and the large round dining table where we played.

"Tom gets here tomorrow!" she crowed. "He's driving down in the morning. Oh my god! I can't tell if I'm excited or terrified."

"Why not both?" said Sister Maria Campos. She was the principal at the parish school and had dark hair and eyes, a few curves, and a merry demeanor.

Esther was a bit jumpy, but you could tell she was looking forward to focusing on something else besides what was bothering her. The only problem was that Sarah Williams accidentally reminded her of part of it.

Sarah, a slim brunette, drew the high card for the first deal and began shuffling the cards.

"The usual five-card draw, jacks or better." Sarah dealt the cards around her three-week-old daughter, Sandra, who was sleeping in a tummy pack. Because we had eight women, that meant the dealer got to call the game, but had to only deal and couldn't play. "So, Esther, are you getting nervous about camp?"

Esther winced. "Why would I be nervous about that?"

We all picked up our cards as Sarah finished the deal. I had a pair of aces and nothing else.

"Lisa, your bet." Sarah asked. "I meant about Wednesday night."

"I'll check," I said.

Kathy groaned. She had to have openers (or a pair of jacks or better, which meant she could open the betting) and didn't want everyone to know.

"I can't open," Maria said.

"I'm betting one," Kathy said, throwing in the chip. No surprise. Probably had something decent.

"I'm in," said Lety.

My sister Mae tapped her cards thoughtfully. She had her new baby, Melissa, with her in a tummy pack. Lissy was just a little over two weeks old. The tapping and thought were just for show, though. Mae had something decent and wanted us to think she didn't.

"I'm in," she said, finally.

So were Esther and Angelique. I tossed my chip into the pot.

"What's Wednesday night at camp?" Ange asked.

"Commitment ceremony," Esther grumbled.

"How many cards, Lisa?" Sarah asked.

"Three, please." I tossed the three I didn't want on the table.

"Oh, come on, Esther." Sarah dealt the cards. "You and Frank? How many, Maria?"

"Three," Maria sighed. "You mean about Esther and Frank getting married at camp?"

"How'd you know about that?" Esther gasped.

Maria shrugged. "Father John told me. Was it a secret?"

"How many cards, Kathy?"

"Two." Kathy smiled. So, she had triple something or other. I had picked up my third ace, so I liked my odds on beating that hand.

"Oh," said Esther. "Well, we are. Big deal."

"I'd say that's a pretty big deal," said Lety, as she signaled for three cards. Nothing much there.

Mae took two, another possible set of trips.

"I'll take three." Esther shrugged. "I just hope Dan's okay with it." She looked at her cards and sighed (nothing there again).

"I'm a little surprised, but he's great with it," said Sarah. "How many, Ange?"

"Going with three." The mild annoyance in Ange's voice meant she didn't have anything either.

"Lisa?" Sarah asked. "You've got first bet."

I debated whether to try to scare Kathy and Mae into folding, which didn't always work, or try to sucker them and take a smaller pot. Mae looked pretty confident, but without that hidden smile when she actually fills out a straight or a flush.

"I'll bet five." I threw the red chip into the pot.

"I'm out," said Maria.

"See your five and raise it five more." Kathy was trying to scare me into folding. She had at least triple something.

"That lets me out." Lety tossed her cards into the center of the table.

"Cost me ten, huh?" Mae smiled. "I'll call."

Definitely confident, not that confident. Esther and Ange both folded, Esther with a curse.

"I'll call," I said. "Whaddya got, Kathy?"

"We three kings." Kathy chuckled triumphantly as she dropped the cards on the table.

"Beats me," said Mae.

I laid my cards on the table. "It doesn't beat three bullets, though."

Kathy groaned as the others laughed. I pulled in the pot, then Sarah handed me the deck for my turn to deal.

"Why the camp wedding?" Mae asked Esther as I shuffled cards.

"Don't want a big one." Esther made a face.

"You seem pretty tense about the whole thing," Sarah said.

"No. It's something else." Esther shrugged.

"Hey, Esther," Lety asked. "Have you heard about that list of engineers that the anti-nuke group put out?"

Kathy and I glanced quickly at each other as Esther turned pale.

"Yeah." Esther swallowed. "It's a stupid joke. What are we playing, Lisa?"

"How about a little five-card stud?"

Because of the number of women at the table, we really couldn't play anything that involved more than five cards, even with the dealer sitting out. Dealing stud meant I had to stay focused on calling the cards as I dealt them, and the last thing I wanted to do was talk to Esther about her reaction to Lety's question. Fortunately, Lety caught on that Esther didn't want to talk about it.

Esther won the hand, and the deal passed to Maria.

"So…" Ange's grin was a little mischievous. "Is Sid enjoying having a new little niece?"

Mae laughed loudly. I would have whacked her, but she was sitting across the table from me.

"Jacks or better," Maria announced.

"He was fine," Mae said.

"After you scared the snot out of him." I glared at her. "Sid's never been around babies before. Sid and I stayed with the kids so Neil could be at the hospital. We left the kids just long enough to visit Mae and Lissy in the hospital. But then Neil brought Mae and the baby home, and Lissy's, like, not even two days old. And Mae goes and plops her right into Sid's arms."

The others declared they couldn't open.

"And we have pictures," Mae said. "Neil made a point of having the camera ready. You should have seen the look on Sid's face. It was priceless. And I can't open, either."

"He picked it up fast enough, though," I said. "And he's got a new little niece to spoil."

"Lisa, can you open?"

I looked at my cards. Bupkes. "Nope."

Maria sighed, and the deal passed to Kathy, who had to call the same game.

Later, Kathy and I stayed behind to help Esther clean up.

"You're not acting okay," Kathy told her as we gathered the snack leftovers.

Esther shrugged. "I'm fine."

"Esther." I put my hand on her shoulder. "You haven't asked once whether I have any tan lines."

Her eyebrows rose. "Do you?"

I rolled my eyes. "I'm not saying, and you know why. But I'm more worried that you weren't bugging me about it."

Esther sighed. "I can't talk about what's going on."

"What about that list Lety asked about?" Kathy asked. "You completely dodged that one."

"I can't talk about it." Esther glared at Kathy. "You both know why. I do top secret stuff at work. I can't talk about it." She looked at me. "You know how it is, Lisa. There's stuff you can't talk about, either."

I sighed. "I know. That's why I'm asking."

"I get that." Esther blinked several times. "You two are closer to me than anybody, except Frank. I can't even tell him that much." She took a deep breath. "The problem is that list is out there. And, yes, I am on it. I can't say why. But I am told by someone who knows that I am safer at camp. And the kids will be, too." She sniffed. "I just hope so."

"We'll see to it," said Kathy. I almost clobbered her, but then the next bit came out. "Both Lisa and I have taken self-defense. We'll be ready."

I grinned. Yeah, acting like an amateur had saved us yet again.

"Sure, we will," I said. "We'll be the Three Musketeers. All for one and one for all."

Esther laughed weakly. "Okay. I'm glad. Thank you, guys."

Kathy and I both held her close.

A couple minutes later, Jesse, Sid, and Frank arrived at the duplex. Yeah, Frank had gotten a snoot-full, but he was in rather good shape, considering.

Sunday, Kathy and Esther went with me to visit my shut-ins. I'm a Eucharistic minister at church and bring communion every Sunday I can to six older men and women who have a hard time getting to church. Then we went to lunch and hit the stores. Esther put her foot down and did not want to wear white.

"I want to wear a happy color," she said, then smiled. "Like red. Red is a happy color."

Kathy sighed. "You know what association we have with red."

"Even better." Esther laughed.

I was so happy to see her looking and acting like her normal self that I didn't care. We found a nice red dress with full sleeves and a knee-length skirt. Kathy took custody of it to be sure that it didn't get forgotten. Esther was wavering about going to camp again, but we got her to agree to go.

Monday morning, I called Angelique to request whatever report there was on the Stop Nukes Now group. She said she'd get it for me in the next couple of days.

Stella got her paperwork signed, then she and Sy ran both Sid and me ragged with getting the condo ready for hers and some of Sy's things. Sid and I had left the couch we'd used there, along with all the dishes and cookware.

Stella had bought a new bed and had it delivered that afternoon, but Sid and I had to assemble the frame and the headboard. I also ran the new sheets and blanket through the washer and dryer in the unit. Then I had to leave for Teen Bible Study that night and was glad to be gone.

Tuesday night, Sid and I took a shift in the recon van. Nick was spending the night with Sy and Stella, who had officially moved into the condo. I first had to go to the Tuesday Night (No Longer) Single Adults group because it was the last meeting before camp (Sid dropped me off). Back when there had actually been more single adults than marrieds, most of the camp leadership had come from that group. That had changed, but the meeting hadn't for some reason. So, we spent the evening working on cabin assignments, going over the schedule, who was doing which talk, and all the last-minute minutiae that needed doing. I gave Esther a ten-minute lead on me, then called a cab to take me to the van.

I took first shift on the monitors since I am a night person more than Sid is. I was about to wake him up around three in the morning when Frank's dogs started yapping and the alerts went off. Sid woke up immediately because he does and grabbed his glasses. There was an intruder in the garage next to Frank and Esther's side of the duplex. As Sid and I got our all-over ski masks on, I held him back and pointed at one of the monitors.

Frank, wearing nothing but his white briefs, was standing and pulled a gun from his bedside table. Sid cursed.

We still had to go in. Heaven only knew what the intruder was up to in the garage. That Sid and I got there before Frank did was probably because of the argument Frank had with Esther (which we saw on the videotape later). Sid and I silently slid into the garage through the door that led to the backyard. We'd gotten around to the back of Esther's aging Lincoln before the intruder spotted us. He (or she) took off, running straight for the side door just as Frank came into the garage, waving a small pistol. Sid and I ducked behind Frank's car, a relatively new Toyota sedan. Frank put a bullet into the wall, then chased after the intruder. A minute later, he came back into the garage, grunting and limping, then went back into the duplex.

I went to the outside door to see if the intruder was coming back, but he (or she) appeared to be long gone. Sid was on his back under Frank's car. I crouched down next to him, and he anxiously waved me away. Another minute later, he slid out from under the car, his hands cradling something. I checked under Esther's car, but it was clean. We slid cautiously outside.

"We need to get that gun from Frank," Sid said as we got back into the recon van. "He's a menace with that thing."

I started checking through the monitors and running video tape back on one of them.

"Well, the intruder went running, as far as I can see," I said.

"And left this behind."

Sid showed me the bundle of several tan paper sticks, banded together with wires sprouting from one end.

I gulped. "That's dynamite."

"Or something close." Sid pulled a camera out and began taking pictures. "It was wired to Frank's car."

"Why Frank's car?"

Sid shrugged, then nodded. "It's the newer of the two and the one he's been driving Esther to work in." He looked more closely at the bomb. "This has Russian lettering on it."

"KGB?" I frowned. "I can see why they'd want to support an anti-nuke group, but why wouldn't they use their own personnel for a job like this?"

"They did, my darling." Sid yawned. "At least, I'm reasonably sure they did. That wiring was a professional job. Red Light is still in town, isn't he?"

"I'm pretty sure."

"I'll have Jesse develop these first thing this morning, then send Red Light straight to New York with it. Ray and Steve have lots of Company connections. Maybe we can get some information on it."

"And what do we do with it in the meantime?"

Sid grinned. "I think there's a dumpster around here worth blowing up."

We hid the dynamite under one closer to Mid-City, then called in a tip to the L.A. Police Department, since we'd crossed over into their jurisdiction.

The week was moving faster than I could blink. Wednesday, Angelique called and said I could pick up the report, although she suggested that I meet her over at Lydia's and Henry's so I could visit with Lydia.

I went over late that afternoon. Ange was on her way from Westwood, but that could take a while. Lydia was smiling and in good spirits, but not doing well.

"There isn't much I can do about it," she said. "There are no more treatments and what there is will only prolong the misery." She sighed.

"I'm so sorry, Lydia."

"I'm making the best of it." She smiled. "How are you doing, dear?"

"It's been good."

I told her about Stella moving out to Los Angeles and my sister's new baby, and Nick's sudden appetite. That last made her really laugh. Well, she had raised two boys.

Ange arrived and had the envelope. She said hello to Lydia just in time for Henry to take Lydia up to bed. We both left, and I held her on the sidewalk.

"You look miserable," I told her.

"It's not been a good week." Ange blinked. "It's mostly Lydia. She's in a lot of pain and not doing well. But then Tom and I had a fight last night."

"Oh, no! What happened?"

"We're trying to figure out if Tom should get his own place or not. Tom wants to give us a few months in my apartment before deciding. Moving costs so much, you know. The only problem is, we're not sure we're ready for living together. We haven't even had sex yet." Ange started crying. "And then he said the scariest thing in the world to me. He's not going anywhere! Even if it's too soon for us to be living together, it's way too soon for us to break up. He wants us to try counseling."

"Okay. I get that it's scary. But that's really a good thing, you know."

Ange swallowed. "You're right. I just don't know how to handle it."

I touched her arm. "You'll be fine. Really. You've got a lot going on. A new relationship, a new job, and Lydia. It's a lot to be dealing with. Counseling's a good idea."

"Yeah." Ange took a deep breath. "It is. Thanks."

"And call me when you need to talk."

"Of course. Talk to you in another hour or so, right?"

We both laughed. I hugged her, then went to my car.

I got dinner on the way home because there was no way I was going to get back to the house in time to eat with Sid and Nick. After I'd eaten, Frank called me on the car phone as I crawled my way down the 405 freeway. It was a good thing the traffic was so heavy.

"Lisa, didn't you used to target shoot or shoot some birds called skeet?"

"Skeet is a type of target shooting," I explained. "Using flying clay disks as the targets. Why?"

"I need to learn how to shoot."

"What?"

"Um. I can't talk about it. But it's important. Can we start tomorrow? I'll need a gun, too. A pistol, I think. Can we?"

"Why are you asking me?"

"Because you carry a gun. Esther saw it in your purse one time. And you talked about shooting this skeet stuff. So, I figure you know how. Can you teach me?"

"Frank, what is going on?" Okay, I sort of knew what was going on, but I had to make it sound good.

"I can't talk about it!" Frank sounded panicky.

"Okay. Well. I'll have to see if I can get a reservation at a shooting range. You want to start as early as tomorrow?"

"Great. Perfect."

"I'll call you later when I have something."

I was a little shell-shocked when I got home and told Sid, who shrugged.

"He's going to have to learn, anyway."

"Yeah, but what brought this on?"

Sid grinned. "His gun may have been replaced with a little note that he shouldn't have one until he knew what he was doing."

I rolled my eyes and went to call the indoor/outdoor public shooting range we sometimes used. There was an opening in the indoor range at ten a.m., so I booked it, then called Frank.

Sid and I looked at the report I'd gotten from Angelique, but there wasn't much in it. Stop Nukes Now was headed by Dr. John Levinsky, a medical doctor with a general practice up in Running Springs, California. There were some concerns that some members of his group were getting a little radical, but there was no sign that they were in any way violent. In fact, Levinsky was a pretty ardent pacifist and had publicly rebuked the guys who had been talking tough.

The next morning, I met Frank at the shooting range. He was nervous and his eyes opened wide when he saw the Smith and Wesson Model Thirteen revolver I'd brought for him.

"That's, um, a really big gun." He smiled weakly.

"Yep. But it will stop an awful lot, assuming you can handle it."

Frank looked away and sighed. "Speaking of, can you not tell Esther about this? She's a little worried I'm going to blow someone's head off."

"That can happen when you don't know what you're doing." I shut my eyes and opened them. It could also happen when you knew, but didn't have time to aim and needed to stop someone, which is how I'd killed my first person. I still have nightmares about it.

I went into an extended lecture on gun safety. It's possible that I shouldn't have brought the Model Thirteen. It's the gun issued to FBI agents and shadow agents working under the agency. I figured no one would really notice which gun it was, and that would be the gun Frank would get when his security clearance finally came in. There was a part of me that couldn't wait and another part that hoped it never would.

I showed him the proper hold and stance, then fired several rounds. Frank was impressed.

"I did a lot of shooting when I was a kid," I told him. "Now, remember, you need to brace yourself. This gun packs a wallop. And just aim for the target. Don't worry about getting it in the center."

Frank staggered with the first few shots, but eventually got the stance. His aim was horrible, though. We worked solidly for the hour we had our spaces, then I paid for another hour, as well.

"Frank, you've got to relax." I swallowed and steeled myself. "You're getting nervy and that will get you killed. This is a deadly weapon you're working with here."

He closed his eyes. "It's just scary, Lisa."

I suddenly realized he was seeing human bodies instead of the small red circle when he aimed, and the Lord knows, I understood how that felt.

"Frank, you want this for protection, right?" I asked softly.

"Yeah."

I closed my eyes. "You've got to be willing to use it, even against people. That's hard to do, I know. But you don't want to hesitate at the wrong time and get it taken from you."

His face grew grim. "Trust me, holding back is the one thing I won't do." He shook his head and looked at me. "I can do this."

I didn't want to tell him he'd have to.

July 19, 1986

S y and Stella brought Sid, Nick, and me to the church that Saturday morning. Frank's mother, who was staying at the duplex to take care of Frank's dogs, brought Esther and Frank. Kathy and Jesse just parked their car in the church lot and left it for the week, as did Carl and Erin MacArthur. It was time for camp, and it all started in the parking lot at church.

Sid was a little perturbed that we couldn't put on shoulder holsters, or even back waistband holsters. But the hugging starts early, and that's not just the goodbye hugs that Sy and Stella got. I'd barely gotten out of their car when several teen girls ran up and hugged me.

That didn't mean we weren't armed. We both had shin holsters and snub nose revolvers on us, under our jeans, and we were wearing our armored running shoes. Kathy and Jesse were likewise armed. All of us, including Nick, had on radio transmitters under our clothes with almost invisible earpieces stuck in our ears.

Still, even with the concern about Frank and Esther, Sid was in a good mood. I suppose the collective glee of over seventy teenagers about to spend a whole week away from their parents is infectious. [Not really. For me, it was the

blissful realization that I was not going to go without sex
for a full week. - SEH]

The parents carpool down to the slip in Long Beach
where the chartered boat waits to bring us to camp. Dan,
who is well aware of the ambivalence most teens feel toward their parents, had made sure that Nick was in a car
with one of the other parents. Sid and I were assigned
to Don Haslip's car, which was kind of interesting. His
wife, Pat, wasn't there, so I sat in the back with Haslip's
older daughter, Renee, and Esme Garcia, and Sid sat up
front with Don. The Haslips were another parish school
family. Renee had graduated from that school and was at
a girl's high school in Brentwood. Their son, Don, Jr., was
a couple years behind Nick, who would be in eighth grade
when school started that fall.

Generally, Sister Maria, Lety, and I try to keep Sid away
from the other parents. Not having been conventionally
raised, Sid is not your conventional parent, which doesn't
go over well with some of the well-meaning but rather
controlling parents one finds at a parish school. Don and
Pat were among the cool parents. Don was also on the
school's Board of Trustees, which made life a lot easier for
Sid and me.

So, the ride down to Long Beach was filled with gossip
about the big Casino Night fundraiser, which was not
only insanely popular, it was more profitable than just
about anything else the school had tried to raise money. Sid
had gotten moved to the Casino Night committee to fulfill
the required volunteer hours after he got bounced off the
newsletter. He'd been put in charge of alcohol sales. Don
had loved the way Sid had scored some significant deals on
some decent booze. Not only had Sid paid less than in years

before, people bought a lot more drinks because the liquor was better tasting.

Of course, there was a group of mothers trying to shut down the Casino Night because it was, gasp, gambling and drinking, gasp. I must give this latest crew some credit. They were trying to say the event wasn't profitable.

"They need to be audited then," Sid told Don. "I know the bar concession was profitable. I counted the drink tickets myself."

Renee and Esme nattered on between themselves and I mostly ignored it. Whatever their issues were, it was not unlikely that I'd be hearing about them later.

At the pier, it was more seeming chaos as carloads of teens and luggage were dropped off. Don pulled his car to the drop off area, then got out and opened the trunk to empty it. He grabbed my suitcase, pulled, then stopped.

"What the hell is in this bag?" he yelped. "Armor?"

"Close enough," I said, grabbing the bag and giving it a solid tug.

"I gave up packing light years ago," Sid said, pulling another couple suitcases from the trunk.

Okay, there were two high-powered rifles, night goggles, a couple more handguns, and plenty of ammo in my suitcase, under all my clothes.

Kathy and Jesse were already on the quay, but I couldn't see Frank and Esther. They pulled up in the car behind us. Almost without having to be told, the teens spilled into a line from the quay to the boat, and the suitcases and sleeping bags began moving along it. Yes, there were more than a few complaints about the weight of my suitcase, but it still got stowed on board the boat.

Don and several of the other parents hung around long enough to see us off. I made my way to the top deck of the boat and Sid followed. He insisted I put a hat on and rubbed sunscreen on the lower half of my face. I got to rub sunscreen on his face, as well. The wind was blowing hard enough that it made it worthwhile to put on windbreakers.

"Nick!" Sid called as the boy ran past. "Sunscreen!"

Nick didn't hear. Sid was about to go after him when I pulled Sid back.

"Let him learn the hard way," I said. "Dan is right. If we treat him like our kid, it will be harder for him to blend in."

Sid made a face, but let it go.

The trip took just over two hours. We watched dolphins jump in the boat's wake. A few sea birds dove and caught fish. Frank and Esther spent most of the trip up on the deck with us. A cheer went up when the island finally rose on the horizon.

Still, it seemed like it took forever for the boat to pull up to the wooden dock in the middle of the tiny bay in front of the camp.

"You gotta see this," I told Sid. I pointed over the side of the boat.

On the camp's beach, another large group of teens waited, many hugging each other, some sniffling, their suitcases and sleeping bags in a pile next to a crew of about twelve camp staffers lined up along a rope tied to the end of a small barge sitting on the edge of the beach. The second the boat had docked, the staffers pulled the rope as a team. Pulleys groaned on the dock and on the beach, and the empty barge slid through the water to a cut-out space on the wooden dock.

"I've gotta go," I told Sid, and ran down below and to the outside door of the boat. Kathy and I needed to be on the first barge trip onto the island. We got on the barge, along with about twelve other kids and Father John, our parish pastor and our retreat's spiritual director.

John and I have a special relationship. He's what they used to call my confessor. Basically, he helps me deal with the occasionally nastier parts of what I do as an operative. I have no idea if he knows that Kathy and Jesse are part of the side business, but I had told them it was okay to talk to him.

The camp staff pulled together, and the barge headed for shore. Once there, John looked a little puzzled when Kathy and I started up the hill into the camp. I waved at him that I'd explain later. As we made our way around the main hall, I looked at Kathy.

"Which side do you want? Boys or girls?" I asked.

"Boys, I guess."

The cabins were grouped on two sides of a little gully. It wasn't a foolproof way to keep the two genders separate, but then, with horny teens, there is no such thing. The vast majority of our kids were pretty good, though, and among those who weren't behaving, they were, at the very least, discreet about it. We hadn't had to send anybody home yet.

Kathy and I went through each cabin and used a flashlight to check underneath. They were all clear, so we hurried back down to the beach, where Sarah called out cabin assignments and teens collected their suitcases and sleeping bags while the camp staffers sent the outgoing teens and their luggage to the boat. There were two finished cabins with three rooms, each near the main hall. Sid and I got assigned to the end room of one, with Kathy and Jesse in the next room. When she saw that, Kathy shook her head and put Sid and me in the middle room.

"More of a noise barrier," she grumbled.

"We'll be keeping it down."

"Your idea of keeping it down registers on the Richter scale."

I sighed. She had a point.

Dan and Sarah, with baby Sandra, and Carl and Erin MacArthur were in the other cabin. Father John usually liked to bunk in with the teen boys. Frank and Jeff Childs, who was a new leader that year, were supervising another cabin. Sister Maria had a girls' cabin and Doreen Lonnergan (Frank's sister who was also serving as our nurse) supervised with Esther. The reason Esther and Frank had to share supervision, even though it was getting a little tight on that front, was that there was going to be a point where they were going to move to one of the finished cabins. Susie Talbot had re-joined us from wherever she'd landed up north, plus a couple other college kids who had been campers in previous years.

We started with mass in the main hall around four-thirty that afternoon. Frank played guitar and Sid played the aging piano. He already played organ for Frank's guitar choir on Sunday mornings. However, Sid had an ugly look on his face as he played that afternoon. The piano was not in tune.

Mass ran really long, so there wasn't much free time before dinner. I chatted with various kids while Sid went to get his tuning tools. He'd been warned about the piano.

Once the dinner bell rang, I went to my usual table. John and Frank were already there, and Tod Wilkins and Jeff Childs both hurried up. Tod had also graduated to leadership status that year, being a freshman at some college back east. Sid went to join us.

"You don't want to sit at that table," Esther told him. "You won't get any food."

Sid looked at her.

Susie laughed. "That's the scarfers' table. It's become a tradition."

"I don't understand," said Sid.

"It's been going for about three or four years now," Susie explained. "I think it was the year before Lisa did her first camp. Tod and Jeff were just regular campers then. But John, Frank, Tod, and Jeff landed at this one table that year and inhaled everything within reach. Lisa came the next year and almost bested them. Now, they always eat together. They tried to split up, but that upset everybody."

Sid sighed. "I am well aware of how fast and how much Lisa eats."

Esther laughed. "Good luck. And you're going to need it."

"We don't go for seconds until everyone has had firsts," I said. "Even at our table."

Which we didn't. That meant Sid got as much food as he was going to eat. He was rather appalled. [Appalled? No. That wasn't it. In shock, yes. I had seen you eat a lot and quickly. Yet I had never seen you chow down like that. But it wasn't just you. All five of you were like black holes. I had never seen so much food disappear so quickly in my life. I couldn't help but wonder if you'd even tasted anything you'd inhaled. And the fact that you guys were on thirds and fourths before most of the tables even took their seconds. It was mind-boggling, and oddly enough, I understood why the rest of the camp cheered you on. It was just that weird. - SEH]

There were seldom seconds on dessert, so by the time that came around, my table mates and I were relaxing over some awful coffee or punch. The camp was pretty strict about alcohol.

"Looks like you've got the best start on the beard growing contest," Tod Wilkins told Sid. Tod, being fair-haired, was at a distinct disadvantage that way.

Sid scratched his five o'clock shadow. "I'm not competing."

"You're not?" asked John. His hair is brown, with gray liberally sprinkled throughout. "Come on. You've got this one in the bag."

Sid shook his head. "I intensely dislike facial hair on myself."

Dan got on the microphone and started the usual announcements about not touching the fire extinguishers, not leaving food in the cabins, and remembering to keep the pig gates up.

"Pig gates?" Sid asked.

"To keep the wild pigs out of the cabins," Frank explained. "They're all over the island. They don't come around here that much, though, except at night."

Sid nodded and sighed. As soon as KP started, he left and got his shaving kit from our cabin and made his way to the sinks next to the guys' outhouses. Finished with shaving, he went back to the piano even though he had less than an hour. The sound of cheering rose from the beach. It was a tradition that the campers dumped each of the male leaders fully clothed into the ocean. I had a feeling they'd gotten their first victim, and sure enough, Frank Lonnergan squelched up from the beach a few minutes later.

"Well, it's better," Sid sighed about the piano as the bell rang to gather everyone to the main hall. As usual, the camp director talked about the camp rules, like not touching the fire extinguishers and keeping the pig gates up. Then the leadership was introduced. Dan introduced Sid, but Sid pointed out that he wasn't really a leader. He was just along for the ride. Then there was the usual chaos as everyone was split up into small groups. Maria and I had a group of about eight high school juniors. Nick landed in a group of freshmen led by Tod and Jeff.

At this point, Dan usually put on a pretty stupid "getting to know the leaders" game, but somehow Frank had helped him come up with a good one. Each of the different small groups was told to send up a representative. Nick's group sent up a young girl named Ming. The representatives were taken outside to wait while the four married couples were set up in chairs at the front of the room. There were eight cards with the different things all of us had done to make money in high school and four cards with how each couple had met. The goal of the game was to hand the right card to the right person or couple.

I felt for the kids. Not one of them got a perfect score. Most of them figured out that I had worked in a souvenir store, that Sid had waited tables at a fancy French restaurant, and that Sarah hadn't worked. But they couldn't figure out who had worked at McDonald's (Dan), who had delivered papers (Kathy), who had cleaned windows

(Carl), who had worked in the auto parts store (Erin), and who had babysat (Jesse).

The how we met was even worse. Since most of the kids knew that I'd started out working for Sid, we repeatedly got the card that read, "Met through an ad in the paper." They believed that Dan and Sarah had met at Bible Study. Jesse and Kathy got "Met in class," and Carl and Erin got "Picked her up in a bar."

Frank laughed like a hyena when the last camper bombed out.

"It's impossible!" Beth Ramsey groaned.

"You guys are forgetting to think logically," Frank said. "There is only one man here who was into picking women up in bars."

"Yeah, but…" someone said.

"But nothing," said Sid, taking that card. "That's how Lisa and I met. She'd ditched a date, then turned me down, and that's why I hired her."

Dan and Sarah claimed the ad in the paper.

"I got fed up dating girls who didn't want to get married," Dan explained. "So, I put an ad in a Christian paper looking for a woman interested in marriage and Sarah answered it."

Carl and Erin had met in calculus class in college, and Kathy and Jesse had met at the Single Adults Bible study at our church.

Dan gave the first talk. The theme for the week was The Journey to Faith, which I thought was a good one. Even if you believe, you can always grow in your faith. And I have to give Dan credit. It was a very touching story about how he had fallen away from the church, thanks to a less than happy family life, but had found peace when he had come to believe in Jesus.

The squirrely kids usually end up at the back of the hall for obvious reasons, which is why we always station a few extra leaders back there. Sid and I were among them that night. It was a good thing. Three boys, Tim Johnson, Tobias Muñoz, and Dean Hartinsky were more than squirrely. They were looking for trouble. You could tell their parents had sent them against their will. Dean had a pocketknife and kept pulling it out and carving things in the air while Tim and Tobias laughed softly. The other kids edged away from the three. Sid quietly stepped up behind them.

"Gentlemen," he said in the tone you do not argue with. "Will you three come with me, please?"

The boys crawled over the half wall and followed Sid outside. I slipped out too. There was a knife, and I did not want to take any chances. I stayed in the shadows, however.

"Let me guess," Sid told the boys. "You three are not here because you want to be."

"So?" Tim glared at him.

"Why not?" Sid asked.

The boys looked at each other.

"Whaddya mean?" Tobias asked.

"Why don't you want to be here?"

The boys looked at each other, confused. That was not the response they'd expected.

Dean recovered first. "'Cause this religion stuff is stupid." Okay, he did not say stuff.

"Yeah," said Tobias. "God is a bunch of B.S."

Sid nodded. "Well, you're certainly entitled to your own opinion."

"So, you gonna make us believe?" Tim stood up, growing still harder.

"Like you're gonna be able to," snorted Dean.

Sid smiled. "I can't make you believe anything you don't want to, and, frankly, I don't even want to try. If you don't want to believe in God, then you have every right not to. And they do respect that here."

Tim snorted a curse word.

"Of course, you have to earn that respect," Sid said. "It might help if you gave them the respect of hearing them out. If you still don't believe, respect the fact that they do and don't go around making life difficult for yourselves and everyone else."

"Yeah, right." Tobias added a couple extra curse words. "And how are we supposed to do that?"

"The same way I do."

"Huh?" All three boys gaped.

"I'm not an official leader because I am not a believer. But I respect their faith, and as a result, they respect my lack of faith. Get it?"

The boys looked confused but nodded.

"Let's get back." Sid nodded at the back of the hall. "Part of the respect thing."

I waited until all four of them were back in the hall before I slid out of the shadows.

The talk wound down around nine-thirty. There was a campfire until eleven, then it was lights out. Sid and I had the first bed check run. I kissed Nick goodnight. He approached Sid and hesitated for a moment, then said something softly to his father.

"If I thought it was that unmanly, do you think I'd do it?" Sid asked.

Nick thought. "No."

"Do you feel like you want to?"

"Yeah, but I don't want to look like a little kid."

"I can understand that." Sid smiled at him. "But ultimately, you're the one who's going to have to decide whether it's childish or not. I don't think so. I'm very proud of our relationship, and I don't mind expressing my affection for you."

Nick smiled. Then the man and almost man kissed each other's cheeks and squeezed each other. Sid looked up and saw me smiling at them.

"Want to join us?" he asked.

We held each other warmly, then pulled apart. I saw one of the boys about to tease Nick and gave him the stink eye.

A little bit later, Sid and I laughed as we really, really worked on keeping the noise level down. We would have succeeded, but the bed creaked. The laughter got worse as the bed in the room next to us began creaking.

July 20-22, 1986

S id was up at five, as usual, and had run a couple laps around the perimeter of the camp by the time the waterfront opened for pre-breakfast activities at six-thirty. I know because that's what he told me he'd been doing when I staggered down to the beach at that hour. Sid eased into the chilly surf and started doing laps around the small bay.

I had given up some extra sleep because Esther had said she wanted to go to the early morning prayer service that John was leading instead of mass that morning. It was Sunday, so we'd do that liturgy instead of the group game and seminar right before lunch. I'd do mass the next morning, and I had also promised to take Nick fishing at least one morning. But beyond that, I was hoping I'd get to sleep until the seven-thirty wake-up bell at least some mornings. I wasn't sure if I was grumpy or worried when Esther didn't show right away, but she did, along with two of the other teens.

Nick was up, also, followed by three girls and another boy whose name I didn't know yet. The five of them walked around the rocky edges of the water on the side of the little bay in front of the camp, their eyes fixed on the ground in front of them. Nick was probably looking for a tide pool or two. I couldn't tell if the others were equally interested or not. I decided it wasn't worth worrying about and re-focused my prayers on Esther and Frank and the retreat as a whole.

Sid climbed out of the water right as we finished our little service and went straight to the hose at the edge of the beach to rinse the saltwater off him. I wandered over to my favorite rock on the water's edge, climbed up, and just basked in the early morning sun for a few minutes. Soon the wake-up bell rang, and sleepy teens stumbled to the sinks to brush their teeth and to use the outhouses. From the main hall, I could hear Sid working again on that piano.

Even Nick, with his accelerated appetite, did not want to chance the scarfers' table. Adam Mencia, a hefty six-teen-year-old, decided to try the sixth spot. I had pity on him and made sure he got seconds, but that was as far as he got.

I got KP that morning and Sid joined me. Okay. It was actually called OTS, or Opportunity To Serve. Yeah, like the teens didn't see through that one. It was KP, and it was necessary. Wanting to serve had little to do with it.

At nine-thirty, the bell rang. The teens gathered. Dan passed out the study sheets for that morning's discussion, and they dispersed to reflect and write. I stayed in the main hall, doing my writing as I listened to Sid continue to wrestle with the piano.

"It's actually a pretty solid instrument," he told me a few minutes before the bell would ring for discussion time. "Given the environment here, it's survived a lot of torture. But there isn't a string out of whack and there's eighty-eight of them."

"*Are* eighty-eight of them."

"Oh, for cripe's sake, Lisa." [That was not what I said. - SEH]

I glowered at him briefly, then the bell rang, and Maria and I went to gather our eight teens.

We had our discussion, then we did Sunday mass, then lunch. Sid flashed me his really hot smile that means he's thinking about us making love, and we hurried out of the dining hall right after dessert and went to our room and actually didn't make much noise at all until we both collapsed onto the bed, feeling pretty satisfied.

It was free time for the afternoon. I found a shady spot and got out a book. Kathy and Esther crashed near me. Jesse followed Frank to the waterfront, where Frank got busy getting into splash fights. Both Jesse and Father John got tossed into the water. Nick went snorkeling with the same group I'd seen him with that morning. Sid went back to the piano.

The waterfront closes at five-thirty. Leaders report to the main hall at the same time for the daily leadership meeting. Sid slipped out and made his second shave while we leaders went over the next day and that evening's activity and talk. Sid came back, played with the piano for another several minutes, then pronounced the job done just as the dinner bell rang. He'd fiddle with the darned thing every so often over the rest of the week. [Well, yes. Given the damp environment and the length of time since that piano had last been tuned, it was inevitable it was going to go out of tune pretty quickly. - SEH]

That evening's presentation really surprised me. It made sense, though.

"If we are going to talk about the Journey to Faith," John announced. "Then we need to start with the journey away from faith. Many of you are here, Catholics in name only, believers because that's what your parents want you to be. Some of you may not even be believers." John looked right at Tim, Tobias, and Dean. The funny thing was, Sid and I had not told John about the night before. "Genuine faith comes when you question, when you seek out. So, let's start with a couple stories about people who lost theirs and one who never had it. Sid?"

I all but gaped. But Sid went to the front of the room and looked at the kids.

"This is pretty weird for me," he said. "As many of you know, I do not believe in God. But I do have a story that John thinks you need to hear, and I respect John. It's about a woman who, in the early nineteen-forties, wanted to escape a father who debased her, who beat her brother, who continually groped her younger sister, and who beat her mother. When that mother went to the priest to seek escape from this man who was hurting her children, the priest condemned her to hell for even thinking about it. When the woman went to the priest to challenge him and tell him the truth about what her father was doing, the priest condemned her to hell. To no surprise, the woman left the town where she lived, left the Catholic Church, and became a communist. Later, her younger sister went to a party and became pregnant out of wedlock. The woman took her sister in, and then took care of the baby that was eventually born and took full custody when her sister was killed two years later. That baby was me. My aunt taught me that there is no God, that religion is the opiate of the masses. As I grew up, I saw little that contradicted what my aunt had taught me. I eventually saw some terrible, terrible things. Some asshole told me that there are no atheists in war. I knew a bunch of guys who became atheists because they fought in the Vietnam War. How could a supposedly beneficent Supreme Being allow that terror to happen? They couldn't answer that, and neither could I. I still see the worst of what religion can do to people. Even recently, people hurt my wife and my son because they couldn't see past their own self-righteous B.S., and I do not take that lightly." Sid paused and took a deep breath. "At the same time, I've also come to see the best of what religion can do. This community has taken me in, accepted me as a friend, and most important of all, respects that I have no faith and am not likely to. There have been few direct attempts to convert me, which is good because I really hate it when people do that. I mean, think about it. How would you feel if I told you that you shouldn't believe in God? That I knew the real Truth, and you didn't? That's exactly how I feel when you say that to me. I started without faith. But I've known an awful lot of people who have turned away from it, and almost always with good reason. Still, faith is the glue that holds my wife together. Faith is what kept her from letting me blow it with her." Sid shrugged. "I have to be grateful for that much. Just don't ask me to believe in something that, as far as I can tell, is not there."

Okay. That one resulted in dead silence. I was not surprised that Sid didn't quite mention the reason he'd known all those guys turned atheist was because he, too, had fought in Vietnam. The war is something he almost never talks about.

"Thanks, Sid," John said, patting him on the shoulder. He turned to the kids. "You guys need to hear the other side if you are going to question effectively. You need to hear the other side to be compassionate. Now, we have a second story of moving away from faith, but this person found it again. Sister Maria, will you come up, please?"

Sid slid down the side of the hall and plopped down next to me.

"I'm amazed," I whispered.

"You made it possible," he said, and squeezed my shoulders. "John's right. They need to hear the other side. I think that's why too many of those self-righteous assholes don't get it. They don't really hear people like me."

I pulled him even closer to me as Maria began her tale. Sadly, she had been molested by an uncle and no one had believed her.

"So, if sex was all I was good for," she told us. "I stopped worrying about it and slept with everybody, and I was only fourteen. How I didn't get pregnant, I do not know. But I had some problems with a couple social diseases that my mother insisted I picked up from a toilet seat. We all know that doesn't happen in real life. As for God, what kind of God would let me be molested by an uncle I trusted? That my parents trusted? I went through the motions, but none of it mattered. And when I got out of high school, I got out of that house, got a job, and kept sleeping around. It took my second suicide attempt for me to recognize that things needed to change. I have been blessed because I ended up at a hospital with a good chaplain, who also happened to be a sister of the Carondelet order. Also, that she understood my story because she, too, had lived it. Some of you may have or be suffering the same things I did. I pray God not, but if you are, I will believe you and I will help you. The rest of you may be thinking, that's not me. How does this affect me? Because you need to know, no matter how dark the place where you end up, there is light to be found. That sister? She helped me get into college, get my degree, and helped me become a teacher. And I have been able to help other children who have suffered what I did. But most of all, Sister Elizabeth helped me find faith in a God that I thought had abandoned me, helped me realize that this same God still loved me and wanted me. Which is why I am now a Sister of St. Joseph of Carondelet. Sid was right. We cannot understand why God allows horrible things to happen. None of that makes sense. It doesn't have to. I don't believe that faith means tossing aside your intellect and ability to think. People who do are almost always the obnoxious, self-righteous ones, and I will tell you a secret. Those are the people who do not have real faith. That's why they're so easily threatened when you challenge what they think is right. But that does not mean we're going to understand the ways of God, either. Sometimes, you just go with it."

As the group cheered, Sid leaned over to me and whispered in my ear.

"Believe it or not, I did not know her before." Meaning before he gave up sleeping around.

I couldn't help laughing, which got a few weird looks.

The next morning, I went to mass on the beach, which is one of those really great experiences. We ate breakfast, did our worksheets, then had discussion. Then there was the group game and Dan got tossed into the water. Then we broke up into four different seminar talks, then lunch.

Right after lunch, I made a beeline to the little window next to the kitchen where the camp sold film, flashlights, batteries, candy, chips, and sodas. After checking that Sid was headed for our cabin, I plunked down some money and bought a grape soda and a Mars bar. It was Heaven. I wolfed down the candy bar and drank the soda so fast, I almost barfed.

During free time, Nick went snorkeling again. Two of the girls had dropped out, but Ming Channing, a cute girl with Asian features, and Armando Espinoza, stuck with him. Kathy stuck with Frank while Esther watched Sid and some others play volleyball. Jeff Childs and Carl MacArthur each got grabbed from the volleyball court and tossed into the ocean. The boys tried to get Sid, but he wriggled free. I was going to go swimming when Barb De-Marais came up. She was in my small group, about sixteen, and this was her third year at camp, so we knew each other fairly well.

"It's about last night," she sighed, shaking her blond curls. "Father John keeps talking about how, like, faith is more than going to church, and there was Sister Maria's story and the other ones. I just feel so lame. I've got it way easy. My parents like me. Mostly. I don't have to worry about food or seeing horrible things. I just keep worrying about stupid stuff, like what the other girls are saying about me, and are my clothes right, and do the boys like me?" She sniffed. "I mean, I do worry about the world. There's, like, that nuclear-armed satellite the government is trying to send up. I'm totally against that. I know I should be standing up against it and going to the protests, but I'm scared to go."

"There are protests going on?"

"Totally. It's this group called Stop Nukes Now. Remember Dave Atwell? He graduated two years ago and is at... UC Santa Cruz, I think. Anyway, he and my brother are still friends, and my brother said that he said I shouldn't go to the protests because that group has some real crazies in it. But how am I supposed to be doing what's right if, like, I'm too chicken, and it's not like I've got any real problems to worry about?"

I sighed. I'd always hated it when people had belittled my problems when I was a teenager. I looked over at Esther shaking her head as Susie Talbot missed a spike. Somebody had tried to kill one of my best friends, and I was about to make things worse by putting her in harm's way. Somehow, Barb's problems didn't seem all that important. Yet they were to her.

"Well," I said slowly. "What do you know about the group? Have you done any of your own research on them?"

"According to the newspaper articles I've read, Dr. Levinsky is, like, a total pacifist." She frowned. "But that doesn't mean some crazies can't be part of his group, right?"

"True. You don't know for certain those crazy people are there." I winced. Just because they'd put out the list Esther was on didn't mean they knew the KGB had tried to wire a bomb to Frank's car. "Making those kinds of assumptions can get you into trouble. Of course, you don't want to get into trouble because you assume they're safe and they're not."

"Like, I know."

"What do your parents say?"

Barb rolled her eyes. "I haven't told them. Dad does not like the whole protest thing. He was doing grad school at Kent State when that big shooting happened. I was just born. He said it was really scary."

"I bet it was."

"It's just I don't want to be one of those people who whine and gripe about the world and don't do anything. Or just worry about how their hair is fixed. I do worry about it because, you know, everyone around me does. But I want to be about real things."

I had to chuckle a little. "You obviously are, Barb. Maybe you haven't found your vocation or niche yet, and that's pretty crazy making. But you're not shallow, I can promise you that."

"What makes you so sure?"

"You're worried about being shallow." I smiled at her and touched her shoulder. "Shallow people aren't worried about that. Yes, you're worried about some shallow stuff, but that is the larger part of your life right now. The big difference is you know that there's more to think about. You'll figure it out. Maybe that's what you need to be praying about this week. Where is God calling you? Protests for good reasons with some potential crazies? Or maybe something equally deep and worthwhile. I can't tell you that part, but you'll find it. I know because you're looking for it, and that's miles ahead of a lot of kids your age."

Barb blinked. "Thank you, Lisa. I knew you'd know what to tell me."

"I'm glad you think so." I smiled and saw Esther again shaking her head as she watched the volleyball game.

I was about to go in the water when Sid came down to the waterfront from the volleyball court. He was wearing a t-shirt, his bathing suit, and flip-flops and still looked dressed up.

"How long have you been standing out here?" he asked.

"Just a few minutes."

Sid shook his head. "That's how you end up sunburned every year. Where's the sunscreen?"

I looked down at my towel. "Right here."

"Alright. Let me get it on your back."

There was a minor problem with Sid rubbing sunscreen on me. I suddenly didn't want to go swimming anymore.

Sid chuckled. "Later. I promise. Let's go swimming. In fact, there's a nice little private cove just beyond that big rock there."

"Sid." My breath caught. "We'd better not."

"Probably not. But I can get you good and worked up for after campfire. We'll just make sure the sleeping bags are on the floor to spare Kathy and Jesse."

"Oh." I swallowed back the excitement and thought about something serious. "I just heard that rumor again about some crazies being affiliated with that Stop Nukes Now group."

"Hm. We'll have to check in with Angelique when we get back home. Want to race to the cove?"

"You'll win."

"Hey, give me one. I can't beat you skiing. I can't beat you shooting."

"You're better at codes and picking locks than I am. And you kill me at racquetball."

Sid gave me a quick kiss, then I broke away and ran into the surf, while he yanked off his t-shirt. He beat me to the cove by a mile.

Later, right before I went to the leadership meeting, I saw Sid getting in his second shave of the day, and about five boys gathered around him, laughing and chatting with him.

Monday night was not as powerful, but filled with stories of coming to faith.

Tuesday, I went from lunch to the little window next to the kitchen and bought another Mars bar and grape soda as Dan Williams and a couple other teens watched.

"No snitching on me, guys," I said, opening the wrapper on the candy bar.

Dan pulled me aside. "Lisa, is it a good example for the kids to be sneaking around behind Sid's back like that?"

"He knows I'm doing it." I rolled my eyes. "Seriously, Dan. He can smell a candy bar on my breath from fifty paces."

"I most certainly can," said Sid, coming up out of nowhere. "And you got one yesterday, too." He winced. "Grape soda?"

"Come on, Sid." I glared at him. "One week out of the year. One week when I do not have to deal with you giving me grief about what goes into my mouth. One week! Is that too much to ask?"

"Oh, so the honeymoon and that trip in June don't count."

"Even you fell off the wagon in June."

"Yes, I did. For a full thirteen-course meal prepared by a master chef. This is cheap candy and artificially flavored sugar water."

Out of the corner of my eye, I saw Dan looking weird. I sighed.

"Here, Dan." I handed him the candy bar and soda. "Enjoy."

I stalked off to our cabin. Sid caught up with me.

"You capitulated awfully quickly."

I looked at him. "So, I'm in trouble for eating something I like and now I'm in trouble for giving it away like you wanted."

Sid winced. "No. I'm worried about you giving in to the expectations because we both know how miserable that makes you."

"Then why are you worried about what I'm eating?"

"It's not good for you." He sighed.

"It's one week. I never get candy."

"You do, too."

"But I don't eat the cheap stuff I like. Sometimes at Halloween. A little at Christmas. It's not going to kill me."

He sighed. "I suppose not. But can you understand that I do care about your health and well-being?"

"I understand. You just take it to extremes. Why can't I make my own decision about it? You might find that I'm a lot more open to staying healthy than you think."

"You can make your own decisions."

"Then why do you nag me?"

He winced. "I'm worried about you." He winced again as I glared at him. "Okay. I don't know."

"You sure? Could it be you're making up for depriving yourself by depriving me, too?"

Sid thought it over. "Possibly. Probably." He suddenly sighed. "You know, it's weird. I have been letting up on you for some time now. Then I went along with you on the honeymoon, and ate what was there, which was really good. Now that I'm having to watch it again, I'm kind of resenting it when you eat. I'm jealous, I guess."

"You want me to give up the scarfers' table?"

"Actually, I don't. But do you mind avoiding the candy bars?"

"How about one a day and I don't do the soda?"

"Can you do it when I'm not around? It's not like I want a candy bar that badly. But just seeing you eat is enough temptation."

I grinned. "Because you always give in."

"Not always, but..." His smile got really hot, and yeah, he was giving in and then some.

July 23, 1986

Wednesday at camp is one of my favorite parts of the week. The walk into Avalon, the main city on Catalina Island. The entire camp goes. Kathy, Jesse, Sid, Nick, and I were all wearing our transmitters. All of us except Nick were carrying small automatic pistols in our back waistbands and had made sure our t-shirts draped over them.

A couple members of the camp staff lead the hike up the steep hill and over the trail through the island scrub. It's not the easiest hike in the world, but it's not that bad, either. We haven't lost a kid yet, never mind all the complaining. I walk at the head of the group, partly because I'm more into hiking and can go fast enough to stay ahead of those few kids who are athletes, and, that year, partly because I was the front guard for Frank and Esther. Jesse took the rear guard.

Jesse and I are the best shots in our little group, which is why we ended up where we did. Sid and Kathy hung with Frank and Esther in the middle of the pack. Nick chose to walk with me, and Ming decided she could keep up as well.

There wasn't much chatter as we went up the hill. It is pretty steep. The march over the island is still hilly, but I kept a moderate pace and Ming walked with me for a bit.

"Nick told me you adopted him," she said, after Nick had fallen back a bit.

"I did."

"I'm adopted, too. My parents got me from an orphanage in China when I was a baby."

"Really."

"Nick is so nice."

"Yes, he is." Something in my gut froze.

I looked back at my son. He didn't seem particularly focused on Ming, and I realized that was a relief.

"It's kind of a bummer that he'll only be in eighth grade next year. I'm starting high school, you know."

"Oh."

"It's really neat talking to somebody who knows what it's like to be adopted."

I sighed. "I'll bet it is."

Ming fell back. I was tempted to give her the stink eye, but really didn't have a reason to. I couldn't fault her that she liked my son. And she had a point about the being adopted thing.

Once in Avalon, we all meet on one of the main piers off the boardwalk. Bag lunches are provided by the camp staff (which they bring around by boat), and Dan goes over the rules for the third time.

That day it was around eleven-thirty when everyone got to the pier. Dan warned them to be back at two, no exceptions. Then the kids were dismissed to enjoy some time on their own. The rest of us who are leaders dispersed as well. Sid had already invited John to have lunch with us at John's favorite restaurant in town and convinced Frank and Esther to join us. Kathy and Jesse already knew they were coming with us and why, but pretended to accept the invite as if it had been freshly offered.

Nick had his transmitter on, and I had to tune out his, Ming's, and Armando's chatter. It was mostly Ming's and Armando's chatter. Nick didn't really say much, which kind of surprised me. He talked up a storm at home.

Sid got us a table on the outside terrace of the diner facing the boardwalk. The nice thing about this place is that it had a bar. Not that any of us were heavy drinkers, but most of us liked a glass of wine or occasionally a cocktail. The problem was a good chunk of the rest of the retreat leadership, especially Dan Williams. He was militantly opposed to alcohol, which I finally understood, given what he'd told us that Saturday. Several of the other leaders were anti-booze, too.

So, those of us who liked a drink tended not to flaunt it. Which meant that there were several rum and colas and gin and tonics at our table, all in regular soda glasses, of course. As we perused the menu, I noticed Frank glancing at the street again and again. I tried to see what he was looking at but couldn't quite. John noticed, too.

"What's going on, Frank?" he asked as soon as we'd ordered our food.

"Nothing!" Frank gulped.

But he kept looking at something across the street. John shot me a glance, and I shrugged. I was taking the lead on the operation that day because it was my turn. We'd already set up some hand signals among the four of us who were on protection duty. It had been Nick's idea before we'd left, based on watching base coaches at the baseball games, and he and Jesse had put them together. I bit my thumbnail. We needed to know what Frank was looking at.

"Esther, you guys look so worried," Kathy said, picking up the ball first. She was good at that kind of subtle questioning.

Esther rolled her eyes. "I can't talk about it!"

"You mean, it's that list again?" Kathy asked.

"You weren't supposed to know about that," Frank yelped.

"Everybody knows about the list, Frank," I said. "And lots of people know Esther is on it."

Esther looked over at John, and I knew darned well he was one of them.

"Esther, we don't have to know what you're doing to be concerned about your welfare," John said quietly. "So, Frank, if you're worried about something, why don't you tell us?"

I thanked God. Apparently, John had figured out that Sid and I were at camp to help Frank and Esther. Well, besides being there anyway.

Frank sighed. "We're being watched. There's a guy across the street who keeps wandering by and stopping and looking at us. There he goes again."

"You mean the guy in the yellow Hawaiian shirt, dark slacks, and white straw hat?" Sid asked.

I heard a quiet groan in my ear, then a cough. Nick was not far away and had made the suspect.

"Yeah, that's him."

I was impressed. How Frank had picked the man out among the hundreds on the boardwalk, I had no idea, but he had.

The waitress brought our food.

"Well," said John. "Unless he does something more threatening, I propose we don't pay him any attention."

I smiled. "Kathy, why don't we take Esther with us after lunch and go get the flowers? The guys can do something else."

"Sounds good," Kathy said.

Esther nodded, but she didn't look convinced.

"Are you getting nervous about tonight?" I asked her.

"No." She smiled at Frank. "That's no big deal."

John chuckled. "You only think it isn't."

Sid and I couldn't help rolling our eyes. We had gotten married because I wanted the Sacrament, and neither of us had thought it would make that much of a difference. We'd made our commitment to each other the year before, had mingled our assets in a business partnership, started raising a kid, sharing a bathroom and then the bedroom. Funny, but being officially married had made a massive difference, largely in how much stronger our commitment felt.

We finished lunch soon after. I almost wished Frank could come with us, but I wanted to split the two up to see who, if either of them, would get followed. I got up and went to the bathroom.

"Big Red, Red Dawn," I whispered. "Make sure you stick with target two and don't let him avoid telling you if someone is tailing you. Tiny Red, you follow me and Red Sky and watch for tails."

Nick coughed again to signal that he'd heard. When I got back to the table, both Sid and Jesse glanced my way, and I knew they'd heard me as well. Esther was gone.

"Where'd she go?" I asked as I sat back down.

"Making a phone call," said Frank.

I frowned. I hadn't seen her. Kathy got up and went to the back of the restaurant, ostensibly to go to the bathroom as well. Suddenly, I heard sobbing.

"Esther! What's the matter?" Kathy's worried voice rang in my ear.

"I called work," she said through her sobs. "My boss. He was killed yesterday. Someone put a bomb in his car."

I really had to fight to keep my face neutral, as did the others. John, however, caught that something was going on. Actually, so did Frank, but he couldn't figure out what. Kathy brought Esther back to the table.

"What's wrong?" I gasped, getting up.

Esther blinked and sniffed. "One of my bosses was killed yesterday." She looked at Frank. "It was a car bomb."

"Who?" asked Frank.

"Gil Woltz."

John looked at her, worried. "Was he on that list that you're on?"

Esther nodded.

I could almost hear John cursing. We somehow finished lunch and Sid paid the bill. As Kathy and I gathered Esther to us so that we could run our errand, John looked at me, then Sid. I'm not sure how, but the priest got Sid pulled away from Jesse and Frank.

"Are you and Lisa involved in this?" John hissed at him through my earpiece.

Sid sighed. "What do you think?"

John cursed, which was a little unusual, but not unheard of.

"I've got a bunch of kids, not to mention leaders, that could be affected here."

"I get that," Sid growled. "Trust me, she's safer at camp with the kids around her than at home. We're on top of it. Okay?"

"No, it's not okay."

"John, just because you know what Lisa and I do does not mean you know how good we are at it. And we have help."

John growled. "And I think I know who."

"Do us a favor. Don't assume until you know. Look. I don't want anything happening to those kids either, and Lisa feels even more strongly about that than I do. Trust us. Okay?"

"You're not who I need to trust." John paused. "But thanks."

Kathy looked at me. She'd heard the same conversation.

"I told you he was safe to talk to," I hissed at her.

Kathy just sighed quietly. Esther, still understandably upset, didn't notice. The three of us headed to the florist Kathy had called the week before. As we left the board-walk, Nick's voice broke in.

"Suspect one is on Little Red and Red Sky."

I glanced back behind us. Sure enough, the man in the yellow Hawaiian shirt was behind us.

I turned away. "Big Red? Red Dawn?"

"Bupkes," said Sid's voice.

"Little Red." Nick's voice sounded a little more anxious. "Suspect one is dropping back. We have a second suspect approaching. Male Caucasian, wearing a white shirt and tan pants."

I saw who Nick had meant, but couldn't see Nick or his friends, who were still chattering in the background. I had no idea how Nick was hiding what he was telling us, but from the background chatter, neither Ming nor Armando seemed to have noticed.

I turned away again. "Stay on suspect two, and thanks, Tiny Red."

"I hate that name," he grumbled.

I couldn't help chuckling and heard Sid doing the same. Still, Nick's observations had been critical. The second suspect stayed fairly close to us while his colleague didn't appear again. I was thrilled that Esther didn't seem to notice that we were being followed. Then Nick muttered that the second suspect was backing off.

"Anyone replacing him?" I asked, looking in the window of a nearby shop.

"Negative."

I went back to walking with Esther and Kathy on the narrow sidewalk toward the florist.

The next couple minutes were possibly the most terrifying I had spent in some time. The thing is, to describe what happened doesn't sound in the least bit scary. A woman walked past us toward the boardwalk. The part that alerted me was that I was hard-pressed to say what she actually looked like. She wore sunglasses, a scarf around her hair, and a big, floppy hat. Her blouse was gauzy and full, and just barely covered her curves and the brightly colored bikini bottom underneath. Then there was the ring on her left hand. It was huge and spiked. Kathy had spotted her, too, and swallowed.

I, Esther, and Kathy walked in file to leave room for the woman to pass.

"Excuse me," the woman said with a smile.

She leaned in toward Esther, then Kathy stumbled, "accidentally" pushing the woman's arm away.

"I'm so sorry," said Kathy. "My shoe caught on the sidewalk. Are you alright?"

The woman smiled blankly. "Fine. Thanks."

She moved on. We got to the florist shop without further hindrance. As Esther looked out the window, I pulled Kathy back.

"Did you get stuck?" I asked.

I heard both Sid and Jesse cursing in my ear.

"No. I wasn't getting anywhere near that ring." Kathy swallowed. "I saw the needle pop out of it."

I swallowed. "I thought I did, too."

"Was it?" Kathy looked scared.

"KGB nerve agent? I'd say yes."

There was more subdued cursing from the guys. They also confirmed that no one had been following them.

Then a friend of ours from Washington, DC, "just happened" to stumble across Sid. That Lillian Ward was there was anything but a coincidence, still she and Sid made it look like one and chatted briefly before moving on.

Close to two o'clock, I looked at Kathy and we both nodded. We'd be on the first water taxis back to the camp and would do a search on the cabins to be sure nobody had tried something nasty, although the odds were against it. Which, after turning Esther over to the guys, is exactly what we did. Having some idea of what to look for did help. However, there wasn't the least sign of any foul play, let alone KGB dynamite, when we finished.

Kathy looked at me as we headed to the volleyball courts after our search.

"I gotta say, this year has not been very relaxing at all," she grumbled at me.

"I know." I sighed. "At least, Esther's okay."

Esther's and Frank's families had not met us in Avalon after all, and weren't due for another few hours. Sid pulled me back into our room and we shut off our transmitters, but he was not interested in fooling around.

"Lillian?" I asked.

He nodded. "Frank's clearance is through, and his and Esther's adoption is official."

"Goody." I sighed. "How do we start training here?"

"I think we can let it wait until we get back." Sid glanced at the room's window. "But it should make things a little easier otherwise."

"Sure, it will."

"Oh, and that device we found on Frank's car was definitely KGB."

"Goody, again."

There were a couple hours of the waterfront being open. Sid, Nick, and I took advantage and brought the biodegradable shampoo down with us and spent some time playing and washing each other's hair. The other boys groaned when they saw Sid was in the water, but finally found Tod Wilkins and got him dunked. It wasn't quite five-thirty when Sid, Nick, and I rinsed ourselves off with the freshwater hose. Sid went to do his second shave and chat with the guys. I'm not sure where Nick went. I got dressed for the leadership meeting.

John, however, cornered me just before it was supposed to begin.

"I talked to Sid this afternoon, but how bad is it?"

"Pretty much what Sid said." I smiled.

John's eyes opened wide. "What?"

"We were wired." I shrugged. "I heard what you said to him, and he's right. Esther's safer here. Look at this place,

John. How is anybody going to approach without one of us seeing him or her?"

John looked up the gully that led into the hills above us, then at the beach. "I guess not."

"John, I'm not going to take a chance on the kids getting hurt."

"That I believe." He looked around. "There are others helping?"

"I've told them you're safe to talk to. Whether or not they do, that's not my business." I sighed. "It wasn't our idea. Nobody is our idea. But it seems to work out rather well." I smiled weakly.

John shook his head. "I can't help worrying."

"Neither can I." I shrugged. "In the meantime, we do have to get Frank and Esther married."

John suddenly laughed. "That is my job."

Sid sauntered into the meeting shortly after it began. There were two significant issues for the leadership that evening, and the good news was, both were under control.

"The commitment ceremony is in place," Dan told us. "Adriana Pacheco will play the piano instead of Sid, so he can help get things ready for later."

"We've got the wedding part set," Kathy said as Sid joined us.

Frank laughed. "You will not believe who showed for that. Esther's father is here."

Frank's mother and his brother had already arrived on the water taxis just before the meeting. That Esther's father was on one of those taxis was saying something.

Esther smiled as Kathy and I gaped happily.

"He's okay with this?" I gasped.

"No." Esther shrugged. "But he loves me. So, what else is he going to do?"

"Be that as it may," said John. "We have one other issue to stay on top of. The reality is weddings lend themselves to a certain amount of off-color humor. That is not necessarily a bad thing, but we all know how easily that can get out of control, especially with kids who don't understand where the boundaries are. So, our job is to be on top of those boundaries." He looked at Sid and me. "And we have at least one couple here who has been pushing those boundaries in the afternoons."

"Just two," said Sid with an evil grin.

"Oh, come on," said Erin MacArthur with an equally evil grin. "Why can't you two do it at night like normal people?"

"But they do," groaned Jesse. "They haven't missed a night yet."

Sid laughed. "Your bed creaks, too, guys."

Kathy laughed as Jesse ducked his head.

"Come on," John groaned. "Neither I nor anyone else really needs to know this. We just need to stem the tide. So, can we all put a lid on off-color jokes? Please?"

Both Sid and Esther sighed loudly.

"It's going to be another boring wedding," Esther grumbled.

"For you, maybe." Sarah glared and grinned at her. "The rest of us will be relieved that we don't have to listen to you and Sid embarrassing us."

"There is no justice," sighed Sid.

Esther's and Frank's families joined us for dinner. Most of the teens didn't notice, but that can be the saving grace of teens. They are wonderfully self-absorbed.

As soon as KP was done, the bell rang for the evening session. John started us off explaining that this was a night of commitment.

"For some of you, it will be your first commitment to a belief system you thought you knew." John smiled at the group. "For others, it will be a call to a deeper commitment to the faith you have already claimed."

He explained that we leaders would be available to pray with individuals while everyone else also prayed and sang as a group. No one seemed to notice that Frank was not leading the singing. He'd left that chore to Jeff Childs, who was pretty competent on the guitar. Sid had already left to collect Frank's and Esther's belongings from the cabins where they'd been staying and move them to that third room in the cabin where we'd been staying. I had asked Sid to promise not to play any jokes with their belongings, and he did. I was a little suspicious of how easily he promised, but there was nothing I could do about it.

In the meantime, Esther and I prayed together over the teens that approached us, as did Frank and Jesse. As always, it was deeply moving, but I couldn't help sniffling worse than usual when I saw Nick approach John to pray with him. Then Tim Johnson came up to pray with Esther and me, and I almost broke down in sobs. Still, by eight-thirty, Sarah came up and took the rest of the kids in mine and Esther's line and I pulled Esther away to Kathy's room. Jesse followed with Frank, and we could hear them in Sid's and my room.

"I don't need help to get dressed," Esther grumbled.

"You're getting it anyway," said Kathy, turning on a portable fluorescent lamp.

"We'll just get your hair looking nice and do a little make-up," I said.

Esther glared amiably. "Only a little make-up. I want Frank to recognize me." She looked at the two of us. "I tell you, this is the only way to get married."

Kathy pulled Esther's dress off the hanger it had been on since we'd arrived on the island.

I laughed. "If only we could have told that to my mother."

Esther suddenly sniffed and blinked. Her family had gotten separated as they'd escaped from Vietnam shortly before the end of the war. Esther didn't know if her mother was even alive, let alone where she was.

I groaned. "I'm sorry, Esther. I shouldn't have said that."

"You can't help it." Esther took a deep breath. "Normally I don't mind. I mean, it's hard, but I can't change what happened."

"At least your father's here," Kathy said. "It's not going to compensate for missing your mother. But it's something."

"It's a lot," Esther sighed. "He still hates Frank. But too bad."

I got out a backless sundress that I'd planned on wearing and pulled it over my head and shoulders. As Kathy zipped Esther into her dress, Esther turned on me.

"Wait a minute." Esther grinned. "How are you going to wear that with a bra?"

I sighed. "I'm taking my bra off."

"And...?"

I pulled the bra off and let Kathy and Esther see the nice, even tan I had over my breasts.

"We do have a private sun deck, you know," I grumbled.

Kathy laughed as she got into her dress.

Hoots of laughter from the next room barely covered the giggles in ours as we focused on getting Esther's hair and makeup done. Kathy looked out the room door, then signaled that it was safe to leave. We brought Esther around to the back of the hall. The guys hovered in the doorway near the front. John was getting into his vestments for mass, as was Frank's brother James, who is also a priest.

"As I told you earlier," John told the rest of the group. "Tonight is a night of commitment. Which is why we have some special guests here tonight." He gently moved some of the kids back from the table we used as an altar. "Frank and Esther's families have come to join us to celebrate yet another special commitment, that of the Sacrament of Matrimony." The kids broke into cheering. "Yes, Frank and Esther are getting married, and they chose to share that with us because this is the community that means the most to them."

He nodded at Jeff and Adriana Pacheco. The two played a simple hymn, and Kathy and I brought Esther to the front of the hall as Sid and Jesse brought Frank to meet her. Nick did the first reading, and Doreen Lonnergan led the psalm. John read the gospel, then grinned as he looked at Frank and Esther.

"I don't have a lot to say to the two of you. We've been talking quite a bit lately." John looked over at the campers and family gathered. "But I'd better say something for the rest of us. This marriage may seem like a surprise, but it's hardly that. Frank and Esther have been working on it for some time now. They may not be the romantic type. But they are committed to each other. It's important to understand that just because we haven't seen the work they've been doing, doesn't mean that work hasn't been going on. I've talked before about making judgments about others when we do not know the facts. This is a prime example of that. Here are two people, committed to building a life-giving relationship under our very noses, and no one knew. But now that we do, our job starts. We are here as a community to pray for and support Frank and Esther. As for the two of you..." John's grin grew mischievous. "Time to make good on what you've told me." He looked at James. "Would you like to do the honors?"

James shook his head. "I don't think Frank trusts me. I spent too many years beating the crap out of that weenie."

"James!" Mrs. Lonnergan started out of the chair where she'd been sitting.

"Okay, Mom." James laughed and took the rituals book from John.

As Frank and Esther made their vows, Sid and I couldn't help watching each other. It hadn't been all that long since we'd reaffirmed ours at our wedding. Mass went on quickly, in spite of a marathon Sign of Peace. Everyone had to hug Frank and Esther. At the end, both John and James gave the final blessing. Then, for the first time anybody could tell, we saw Frank and Esther kiss each other. The cheers went through the roof.

We adjourned to the dining hall from there. The camp staff had made a wedding cake and put out punch. Sid didn't make it terribly obvious, but he had some Champagne in a Thermos to pour into the glasses that Mrs. Lonnergan had brought from her own wedding.

"Frank," Sid began casually after pouring some wine into the glasses. "I owe you one. Actually, I owe you several ones. My good friend, you have pulled many a dirty trick on me. Like the time you converted the girl I was hitting on right out from under my arm. Then there was the grass clippings on my bed. The way you changed all the covers on my sheet music. Or the time you blew air bubbles into the waterbed. Yeah, I've gotten you back for some of those. But then there was fooling my aunt into playing a Billy Joel tune with a mildly salacious title for communion meditation at my wedding just because it also happened to be Beethoven. Or that amusing little message you painted on the bottoms of my shoes that same day."

"I didn't do that!" Frank yelped with a laugh.

"Uh-huh." Sid shook his head. "And I'm not even talking about that big bet you rigged on me last fall. But I am feeling generous right now. As of tonight, I am counting everything as paid up."

"That's very gracious of you, Sid." Frank may have been grinning, but he did not trust Sid for one second.

Nor should he have. It is not like Sid to give up his revenge.

Sid raised his cup. "To Frank and Esther. May their lives be truly happy."

Everyone drank.

"Oh, that is good!" Frank sighed.

"I know." Sid grinned. "Here. Let me top you off."

As he reached over to refill Frank's glass, he knocked Esther's into her lap. Several of us jumped up to mop up the mess. However, in all the confusion, I was fairly sure I saw Sid palm something into a paper napkin.

I didn't get a chance to ask Sid about it, though. The gaiety accelerated. Many of the usual traditions, such as the cake cutting, the bouquet and garter toss, were foregone in favor of general eating and laughing. It was past ten o'clock when everyone trooped down to the beach and the waiting water taxi to say good night to Frank and Esther's families. Then the campfire was lit, and the kids shared about their experiences during the commitment ceremony and the wedding. Finally, we all followed Frank and Esther to the third room in our cabin.

Dan called lights out and he and Sarah took over the bed check run. Inside our room, I couldn't help kissing Sid and enjoying him kissing me. I went to unbutton his shirt, but he caught my hands.

"I wouldn't do that just yet," he whispered, mischief glinting in his eyes.

I couldn't help glaring. "What did you do to Frank and Esther?"

"Hackbirn!" Frank hollered from the room next to us.

"Nothing serious." Sid grinned.

"Hackbirn! This isn't funny!" Frank may have added several expletives.

"Sid." I left our room to the wood terrace that ran the length of the cabin.

Kathy and Jesse were already out of their room, and Frank was outside ours, getting ready to pound on our door.

Sid followed me. "Problem, Frank?"

Several of the kids had heard the hollering and wandered down from their cabins. Dan and Sarah were on the terrace of their cabin, with Carl and Erin close behind. Frank let out a few more obscenities.

"What's going on here?" Dan yelled.

"He Crazy-Glued my pants shut!" Frank screamed, pointing at Sid.

Okay. Even Dan had trouble not laughing. We all knew it had to have happened when Sid had knocked the Champagne into Esther's lap.

"Has anyone got any nail polish remover?" I asked, swallowing back my giggles.

Maria was still laughing but nodded. "One of the girls must."

"How is that going to help?" Sarah asked, trying to soothe baby Sandra, who was screaming.

"It's acetone," I said. "It's the one thing that dissolves Crazy Glue."

Sure enough, there were several girls with nail polish remover. Maria got a bottle and some cotton balls and surrendered them to Esther, who had also called Sid any number of foul names in two languages. Peace eventually settled on the camp again. Until the bed started creaking in Kathy and Jesse's room. Another started creaking in Frank and Esther's. At that point, Sid and I let our bed creak, too.

July 24 – 25, 1986

F ive-thirty the next morning came a lot faster than I'd wanted it to. I had promised Nick and a couple of the girls that I'd take them fishing before the wake-up bell that morning. Sid, of course, was in his bathing suit, a t-shirt, and running shoes as I sleepily pulled myself out of bed.

"We should stay wired as much as possible today," Sid told me, getting his towel from the rack next to the window.

I sighed. "Yep. Have you told Nick?"

"Last night when we went to bed. I'll have to get mine on after I swim this morning."

"Okay." I got on my shorts and t-shirt, took my Model Thirteen out of my daypack and put it into my suitcase, then got out a pair of binoculars. "I'll see if we can get far enough out that I can check out the next cove or two."

"Good idea."

Vanessa Ayala and Marti Carranza met me and Nick on the beach. I'd reserved one of the rowboats, and it and all the tackle were waiting for us on the beach, with a second boat and tackle nearby. Carl, Eddie Valentino, and Phil Meeker came up to claim the second boat.

"Hey, Nick," Eddie called. "You sure you don't want to come with us? Like, what are the odds you'll catch anything in a boat full of women?"

"Better than trying to catch something with you doofuses," Nick called back amiably.

I smiled warmly at my boy. Vanessa, a senior who'd gone fishing with me before, offered to shove us off. I accepted, glad that Nick and I could get into the boat without worrying about messing up our transmitters. I did the rowing, and I pulled us just far enough out that I could see into the next cove. Supposedly scanning the surface for fish, I aimed the binoculars at the other cove's shore, but didn't see anything.

Nick helped Marti, a sophomore who had never fished before, bait her hook. Then Vanessa, a tall, slender young woman with thick, black hair, showed the petite brunette how to cast. The hook had barely sunk when the pole almost jerked out of Marti's hands.

"You got one!" Nick gasped as he helped Marti reel the fish in.

It was a decent-sized bass. I got the net underneath it, then had Marti hold up the line with the fish dangling from it.

"Hey, guys!" I called across the water. "Look what Marti reeled in. You got anything yet?"

They hadn't. Nick reeled in the next fish, then Vanessa hooked and got a massive bass. I caught a couple, myself, but spent most of my time enjoying watching the kids and scanning the cove and water for anything suspicious. Carl and the other boys rowed back to shore well before the wake-up bell was due.

We caught up with them on the way to the dining hall. Nick held up our collective catch.

"Guess what we're having for lunch." Nick grinned. "How about you?"

Eddie just shot Nick an evil look.

"We didn't get anything," Phil sighed.

"We'll share," Vanessa said.

The four of us went to clean our catch and Nick showed Vanessa and Marti which fish innards were intestines and which were the hearts and other organs. Marti was grossed out, but Vanessa was impressed.

"I took biology last year and didn't remember all that," she told me.

"He's a smart kid," I said, smiling. "I'm so proud of him."

Vanessa suddenly sniffed. "He's lucky to have a parent like you. I'm never good enough for my mom."

"That must feel really bad."

Vanessa shrugged. "I know she loves me. I just don't think she likes me very much. Guess I'm a little too radical for her."

I let her continue on, not knowing how much of her pain was the usual teen-age conflict and how much of it was a mother who really did not like her daughter. Then the breakfast bell rang, and we had to go inside.

I did get a moment with Esther before grace.

"How are you doing this morning?"

She smiled. "Okay. My boss dying. That still gets me. But it's nice being married to Frank." She sighed. "It's weird being so happy and so sad at the same time."

"Know that one." I looked around. "Is Frank still mad at Sid?"

"It's worse." Esther shuddered. "He thinks it's funny now."

"Oh, no! Think we can keep them from an all-out war?"

Esther made a face. "I sure hope so."

Then we were called to join the group.

After small group discussion, we have a group game, and Thursday, we did the people pass. We all line up in two lines facing each other and shoulder to shoulder, then one person at the end of the line gets lifted above the two lines and, with everyone helping, gets passed along the lines to the other end. Sid was one of the last to be passed, and when he got to the end of the line, the guys saw their chance and started running with him to the ocean. At the last second, Sid wriggled free and remained dry.

"Maybe you should just let them do it," I whispered to him.

"Can't. Got to stay wired."

Now, on most days, the second session of the morning is when we do seminars, usually four smaller talks on specific topics. There is one seminar that is so popular that everyone wants to go to it. I credit the topic. It's also the one I give, "Sex and the Problem of Temptation." When everyone wanted to hear the talk my first year at camp, our former youth minister gave up and just had me do it for everyone, and it's been that way ever since.

This year was going to be really weird, though. You see, Sid's infamous former lifestyle figured prominently in the talk. He knew about that, in fact, had cheerfully offered himself up as a bad example the first year I did it. That he'd given up sleeping around made the talk the previous year. This year, he was there.

He sat on the side of the room, smiling softly. I looked over at him. He just chuckled and nodded.

I took a deep breath. "Okay. The reason I got the talk on sex three years ago was that, at the time, I was working for a man who was randier than a British Royal. Sid, as most of you know, was and even now still is, a firm believer in free love. That sex is a really good thing and natural, healthy and to be indulged in as often as possible. Even back then, I said that Sid wasn't wrong. Sex is a good thing. But for me, and for most of us here, sex is also something sacred, a special, joyful way of connecting to a life-time partner. It's how life begins. It's important to understand that. I've said this every time, and I'm saying it again. This talk is not about judging Sid because he slept around. It's about how we deal with the temptation to have sex when we shouldn't. Sid was the first real threat to my honor I have ever known. He was and is incredibly sexy and hot. And then I started falling in love with him and that did not make things any easier."

The rest of the talk focused on staying out of trouble, which had not been easy back when Sid was still sleeping around. It was a lot of not getting yourself into a situation where it was easier to give in. That much, I had a lot of experience with. As I pointed out, Sid is and was a really sexy man.

I finished by pointing out that the best reason not to have sex too early was that the kids deserved the commitment. Sid, naturally, had to affirm that committed sex was the best there is, which drew a chorus of cheers and a few knowing grins. I flushed. Well, Sid and I are pretty oversexed. I looked over at Nick, expecting him to be trying to get under the floorboards and away, but he just rolled his eyes in adolescent disgust, then grinned at us.

Lunch was fun, even though Sid sat at another table than mine. We kept grinning at each other as I kept up with the other scarfers. Sid waited until dessert, when there weren't any seconds available, to rub the back of his neck. It was the signal that he wanted to be kissing the back of my neck, which was one of those things that really got me excited. I flushed, shifted, then rubbed the inside of my wrist. The way he caught his breath was very gratifying. John sighed, Frank chuckled, and Jeff and Tod both gasped.

"I'll be at the waterfront when it opens, or not much later than that," I said.

"Too bad," said Frank with an evil glint.

John just rolled his eyes. "You know, I have told both of you that I do not care, nor do I really want to know what you are doing. I really don't!"

Frank and I left the dining hall together. He was about to head for the beach when he stopped.

"You okay, Frank?" I asked.

He winced, then looked at me. "There's a boat out there that shouldn't be."

"Where?" asked Sid's voice in my ear.

We were still wired. Kathy and Jesse had also heard us. I could see them on the terrace of the main hall, scanning the small bay below. I didn't know where Nick was, but I knew he'd heard, too.

"Which one?" I asked. There were several boats passing through, plus the ones that were part of the camp.

"That one." Frank pointed. "Just a ways beyond the dock float. It's anchored. The others are either tied up or moving."

He was right.

"Frank, that doesn't mean anything," I said. "Lots of boats anchor here. It's a nice cove."

"Yeah. Right."

I glared at him. "And what are you going to do about it?"

Frank sighed. "Probably nothing. But I'm not going to let anybody hurt Esther. I swear I won't."

Sid's curse rang in my ear. I looked around but couldn't see him.

"Frank, don't be stupid," I said. "You don't know what's going on with that boat. Yeah, I know things are scary for you and Esther right now, but you don't want to make a major mistake."

Frank huffed, though he didn't argue. I hurried to Sid's and my room as I listened to Sid tell Kathy and Jesse to keep an eye on Frank and Nick to keep an eye on Esther, and that we were going to tune out for a few.

"We can wait," I told him as I shut the door to the room.

Sid's hot little grin popped out. "Yeah. But I have just spent past the couple hours thinking about the best sex I have ever had in my life. Do you still want to wait?"

I couldn't help laughing. Yeah, we had to keep a lid on the noise, but Sid was in a mood, and come to think of it, so was I. Afterward, I ran to the outhouse to clean up a little, then came back to the room.

Nick was there. Apparently, the transmitters were still off so that they could have their debate in peace. My arrival did not help.

"Dad, nobody is going to notice a kid."

"What's going on?" I asked.

"Our son," Sid said with great resignation. "He wants to go snorkeling out by that boat that Frank spotted and see if he can find anything out."

I shut my eyes and groaned. "There's only one problem, Sid."

"What?"

"He might be able to find something out and the risk level is relatively low. He's right. There are kids all over the place here. Why would anybody on that boat notice one who accidentally got too close to them?"

Sid shook his head. "He'll be in the water. He won't be able to wear a transmitter."

"Dad, you were going to let me go swimming without a transmitter, anyway."

Sid looked at me. I made a face and shrugged. The last thing Sid wanted to do was put our son or any other kid at risk. Neither did I. But with Nick, we knew we didn't always have that option.

"Alright. But you wait to go in until your mom and I are on the beach. Okay?"

"Okay." Nick ran off.

Sid looked after him with a sour look on his face, then switched on his transmitter and called Kathy and Jesse to the room.

"Your turn for lead," I told him, and he nodded.

To Breanna, 1/3/01

Topic of the Day: My first kiss

Okay, this is a fun one. It was kinda scary, too, as it turned out. It was the first time Mom and Dad let me run an operation on my own. I was thirteen, and it was the summer right before I went into eighth grade. Someone was trying to attack some friends of ours, and the three of us had to protect those friends without letting them know we were.

So, we went to that church camp I went to a couple times. I was the only eighth grader there, but it was lots of fun being with all the high school kids. Most of them didn't even realize I wasn't going into high school yet, and a couple thought I had to be a sophomore because I knew so much stuff.

Anyway, this boat had anchored in the small bay in front of the camp, and the way things had been going, we figured it needed checking out. So, since I'd been snorkeling all over that bay that week, I talked Mom and Dad into letting me snorkel out near the boat and see if I could find anything out.

There was this really cute girl, Ming Channing, who had been hanging out with me that week. She was a freshman, real small, with long black hair. She'd been adopted, too, only as an infant from China, and her parents were Anglo. So, I go down to the beach, get my mask, snorkel, and fins on, and start swimming out in the general direction of the camp's little dock, and beyond that, to the boat. I didn't know that Ming was behind me with her snorkel, mask, and fins. Hell, my parents were on the beach watching, and they didn't spot Ming until it was too late. Wait. Mom was on one of the hillsides, watching from there.

So, I started floating around the boat, with my ears just above the water, and I hear a woman's voice coming from a radio. I couldn't tell what she was saying, but a man on the boat said that they were going onshore that night after the camp was asleep. Another man said something else, but I couldn't hear what it was.

"Hey, Nick," Ming called as she swam up.

"What are you kids doing here?" A man appeared on the deck, and he was really angry. I'd also seen him the day before, tailing our friend.

"We're just snorkeling," I said. Ming was treading water and looked terrified because the guy was damned scary.

"Get out of here!"

I heard that ominous click of a shell being chambered.

I got a hold of Ming's arm. "Okay."

I pulled her from the boat and started her swimming for shore. Once we got past the dock, Ming started crying.

"We weren't doing anything. Why was he so mean?"

"I don't know. Uh-oh. My dad's calling me in. Come on."

Dad wanted to know if I'd found anything out and if Ming was okay. So, I told him what had happened. He told me he was proud of me, then handed me the sunscreen and told me to get some more on. I told Ming it was about the sunscreen when she asked if I was in trouble. I helped rub some on her back. She rubbed some on mine. I was surprised how fun that was. Then we went back toward the cabins, and behind the one where my parents were staying, Ming kissed me.

It was nice. The problem was that was all she wanted to do after that, and she got mad when I told her I wanted to do other stuff, too, which I did. The other problem was that I couldn't tell her that I had to keep my transmitter on when I wasn't in the water, and I did not want my parents to hear us.

From my hillside perch, I saw and heard Sid send Nick on his way. Then Sid called Jesse and me in. Kathy came up from the volleyball court where she and Esther had been watching Frank play. The four of us got some chairs from our rooms and sat on the terrace, where we could watch the waterfront. Nick and Ming had disappeared, which had me mildly concerned.

Kathy looked pained. "They're coming in tonight, huh?"

"We've got at least two of them," Sid said, gazing out toward the volleyball court. "Here's the plan for later."

The plan was pretty simple. Shortly after lights out was called, Jesse and I got into our black clothes, put on the night goggles and took up our positions on the two slopes on either side of the bay. Jesse was turning into a pretty decent sniper. We'd told Nick he could turn off his transmitter and didn't hear any chatter from his cabin mates, so we figured he had.

Sid and Kathy had night goggles around their necks and night vision binoculars. They sat outside the cabin, waiting. Jesse and I each had a high-powered rifle with a silencer. The silencers wouldn't actually silence the shots, but they would make them quieter and, I could hope, less likely to wake someone in the camp.

The crew from the boat waited until after one a.m. to push off the boat in a small rubber dinghy. As I looked through the night vision site on my rifle, I saw something.

"Hold fire, Red Dawn," I whispered into my transmitter. "Big Red, suspects are using night goggles and what looks like AK-forty-sevens."

"I have eyes on them," said Sid's voice very softly. "You may be right about those guns. Let them get to shore before firing. Maybe they'll drop something before you scare them off."

If we scared them off. I was praying we would. I was not looking forward to having to make someone a corpse, let alone moving said corpse from the camp. Assuming we could do all that and not wake anyone.

The two men slid onto the beach quietly. I wasn't sure what they thought they were going to do, although if they had night vision binoculars and goggles, they could have seen Frank and Esther go into their cabin room earlier. One pulled the automatic rifle off his shoulder and got it into his hands. I shot two rounds at his feet. Jesse let off another round and the man's partner crumpled. I heard Jesse cursing.

Fortunately, the first man dropped his gun and ran to get his partner. The second man didn't quite get up, but was still moving. The first man got him on his feet and the two headed toward the dinghy. I let off another round. The dinghy headed for the boat.

"What's going on?" someone called from the boys' side of the camp.

"I heard gunshots."

Jesse and I froze in position.

"Those weren't gunshots. Probably someone shooting firecrackers off their boat."

"Boys," Dan called grumpily. "Go back to sleep!"

The boat suddenly started up and roared away toward Avalon.

"What are you two doing out here?" Dan's voice hissed in my ear.

"Just getting some air," said Sid.

"Did you hear anything just now?"

"Firecrackers, I think," said Kathy. "Must have come from that boat that's getting out of here. I thought I saw something flashing out that way just now."

I wasn't sure, but I thought I saw Dan go back to the other cabin.

"Clear," Sid's voice muttered.

I hurried down to the beach, got the gun I'd seen dropped and swept the sand clear of tracks. Sid was not happy when we examined the gun the next morning. It wasn't specifically an AK-47. It was another version of the Russian automatic rifle and one frequently used by the KGB.

The good news, the boat was gone and none of us saw anything that might be a threat to Esther and Frank the next day. Nick seemed to be dodging Ming a lot, too.

"I wonder what's going on with that?" I grumbled just after lunch.

"What?" Sid asked.

"Nick and Ming. One minute they're together, the next he's taking off." I frowned. "She'd better not be playing games with him."

Sid laughed. "Lisa, my dearest, you are your father's daughter."

"What's that supposed to mean?"

"You know how protective your daddy is of you. And now, you're trying to protect Nick."

I just snorted. Sid went to join the other leaders who were playing in the staff versus leaders volleyball game. Our team of leaders killed the staff, never mind that they had a couple college-level players. We had a couple athletes on our side, plus Sid, whose serve scared even the college players. And I got my shoulders sunburned while watching the game. Sid just sighed.

July 26 – 27, 1986

The last day of camp is bittersweet. The campers are usually ready to go home, no matter how much they protest otherwise. Most of them have been touched by the experience. A couple, at least, have turned their lives around. I have always been ready to go home.

That year, if I could have stayed the rest of the summer and kept Esther there, I would have. Esther, for her part, really wanted to get back to work, although I didn't know exactly why. Saturday morning was devoted to cleaning up, packing, then final discussions and sharing, then the big group photo. Somewhere in there, I was on the veranda of the main hall and Sid was walking along in front, when five of the senior boys snuck up on him.

"Hey, Sid!" one called.

Sid turned and got five buckets of sea water in his face.

"We couldn't get you into the ocean, so we brought the ocean to you!" another boy called.

"Touché," Sid said calmly.

I was laughing, as was pretty much everyone else.

"Sweetheart?" Sid looked up at me. "Do we have a plastic bag?"

"Yes, darling. Let's get you into some dry clothes."

I was still giggling when we got into our room. "Is your transmitter still working?"

"I think so. Turn yours off." Sid unbuttoned his sport shirt. "What a mess."

"Well, maybe you should have let them dunk you early on," I said.

"Still broadcasting," said Jesse's voice in our ears.

Sid got redressed in a new sport shirt and jeans.

Soon, we were the group gathered on the beach watching the camp staff pull the barge in and out to the charter boat. A new camp came in, filled with teens nervously giggling, a couple looking for trouble, and leaders carefully checking lists. Our camp got on the boat, kids singing, many of them arm in arm. Sid made sure he kept his arm around my waist and not my burned shoulders. Well, it wouldn't be camp if I didn't get a sunburn.

Back in Long Beach, Sarah Williams was everywhere, checking lists and re-checking them, terrified that a camper would get left behind. But she got us all into the various cars the parents were driving. At the church, other parents had barbecues set up, meats grilling, and plenty of salads and other tasty things. Sid made a couple of phone calls from the church office. Frank and Esther's place was clear, and the recon van was in place with the local Yellow line hub team.

"The only problem is the van has to be back in the FBI parking lot before Monday morning," Sid told me as we ate and waited for Sy and Stella to come pick us up.

"Why?"

"As Lillian put it, we don't have unlimited resources. Looks like we get to worry about budgets, too." Sid rolled his eyes.

"At least we get a little downtime. So, when are we going to spring it on them?"

"Haven't thought that far ahead, and we do have to consider Sy and Stella."

Both Sy and Stella arrived shortly after and hung around long enough to get something to eat, but then bundled Nick, Sid, and me into the car Stella had bought that week. She'd picked out a steel blue Honda Civic sedan that was only a couple years old. At least, it had four doors.

"You're really settling in," Sid said as she drove us to our house.

"Oh, yes. I even have a couple students set to start in September. Now, how much longer before you have your master's degree?"

Stella had been pleased to find that Sid was working on a master's degree in music at a small arts college in the area. The program was for working adults, which helped, because Sid had a little problem with attendance, thanks to our side business.

Sid sighed. "I have no idea. I was lucky I was able to pass the course I took last semester, what with the honeymoon and all."

"You might just consider focusing on your degree for a year or two. I'm sure you could afford it."

"Why do you care?" Sid suddenly shook his head. "You're not assuming I'm going to just jump in and start teaching with you, are you?"

"I'm not assuming anything. But it would be nice. Besides, when you chose music education as your emphasis, what else were you intending?"

"Not having to worry about attendance because Lisa and I travel so much. We'll see about the teaching."

"You always were stubborn."

"Gee, where did I learn that from?"

Sy chuckled as I tried not to sigh. Sid's relationship with Stella had never been an easy one. Stella was getting better about not putting Sid down, but she'd never learned how to be kind from her family, so it was not entirely surprising that she was pretty hard on Sid. It was going to be interesting to see how well living so near was going to go.

However, as Sid later put it, Stella's expectations were the least of our problems. Since we had the personnel and the van through Sunday evening, we decided not to make any plans regarding Frank and Esther until Sunday afternoon. That way, all of us could get some rest. At least, we hoped we could. It would depend on whether things stayed quiet at the duplex.

Sy and Stella only stayed late enough at our place to invite Nick and Darby to go camping with them in the next few weeks and to listen to Nick talk about his week.

"Did you meet any girls?" Stella asked.

Nick giggled and flushed. "Yeah. I mean, they were all in high school, but Ming was really nice. Mom, why are you making that face for?"

Sid laughed. "You and your dad."

"I just want to be sure she didn't hurt your feelings this morning." I sighed.

Nick grinned. "No! I was relieved." He looked over at Stella. "Ming told me that she didn't want me to call her after we got home because she's in high school and I'm not yet. I was trying to figure out how to tell her I didn't want to call her." He sighed. "She was getting boring."

Still, there was something about the way Nick had flushed when Ming's name came up that had both Sid and me wondering. In fact, as soon as Sy and Stella left, Sid went and talked with him.

Sid came back upstairs to our room with an utterly befuddled look on his face.

"Oh, my god!" I gasped. "Did he...?"

Sid laughed weakly. "It would actually make sense if he had. But no. Our boy is still a virgin. I'm not sure what exactly happened, but he confirmed that much." Sid sat down on the bed's edge. "He said we'll know when he takes that step because he has no idea how to have sex and he's going to have to ask me when it's time."

"That's odd. Good, but odd." I sat down next to Sid.

"He says he doesn't want to sleep around, either. He doesn't know why, but he doesn't."

"I can't complain about that."

Sid snorted. "Neither can I, really."

"But what happened?"

"He didn't say." Sid shrugged. "I mean, when you think about it, how much of that is his business and not ours?"

I winced. "I suppose that's true." I flopped back onto the bed. "But how do we know how much is his business and how much we need to be on top of?"

"You're asking me?" Sid sighed. "I can't help thinking there's got to be some point where we get a handle on this."

"Not according to Mae. She told me she keeps thinking Lissy is going to be an easy kid because she's done this already four times, and with twins that last time. Only Lissy wasn't even two weeks old and was still doing stuff none of the others did."

Sid shook his head. "How the hell did I end up here?"

"The condom broke, dearest."

"Overall, I have to say that was a good thing. Still..." Sid looked down at me. "I suppose I could continue lamenting the intricacies of being a good parent. On the other hand, seeing you laying there like that is quite pleasantly distracting."

I grinned. "I could use some distraction."

Sid just chuckled.

The next morning, we were pretty tired and overslept, but somehow Sid, Nick, and I made it to church in plenty of time. Frank was there early, too, with Esther along for the ride. Frank directed the choir at ten-thirty mass and Sid played organ and piano for them. Nick and I left them in the choir loft. Nick got his seat in a pew near the front, next to Kathy. Jesse and I were both serving as Eucharistic Ministers that day, so we went to the sacristy to meet with the other ministers.

"I've got my shut-ins," I whispered to Jesse. "But after that, we'll have lunch to figure out what we're doing about Frank and Esther."

"What if they don't go home?" Jesse asked.

I shrugged. "We've got a team on them. If Frank ditches them, he's ditching the bad guys, too."

Jesse nodded.

Jesse and Kathy took Nick over to see Sy and Stella while Sid rode with me to take communion to the several seniors I visited when I could. Then Jesse, Kathy, Sid, and I went to lunch at our preferred Mexican restaurant, where we decided that delaying things was only going to make life harder for all of us. Fortunately, Frank and Esther had gone back to their duplex after mass, which we knew because we'd called the team watching them.

Frank answered the door when we rang the doorbell, accompanied by continued high-pitched yapping. Frank's mother and brother had returned to Chicago earlier that morning. Frank and Esther were a little surprised to see all four of us, but offered us a seat in their living room. Coco and Reilly, Frank's two dogs, yapped for a couple minutes more.

I honestly think the reason the Ladies Night Out poker game has stayed at Esther's place is that the decor resembles that of a frowzy bachelor pad. Nothing in that place matches and much of it looks like it was handed down from someone else. Sid stayed standing while Jesse, Kathy, and I sat on the frayed couch. Esther stood, as well, and Frank sank into one of the two beat-up recliners facing the side wall and the TV. Coco and Reilly jumped into the other recliner.

Sid took a deep breath. "Frank, Esther, there is no easy way to start this, but the four of us know about the Cat's Paw satellite."

"How could you know?" Esther glared at us. "You're not cleared for that."

Sid smiled. "Actually, we are."

"You're them." Frank started chuckling. "I told you, Esther."

"What? How?" Esther demanded, then cursed and glared at Frank. "Just because she had that gun doesn't mean she's it."

Sid, Kathy, Jesse and I all looked at each other.

"What?" Sid asked.

Esther rolled her eyes. "Your friend Henry from the FBI. He talked to me last spring after the wedding. He heard the Soviets were really interested in the Cat's Paw project and asked me if I'd mind doing some top secret work to help protect it. I said sure. Then he asked if Frank would help, and told us there might be more of this sort of thing to do if we were okay with it. Which we are. But then me and my co-workers got a bunch of threats, and Henry said we'd be protected, but we also needed to wait for our training team to contact us."

Frank grinned. "And that's gotta be you, Sid and Lisa."

"I'm afraid so," I said.

"You two?" Esther gaped. "You gotta be kidding me."

"So are Kathy and Jesse." Sid glowered at Frank. "We four have been watching out for you two since the beginning of this month."

Esther exploded. "You're the best that Henry has to offer?"

Kathy was on her feet in seconds. "Hell, yes! We've been busting our asses keeping you two safe! You get a little bit of trouble, and you think we're not doing our jobs? Well, excuse me! I almost got my butt killed last Wednesday trying to keep you from getting shot up with nerve agent."

"Kathy!" I grabbed her arm and pulled her back to the couch. I looked at Frank and Esther. "Yeah, Frank, you may have made a tail or two. You are obviously good that way. But we scared off that guy in your garage right before camp and dismantled the bomb in your car. And that operative with the nerve agent. We also took care of that boat you were so worried about."

Frank frowned. "So, those were gunshots the boys heard Thursday night."

"They were," Sid said. "The thing is, this isn't just about protecting you. Not only are we your training team, you two have officially been adopted into the organization as of earlier this week."

"What?" yelped Frank, leaping out of the recliner. "You mean it's not just 'til Esther's safe from those anti-nuke crazies? No!"

Esther laughed and cursed. "Are you serious? Permanently?"

I sighed. "For better or worse, yes. Esther, your previous security clearance has been upgraded. Frank, you now have one."

"What if I don't want to do this?" Frank glared at me.

"Frank, we talked about this," Esther snarled.

"But I thought it was just going to be an odd job or two." Frank's voice stopped just short of a wail. "I'm not ready to be a spy."

"You will be ready," said Sid. "We'll make sure of that. Trust me. You wouldn't have been recruited if we didn't think you were up to it."

"You're good, Frank." Esther laughed. "This will be awesome."

Frank swallowed and looked at us. "You really think I can do this?"

"Hell, yes," said Jesse with a laugh. "The way you made us all crazy ditching us when we were following you to protect you? And that guy in Avalon that was following Esther. You spotted him, Frank. We didn't."

"And you will be fully trained," I said. "Sid and I are good at this, and we'll be sure you have the same skills we do."

Sid looked at Frank, his eyes narrowing. "We need to be sure you're fully on board with this, Frank, before we can go any further."

Esther's eyes opened wide as she gazed at her husband. "Oh, please, Frank!"

Frank looked at all of us, then his eyes finally settled on me. I nodded.

"Well," he said slowly. "If you guys believe I can, then I'm in. I just hope you don't regret it."

I already did, but that had nothing to do with Frank. Sid smiled.

"We won't," Sid said.

"Oh, hot damn!" Esther all but bounced up and down. "This is going to be fun."

I glared at her. "You only think that now, Esther. You have no idea what you're really up against."

"Yeah, I do," said Esther. "I've been doing top secret work for years."

Kathy smiled. "But now you got some folks you can talk to about it."

"She's right," I said. "I know how hard it is to keep those kinds of secrets. I've been doing it, except for Sid, for years, too. It was tough sharing it when Kathy and Jesse got recruited, but it is easier to deal with."

Esther's eyes penetrated mine. "You always had something you couldn't talk about."

"This is it," I said. I looked at Sid, then took a deep breath. "Within the structures of the FBI and CIA are several smaller organizations so secret that mostly only their members know they exist. We belong to one under the FBI called Operation Quickline. We mostly do courier work, but little chores like protecting you and that satellite are all part of it."

"Tomorrow we will start your training," Sid said. "It's going to be tough with Esther's work schedule, but we'll get it together."

Esther looked at Sid. "When did you start?"

"Almost seventeen years ago," he said softly. "And, yes, it was while I was stationed in Saigon and elsewhere."

Esther nodded. She was one of the few people we knew who really understood about the war in Vietnam. Still, both she and Sid danced around it and never really touched on that connection they had.

Frank swallowed, still not entirely sure. "Now what?"

"We start with physical fitness training in the morning," said Sid. "Given the threat you're dealing with, we'll start you at the gym at six a.m."

Both Frank and I groaned.

"I have to go to work tomorrow," Esther said.

"That's why we're meeting at six," said Sid. "We've got to get you two into prime physical condition as fast as possible."

Esther made a face. "I work at a desk."

"But you won't always be," I said. "As much as I complain about the early morning run and doing the weights and all, trust me, it's saved my backside more than once."

"We'll have code work in the evenings," said Sid.

"We can't tomorrow night," I said. "Camp follow up."

Sid sighed. "We'll also need to get you guys working on spotting tails and tailing others, weapons, hand to hand self-defense, drops and pickups."

"And more codes," grumbled Jesse. Like me, codes were not his strength.

"And how to do break-ins," Kathy sighed. She was good at break-ins. She just had some trouble because they were sort of illegal.

I looked at Sid. "We also have to figure out security on these two for tonight."

Esther jerked her thumb at the front window. "We've got that van outside."

"We have to have it back where it belongs before tomorrow morning." I winced.

"What?" Frank gaped. "What about our protection?"

Sid sighed. "That was just until we could teach you two to protect yourselves. Esther, we'll have to get time on the shooting range on your lunch breaks. Frank, you and Lisa will practice during the days."

"I already know how to shoot," Frank said. "Lisa, you took me out right before camp." He stopped. "You knew this was coming."

"I'm afraid I did, Frank," I said. "But you're going to need a lot more time on the shooting range before I'm comfortable with you and a firearm."

Kathy looked at me. "He's that bad?"

"What's the cliché?" I looked at Frank. "Can't hit the broad side of a barn."

"I hit that target a few times," Frank grumbled as he sadly collapsed into the recliner.

"You'll get better," I said. "I promise."

"What's the broad side of a barn?" Esther asked.

"Something completely irrelevant at the moment," said Sid. He looked over at me. "You okay if we take them home tonight?"

"What about my dogs?" Frank asked.

I sighed. "We'll bring them. They've met Motley before."

"Then we're keeping the cats out of the bedroom," grumbled Sid.

We still weren't sure which of the three cats was the guilty party, but when they got peeved, one of them tended to poop in Sid's dress shoes. Strange dogs would not make any of the cats happy, even dogs almost smaller than they were.

"The other thing we need to do tonight is for Esther to tell us everything about the Cat's Paw project," I said.

Esther frowned. "I'm surprised you even know the official name."

"We're cleared," I said. "Sid and I have been hearing about it since around April. We're not sure how it leaked, though."

"I don't know." Esther sighed. "Probably the usual chatter. That's why nobody cared when the protests started. That group got it all wrong. There's no nuclear arms on that satellite. There's no arms at all on it. We can't do that yet. We can change its orbit, but the real payloads are its ability to triangulate a position with one of the other satellites already in orbit. And data compression."

"What's data compression?" Kathy asked.

"It's how you get pictures from space to the earth." Esther smiled and sat down on the arm of the recliner Frank was sitting in. "You see, most of the satellites up there can take some really good photos of what's on the ground. The problem is those pictures are made up of a lot of data. That's really hard to send from space. Well, anywhere, really. I mean, think about it. One picture is like twenty or thirty Sunday newspapers all bundled up and we're trying to stuff that bundle through the mail slot on our front door."

Jesse frowned. "They got us video from the moon, and that was back in the sixties."

"Yeah, but it was all grainy and hard to see. And it took a really long time to get here." Esther was just warming up. "But data compression means that we can compact all those newspapers so that they fit better through the mail slot. People have been working on it for years and years. Only now we have a better way to do it, and that's why the Cat's Paw is so special. I mean, it's not as sexy as nuclear warheads, but it's a lot more dangerous to bad guys because it's a lot easier to see what they're doing."

"You mean bad guys like the KGB," I said.

"What?" Esther looked at us.

"The Soviets seem to be backing that group that's protesting the satellite," Sid said.

"What makes you so sure they are?" Kathy asked. "They could have gotten that equipment someplace else."

Sid shook his head. "Trust us. This is not the first time we've seen the KGB use local amateurs. And we're probably doing the same thing over in the USSR."

"What equipment?" asked Esther.

"The bomb that they planted on Frank's car," I said. "The guns those guys on the boat were carrying. They were also wearing night goggles. You don't just pick those up at Kmart. And I'm willing to bet the bomb they used to kill your co-worker was KGB, too. We just haven't gotten the official report on it yet."

"But you two do not have to worry about that part," said Sid. "You just have to focus on training. Lisa and I will worry about the investigation part of it."

"And we'll be here, too," Jesse said.

Kathy gestured to include Sid and me as well as Jesse. "All of us will. We know what you're going through."

"Trust me," Sid said, looking at Frank. "I know how it feels to get roped into this business. It happened to me twice."

We got Frank and Esther packed, reminding both of them that they really, really had to keep the business an even bigger secret than the satellite.

"What about my folks?" Frank asked, as we rode with Kathy back to Sid's and my house.

Jesse and Esther were riding with Sid in his car.

"You can't tell them, Frank." I looked at him. "My family doesn't know I do this."

"Neither does mine," said Kathy. "And I don't want them to know. I don't want to think what could happen if they let something out and got hurt because of it."

"We're safe because no one knows about us," I said. "And our families are safe because they don't know."

Frank sighed and nodded.

July 29 - 30, 1986

We took Frank and Esther to our martial arts dojo the next morning instead of the gym, then Sid took Esther to work, and I took Frank with me back to the house. There was a mildly unpleasant surprise waiting for us in Josie Prosser and two of her pre-teen friends. Well, I still wasn't sure who was who yet, but I was reasonably sure one of them was Josie.

They scattered when they saw the garage door open as I pulled up, but they came right back once I had pulled into the garage and closed the door.

"What's that about?" Frank asked as I checked out the front windows.

"Something we don't need." I shook my head and went over to my desk. "The girls are chasing Nick. It's why he's over at Sy and Stella's for the time being."

I checked the answering machine just as my pager went off. I paged Sid first to let him know that I'd take the call, since our pagers tended to go off together. The call was for a pickup addressed to us from the Green line. I set it up, then decided to bring Frank with me. We needed to go to the shooting range, anyway. There weren't any urgent calls on the answering machine, either.

The weather outside was warm, and I was wearing a pair of lightweight mint green linen Bermuda shorts with sandals and a sleeveless polo shirt in a flowered print. The pickup was a priority three, code three, and I'd set it up for a donut stand that was not only well known, it was a favorite of mine and Frank's. In fact, he'd taken me on a date there shortly after we'd met.

I explained the priority and code system to Frank as I drove us there.

"Priority is pretty obvious," I said. "One doesn't happen that often, but you know it's hot if you get one. Code is the level of contact we can have with the other courier. Code one is no contact at all. Code five means you can hang around and maybe even talk to each other. This pick up is a code three, which means we'll probably see the other courier, but not really talk to him."

"Him?" Frank asked. "I thought we weren't supposed to know anybody."

"Well, after a while, you can't help but recognize people."

In fact, I had seen Green Lantern, the mover on the San Francisco stop of the Green line, any number of times, and the nondescript man had seen me, as well. I ordered several donuts and coffee for both Frank and me, then we sat outside at one of the cement tables. Green Lantern wandered past us on his way to the parking lot. Some minutes later, Frank and I had finished our donuts and took the remains of our coffee back to the truck.

"That's it?" Frank asked as I started the engine.

"Be thankful that's it," I said. "When it isn't, it's ugly. And speaking of, we need to spend some significant time at the shooting range today."

Frank grimaced. According to Sid, the previous day's session had not gone well. The range we went to was a special one for undercover operatives and others who needed a discreet place to practice. The targets were the human silhouettes one associates with law-enforcement. That didn't seem to bother Frank.

I let him squeeze off a few rounds and saw that Esther had been exactly right. He was rushing his shots. It was probably not one of my finer bits of inspiration, but there was the movie The Karate Kid. I'd seen it several times with Nick, who really loved the film. Wax on, wax off.

"Alright, Frank, we're going to try something different," I told him. "Before you shoot, I want you to take a deep breath, hold it, take your time sighting down the barrel at the target, let out your breath, then slowly squeeze off the shot."

"That's not going to help if somebody's shooting at us."

"Just do as I say."

Frank shook his head, put his ear protection on, then followed my prompts, and hit the target right in the chest. He gaped.

"Wow."

"Let's try that again. Slowly."

He kept trying to rush my prompts, but I wouldn't let him.

"But what are we going to do if we're in real trouble?" he asked as we finally left the range. "I can't shoot that slowly and expect us to come out alive."

"I'm not worrying about that right now," I said, starting my truck.

"You don't understand, Lisa."

"What do you mean, I don't understand?" I couldn't help glaring at him. "How many gunfights have you been in, Frank?"

"I haven't, but—"

"Frank, I've been in plenty." I wasn't sure why I was so irritated by him at that moment. I looked over at him and finally saw that there was something else gnawing at him. "I'm sorry. I shouldn't be so cranky, but this is something I really know, and it feels like you don't believe that I know what I'm doing."

"That's not it." Frank's face grew even more pained. "I'm just scared, Lisa. I need to be there for Esther, and what if I'm not?"

"That's not the way to be thinking about this." I sighed. "Look, Frank, I worry about the same thing. What if I'm not there to save Sid, or worse, Nick? Sid, at least, has years and years of experience. But my son. He's just a kid. The worst of it is, no matter how much training or experience you have, things can still go wrong. Which is why you can't be worrying too much about being there for Esther. There are no guarantees that things won't go bad in spite of your best efforts."

Frank snorted. "Oh, I know that. I really know that." He looked at me, then blinked. "My dad was a cop, you know."

"That's right." I frowned as I remembered. "Didn't you say he was killed in the line of duty?"

"I did."

"That sucks."

"You have no idea."

"I'm sure I don't." I glanced over at him, then focused on the freeway ahead of us.

"It's not just about being there for Esther." Frank took a deep breath. "My brother Patrick thinks I'm a major screwup."

"I thought your brother's name is James."

"James is the second oldest. Our older brother is Patrick. He's a special agent for the FBI. He always says I should have gone into law enforcement, that it would straighten me out." Frank sighed and shook his head. "He never got me wanting to play the flute. None of my family does. Doreen sort of gets the music thing, and Mom doesn't understand it, but she's okay with it. But the rest of them, James, Sean, Colleen, Joseph, and especially Patrick, they love me, but they just do not understand. That's why I came out here for school, then stayed."

"Frank, you're not a screwup. You've got some impressive talent, especially spotting tails."

He gazed out the window ahead, then at me. "You know, Lisa, I did sort of have you and Sid figured out. I knew you were doing something for the FBI. At least, I was pretty sure you were. The way you ditched people following you, and the way you'd clam up about things. I'm good at figuring things out. I just don't say anything about them because I used to get in trouble when I did. But I'd seen your gun, too, and I knew what it was. A Smith and Wesson Model Thirteen, standard FBI issue. It's the one Patrick carries. That's why I choked when you brought me that one week before last. The funny thing is, I could never figure out that thing you have about corpses."

"My little phobia." I sighed. "It was the business that did it to me."

Frank shrugged. "Okay." He waited a moment, then realized I was not going to say any more about it. "Anyway, if you can have a phobia of corpses, then I don't have to be the best marksman out there." He put his hand up as I started to protest. "I have to get better. I'm not saying I don't. But I don't have to be Dead-Eye Dick. Which means I'm not a major screwup."

"I already said you're not." I sighed. "If I'm being a hard nose about the shooting thing, it's because right now, you're more of a danger than a help. I'm sorry. That's the hard truth, and it's not helping you to say otherwise. But darn it, I will get you shooting straight if it's the last thing I do. I owe you that much and I owe it to Esther, too. And it will happen before we're both senile."

Frank closed his eyes and started chuckling. "I'm not that bad."

"You're not and you showed some significant improvement today. We'll just keep on working on things slowly and the next thing you know, it will speed up and you'll be hitting the target without even thinking about it."

"I sure hope so."

I didn't say anything, but there was part of me that was hoping the same thing, preferably before Frank got his backside killed.

Nick called the car phone to say he wanted to come home that night and asked if I'd mind if Kathy and Jesse gave him a ride over since they were coming over to the house. I said yes. Frank looked at me funny.

"Sy and Stella are staying in that condo Sid and I bought last year when we were remodeling the house," I explained. "The one right across from Kathy and Jesse's."

"Oh, right."

Nick, Kathy, and Jesse were already at the house when Frank and I pulled into the garage. Sid showed up with

Esther soon after. I told Sid about the pickup I'd made earlier that day, which confirmed that the bomb that had killed Gil Woltz had been of KGB origin and pretty sophisticated, not unlike the bomb we'd taken off of Frank's car before camp. Esther and Sid both had some interesting news, too.

"Leon Thomas will be the new hire on the Cat's Paw project," Sid said with a grin as we all gathered in the living room.

I was thrilled. Leon was really Desmond Moore, our Red Line mover in Phoenix, and, yes, keeping all the aliases straight could be insanely confusing.

Esther grinned. "And I found out what happened to Gil Woltz's ID last spring. He filed it as missing on May thirteen, then found it again on May sixteen. He got into the plant the night of May thirteen and stayed several hours, and also in the security logs were the sign offs on IDs for about eight different people, five men and three women." She plopped a piece of paper into Sid's hand. "Here are the names, but it won't make much difference. I disabled all of the IDs and added a warning to hold anybody who has one of them."

"How did you get this?" Sid asked.

Esther shrugged. "Gil was stupid. He put his passwords under the desk pad. Everyone knew they were there. And I have to get into the security admin files every so often because the guys play games with them. They think they're being funny. I have to go through personnel files pretty often, too."

Sid looked thoughtful. "If you weren't so busy with that launch, I'd have you go through those personnel files. We might find something."

Conchetta had left a nice taco salad for dinner, and Kathy and Sid saw to filling it out so that there was enough for all of us. After we ate, we started in on code work, never mind that there was Bible Study that night. We probably did more talking than code work. As Kathy put it later, we all needed some time to deal with the sudden change in Frank and Esther's lives.

If I held Nick somewhat closer to me than usual that night, well, there was the conversation I'd had with Frank earlier. Not that Nick entirely noticed. Bless him, he was absorbed in his usual pre-teen fog of doting grandparents, adventures with his buddies, and how to get away from annoying girls. For that, I was immensely grateful, and squeezed him yet again.

Sid and I sent Nick to bed around nine-thirty with the usual kisses and hugs. Kathy and Jesse went home shortly after that, and Esther was in the guest room somewhat before ten. Leaving Sid and Frank talking in the living room, I went upstairs to Sid's and my bedroom.

I love to read in bed. I wasn't sure what time it was when Sid finally made his way into our bedroom that night, but I was well into the book I was reading when he did. He went into our bathroom and dressing room to get undressed and otherwise ready for bed. The waterbed rocked a little as he finally slid underneath the covers.

He squinted at me and the book I was reading. Sid is very nearsighted, but wears contact lenses, so most people don't really notice.

He grinned. "Is that from the dirty books bag?"

I chuckled. "Uh, yeah."

Library book sales are one of my Achilles' Heels. I'd been to the Beverly Hills Library sale about a month or so before and somehow ended up with a bag of books filled with sexy best-sellers from the nineteen-seventies, including Fear of Flying, by Erica Jong (which I'd really liked), Jaws, by Peter Benchley, the Godfather, by Mario Puzo, and several Harold Robbins books (which were boring me to tears, although the sex scenes were decent), and the book I was currently reading.

"And...?" Sid asked.

Okay, he was a little hopeful. Some of the books I'd read had... Well, led to some intense connections.

I sighed. "I'm not liking it."

"Which one is it?"

"Once is Not Enough. Jacqueline Susann."

"Ah. I've read it. Once was too much."

"You're right. Good lord, this girl is pathetic."

Sid rolled onto his back, then blinked. "How close are you to done?"

"Almost." I flipped through the last few pages. "They're doing LSD and there are a bunch of hippies... Sid, did you ever try doing it during a people pass?"

Sid groaned. "That scene is a joke."

"Oh."

"Folks who are that strung out are probably not standing." He sighed. "But, yes, there was a party, and we tried to reenact that scene."

"And...?"

"Sweetie, you know how hard it is to pass people who are keeping still along a line. What are the odds two people are going to be able to hump in that situation, even without being passed?"

"Um, it didn't happen?"

"Let's just say I damned near broke my neck, and the folks holding us were mostly sober."

I read a few more lines, then threw the book across the room. "Okay. I'm done with this one."

He looked at me, then pulled me next to him. "Are you okay?"

I winced. "I got cranky with Frank today. It wasn't entirely fair. He was panicking a little about the shooting thing."

"Hm." He sighed. "Your mood has been a little off for a while now. Are you happy?"

I put my hand on his cheek. "Yes. I love being with you, Sid. More than anything."

"And you don't have any regrets about getting married."

"It was totally the right thing to do." I looked at him. "Do you miss your old life?"

"Not in the least." He gave me a quick squeeze. "How about you? Do you miss your old life?"

I winced. "Maybe a little. I liked being able to schedule a lunch date without worrying about what you're doing or whether I have to pick up Nick somewhere. Maybe I wasn't all that independent because of working, but it was nice just being on my own."

"Ah." Sid rolled onto his back. "My darling, when was the last time you had any significant time to yourself?"

"Ummm." I counted back. "Well, there was camp. That was pretty much wall to wall social contact. Then the craziness watching Frank and Esther the week before, and the week before that, not to mention Henry's retirement party."

"Then there was the Fourth of July, and the reunion. And before that was getting over the jet lag from the Travel Club meeting."

The Travel Club was visibly a group of people who liked to travel and visit with each other, and there were several civilians who were part of it. However, the meeting, apart from various spouses, was actually about the operatives in the group having a small conference on what was going on in their various parts of Europe and South America so that we could be sure to get the right intelligence to the right agency.

"And the Travel Club meeting itself. Good lord, Sid. I don't think either of us has had any real downtime since before we left for England."

"At least, I've had morning practice time up until camp happened." He shuddered. "No wonder you're cranky. I'm just about there, myself."

I flopped onto my pillow. "And we're not going to get any quiet time for the foreseeable future."

"Honey, we've got to take some time. If we don't, we won't be good for anything."

"When are we going to do it? We've got Janey's birthday party tomorrow night."

Janey is not only my niece, she's very close to Sid.

He sighed. "We can't miss that."

"And it will not be a nice, quiet little party. We're way behind on code work with Frank and Esther, let alone all the other training they need." I sighed. "We'll just have to gut through. At least, I know what's getting to me. That's a big help."

"Yeah, it is." He rolled onto his side and smiled at me. "How do you feel about the two of us making some noise right now?"

I grinned. "I always love that."

The next morning, Sid insisted I sleep in while he took Frank and Esther to the gym.

"I need to take Frank to the shooting range," I muttered.

"Fine. I'll bring Frank back here after we take Esther to work."

"You're leaving her there?"

Sid shrugged. "With the extra security and the way she killed those IDs, there's not much risk. And Desmond starts there today. Besides, Esther knows to call us if anything weird turns up. In the meantime, get some extra sleep and quiet time. I'll leave a note for Nick not to bother you. Okay?"

I blinked and smiled. "Thanks, lover. What are you doing for yourself?"

"I'll figure something out after you take Frank to the shooting range."

We did still have work to do for the October issue of the magazine, some of which was primarily mine because while Sid was getting better at the grammar and spelling thing and he was very good at working through any logical lapses in an article, I am the better editor.

The extra rest, though, helped a lot. I was up and dressed by the time Sid got back with Frank. We all ate breakfast together with Nick, who was still inhaling plenty of extra food. I think we went through a whole loaf of whole grain bread that morning between Nick, Frank, and me, and Frank and I did not get the lion's share.

I took Frank to the shooting range after that. Slowing him down was helping a lot. I didn't rush anything but let him make several shots on the same deep breath and they all hit the body area of the target. We worked until lunchtime, when Sid and Esther showed up. I worked with Esther while Sid took Frank back to the house.

"So, anything going on at the office?" I asked Esther as I drove her back to her office.

Esther rolled her eyes. "Just a bunch of managers wetting their pants over whether the systems will be functioning by the launch date. They will. They always do. But that doesn't stop the managers."

"How much time do you have?"

"It's supposed to go up the twentieth."

"Of August?"

"Yeah. Everything will come together at the last second. It does every time we do a satellite."

I made a point of going through a drive-through so that Esther could have something to eat. She finished her lunch before we got to the defense plant. I had gotten my wig on and flashed my ID at the guard at the gate before dropping Esther off at the door to her office building. I waited just long enough to be sure she was inside.

Back at the house, Sid had Frank working on codes. My sister Mae called to ask me a favor.

"I can't believe I'm doing this," she told me. "I'm stuck here at work until five. Neil's going to pick up the cake and the food. But we could use an extra salad or two. Do you mind?"

"It shouldn't be a problem. What kind of salad?"

"We're getting tamales and enchiladas, so maybe a cole slaw and maybe some green salad. I should have ordered them from the restaurant, but I didn't think ahead."

"Oh, shavings! I didn't think ahead, either. What am I going to feed Frank and Esther?"

"Why are you feeding them?"

"They're staying with us. There's a plumbing problem at their duplex and they don't have any water." Okay, we'd planned that excuse, never mind that the plumbing was working just fine at their place.

"Darby loves Frank. Bring them along, too. And add a potato salad. I know how Frank eats. Is Nick still chowing down?"

"Like nobody's business," I sighed. "I'll see if I can convince Esther to leave work early or we're going to be really late. I'll call you once I know."

I called Esther and convinced her to be ready to leave work at three-thirty. Sid heard about the salad request and immediately called another restaurant to order enough for everybody. The expected articles for the October issue had finally arrived, and I went over them with my red pen. By the time I was done, it was time to gather Janey's presents together and Frank and Nick, and swing by the restaurant, then Esther's office. It felt like it took forever to get to Mae and Neil's place in Pasadena, but in truth, we got there right around five-thirty. No surprise, Sy and Stella had beaten us there. Of course, they'd been invited. Sy was mentoring Darby on the violin and Stella loves Janey almost as much as Sid does.

Once we pulled into the narrow driveway, Darby, a redhead who was about Nick's age, came running out. He and Nick chatted for a second. Darby gave me a hug, shook Sid's hand, and said hi to Frank and Esther, then he and Nick disappeared into the house and Darby's room. Janey, a brunette celebrating her tenth birthday, was already on the porch, ready to give Uncle Sid his own special hug. Ellen, who was eight and looked like her older sister, bounced just inside the living room, dying to tell me and Uncle Sid about her latest science experiment. Twins Marty and Mitch, two other red heads who would turn six in September, were intent on doing some rough housing with Uncle Sid, only they couldn't because Sid and I were bringing salads into the house.

Ellen glommed onto Esther, who was all ears about the latest experiment. After hugging Sid, Janey hung next to me, telling me all about her summer thus far, especially about all the books she'd read. Lissy, like any decent one-month-old, was sort of awake as Stella held her. Stella, we'd discovered, really liked babies.

In short, it was the usual noisy chaos that prevailed when my family got together. We ate dinner, sang Happy Birthday to Janey. She opened her presents. Mae asked me to tell her about the trip to England at the end of June. I couldn't tell her that the trip was about connecting with a variety of other operatives and Quickline colleagues. But it had still been a very nice time, and I was able to share that and the wonderful dinner we'd had while in the Lake District in Northern England.

Sid and Stella traded off time on the family piano as we listened and sang. And, of course, Sy and Darby played violin together. Frank had brought his flute, too, and the music just went on. It was lovely, but also very wearing.

Nick wanted to talk about the day in the car on the way home, but I shook my head and insisted on silence. It was what I really, really needed.

July 31 –
August 4, 1986

I was not a happy camper the next morning. I'd driven Esther to work and got back to the house only to find Sid packing an overnight bag.

"I'm only going in, getting the drop, and leaving," Sid told me.

"We should probably go together," I grumbled.

"Do you really want to?"

"No."

"We've got too much going on here, anyway. I hate dumping the training on you, but you seem to have a handle on getting Frank's shooting skills in place. Kathy can help them with the codes tonight and tomorrow night. I may even be home by then."

"If you're lucky."

Sid pulled me close to him. "I've got to run if I'm going to make that flight. Look at it this way. You'll have a little time alone."

I nodded sadly. Sid gave me an extra passionate kiss, then ran for the garage. I didn't like it, but it was part of our new responsibilities. Someone in Europe had left some information at a safe house in Athens, Greece, and we'd been tagged to go get it. As I'd noted, we could have gone together, but Sid was right. There was too much going on with the upcoming launch, trying to find the leak, and getting Frank and Esther trained in all of that for both of us to go.

Nick didn't really help, either. Part of the problem was that the girls were watching from across the street, which meant he couldn't leave the house without Frank or me guarding him. Also, he was getting a little down and I couldn't figure out why, even though it felt like I should have been able to.

Kathy and Jesse came over for dinner that evening (I thanked God that Conchetta had cooked enough), and Kathy pushed Frank and Esther on the code work. I retreated to the library and Nick watched a movie in the rumpus room.

The next morning, I drove Esther to work, then pushed Frank on the shooting range. He was getting better, but that afternoon, I couldn't take anymore. Right after lunch, I got on my gear and headed to the riding club. Sid had bought me the membership the winter before. The nice part about it was that I didn't have to own a horse and keep it up, and all that went with it. But when I wanted and had the time to go riding, I could. I was able to get one of my favorite horses, a chestnut gelding named Thor, and took him out on a trail in the Santa Monica mountains. The weather was pretty warm, even with the breeze from the ocean, so all I could do was walk Thor, but it was something. I was feeling a little better by the time I had to pick Esther up from work.

Esther and I got a couple pizzas and brought them home for dinner. Frank complained that his brain was mush, and while I shouldn't have, I let them off code work. Instead, we watched Star Wars again. Sid has a really good pirate video of the trilogy that we really shouldn't have been watching, but we did. Frank and Esther love Star Wars and Nick got a kick out of watching them enjoy it. But I put my foot down after the first film and insisted that Nick go to bed. I walked him to his bedroom and kissed him goodnight.

"Do you want me to tuck you in?" I asked.

"Nah. I'm okay." He frowned. "When's Dad going to be home?"

"He called me this morning that he was getting on the plane. But it's a really long flight. Eleven hours, at least." I ran my fingers through the hair flopping over Nick's forehead. "He should be home soon."

Nick nodded, kissed me again, and I went upstairs. The night before, I'd gotten my copy of Gaudy Night, by Dorothy L. Sayers, from our personal library and started re-reading it. It was still on my nightstand because there was no way I was going to get through that massive tome in one night. I stripped and washed up and slid under the covers of the bed, breathing in the room's silence. But I picked up the book only to see the red light of the security system flashing. I got up and checked the readout. The garage door had opened.

I smiled and got a robe on. Our bedroom is soundproof, but I had a feeling Nick had heard the garage door. His room is close to the door from the house into the garage. I hurried down the stairs and found Nick hugging his father in front of the utility room.

Poor Sid looked exhausted, but he smiled at me as he held his son.

"Alright, son." Sid gave Nick one more squeeze. "It's time you went back to bed. We'll talk in the morning. Okay?"

"Sure, Dad." Nick scampered away, and I suddenly realized he'd forgotten to put on a robe. Nick, like his father and I, preferred to sleep in the raw.

Sid scooped me into another warm hug, then kissed me with even more warmth.

"How did it go?" I asked when I could.

"In and out," Sid said. "I spent more time on the planes there and back than I did in Athens." We started up the stairs, arm in arm. "We'll get it all processed in the morning. How did it go here?"

"Well enough. Frank's getting a lot better on the shooting range. Esther has most of the codes down cold. We're still way behind on tailing and spotting tails, but we'll have the weekend to work on that. I've got all three of our October articles edited and you just need to review them. There's still no more information on Levinsky."

"We may want to go up to Running Springs to check him out, but we can figure that out later." Sid nuzzled my ear, and we paused in front of the bedroom door. "Do you realize it has been almost forty-eight hours since we last had sexual intercourse?"

I couldn't help giggling. "Yeah. Forty-seven hours and twenty-three minutes since we last had sex. Not that I'm counting."

We got inside the bedroom before I started pulling Sid's clothes off. However, he had to use the bathroom and get his contacts out and teeth brushed.

"When was the last time we went this long without making love?" Sid asked me as he slid into bed next to me.

I paused, thinking, as we kissed. "I don't think we have since the wedding. Before that, we may have skipped a night or two."

"Honey, since we started the oral thing last year, we've maybe missed a night here and there, but not two nights in a row." He kissed me again and his hands went wandering, as did mine.

"I guess we'll have to make up for it."

Sid chuckled lecherously, and I thanked God once again that we'd had the bedroom soundproofed.

To Breanna, 7/31/00

Today's Topic: Something I've Never Told Anyone Before

Hey, Love -

Good timing on this topic. Yeah, I'm getting a little down. It's that time of year again. The anniversary of my first mom's death has always been hard on me. I'm only now coming to realize that it's because my feelings about my first mom are so mixed-up.

Don't get me wrong. I loved her and knew that she loved me. We had a good time together. I like to think she'd be proud of me, of my PhD work, stuff like that, although neither she nor Grandma were prone to that kind of expression. My first mom could also be really nasty, especially about Mom Two. She hated Mom Two and would tell me that Mom Two didn't really want me and other mean stuff. I think now that she was afraid that I'd love Mom Two more than her, which was ridiculous.

The embarrassing thing is that I let my first mom's attitude get under my skin the way it did. Even after I'd been with Dad and my second mom for that first year, I sometimes still questioned whether Mom Two really wanted me. I couldn't say anything about what my first mom had said. I did not want to hurt Mom's and Dad's feelings, and probably did not want to admit it was getting to me that much, especially in the face of overwhelming evidence that my first mom had not told the truth. And I suppose if I'm being honest, life with Dad and my second mom made me so happy. Yeah, it was scary sometimes. I worried a lot and still do. As horrible as it was to lose my first mom, I was happier with my dad and second mom, and that still makes me feel guilty.

Nick was even more out of sorts at breakfast the next morning. Sid not only spotted it, he put his finger on what was driving the boy's mood. After Frank and Esther had gone to their room to get ready for the day, Sid asked Nick if he was okay.

"I'm fine, Dad." Nick's voice had the rhythm and tone of pre-teen angst, but was far too lackluster for that kind of deep annoyance with life.

"Come on. Let's go to the office." Sid nodded at me to follow, then put his arm around the boy's shoulders and steered him in that direction.

Once the three of us were inside, Sid shut and locked the door.

"Did you have a nightmare last night?" Sid asked.

Nick winced. "It wasn't any big deal."

"It was your all-alone dream again, wasn't it?" I said softly.

"Yeah." Nick squeezed his eyes shut.

Sid sighed. "I suspect you're going to be having problems with those over the next few days."

"I guess." Nick blinked. "It's been almost a year."

I nodded as my chest squeezed shut. That coming Monday would be the first anniversary of the death of Nick's first mother, Rachel. That's when Sid and I had taken custody of Nick, but unfortunately, that had also meant taking him away from his friends and the house he'd grown up in, and pretty much everything he'd known. Nick had wanted to come live with us, which had helped. Even with a little acting out, he'd adjusted extremely well. Still, he missed his first mom, and that was as it should have been.

"I am not going to invade your privacy." Sid smiled softly at Nick. "But why don't you put your intercom on to go to our room for the next week or so? That way, if you have another nightmare, we can be there for you."

Nick made a face. "I'm not a little kid."

"Neither am I," said Sid. "This isn't about being grown up or not. This is about getting over trauma, and losing your mother was traumatic. I have nightmares, too, Nick, and the only thing that makes them better for me is having your mother there to hold me."

"And right after that kidnapping, your father made a point of sleeping in my sewing room so he'd be there for mine," I told him. "It's how we take care of each other."

Nick nodded and we let it go from there. He would either talk about what he was feeling, or he wouldn't, and he was at the age when it's important for kids to start parsing these things out on their own. Sid and I just had to trust that we'd left the door open for him to come to us.

The good news was that we had a lovely day. We spent it on the Venice boardwalk, training Frank and Esther how to spot and evade tails. The reality is, if you're expecting a tail, it's pretty easy to spot one, which is part of why Frank was so good at it. He was always watching for something. Even a full team, with people changing clothes, can be made by someone who's expecting it. That being said,

Sid and I had a secret weapon. Nick was insanely good at tailing people and not getting made. He did have a slight disadvantage in that he could only tail on foot. But it took Frank a good fifteen minutes to make Nick, and Frank had caught me in my wig in almost five minutes. It took somewhat longer for him to spot Kathy.

The next lesson was, of course, how to tail, and Esther did somewhat better than Frank, although both were darned good. Not as good as Nick, but still pretty good.

For dinner, we found a nice little seafood restaurant just south of Venice and had a good time eating and being friends. We got home late and sent Nick straight to bed. That night, neither Sid nor I slept all that well. We were listening, although there wasn't that much to hear. I was fairly certain Nick had turned his intercom on, though. I heard some almost snores and a few sighs.

The next day, after church and my shut-in visits, there was more tailing and evading practice, this time in cars. We ended up in San Juan Capistrano, had dinner down there, then chased each other up the freeway home. Kathy and Jesse went on home. Frank and Esther followed us to our house. We got there around eight-thirty. The others went to the rumpus room where Esther hooked up her Nintendo console to the television and everyone started playing some adventure game. I went to the office to get the week laid out.

Just before nine, the phone rang, and I picked it up. It was Marlou Parks. She had been Rachel Flaherty's best friend and had not only taken care of Rachel during the last months of her life, she took care of Nick, too.

"Good to hear from you, Marlou," I said. "Do you want me to get Nick?"

"Um. No. Please don't." She sounded nervous.

"Is everything okay?"

"Well, we're officially in escrow on Rachel's house." Thanks to Rachel's will, Marlou had been given the job of selling the place.

"That's right. Sid had mentioned there had finally been an offer." I didn't remember when and hadn't really paid it much mind. Marlou had moved in the year before to take care of Rachel and Nick and had continued living there, partly because the mortgage payment was somewhat smaller than her rent had been and partly because a lived-in house was more likely to sell. "Have you got a new place yet?"

"Yeah. I found one this morning." She paused. "Um. Nick tried to call me on Friday. I wasn't in and I haven't returned his message."

"Oh."

She took a deep breath. "This is tough, but I'd really rather not be talking to him right now. It's not his fault. He is a terrific kid. It's just that... I've been in counseling these past few months, and it came out that I'm really angry at Rachel for what she did to me and to Nick, making us keep the leukemia a secret, and having to take care of her and Nick, and then only leaving me half the house." She choked a little. "I'm sorry. It's just been so hard. That's probably why it took so long for me to get the house listed."

"I can imagine."

"Anyway, I don't want my anger at her getting turned onto Nick. He doesn't deserve that. Honestly, Lisa, I never wanted a kid in my life, and I never knew what to say to him. I think the best thing to do for now is just avoid contact for the time being. We should probably stay on each other's Christmas card lists, just in case things change."

"Alright. I'll talk to him about it."

"Please, Lisa, it's not him. I'm just so furious at her. And, really, I know Nick loved her, but I've got a feeling he's got some seriously conflicted emotions going, too. It was not the best of relationships. Rachel tried, but she was not the touchy-feely type her mother was, and even then her mother was pretty critical of the both of them. That whole family was really messed up, between Rachel's father being a drunk, then her brothers and sister disowning her when she got pregnant." She sighed deeply. "I'm glad he's with you guys. I remember when Rachel took him to meet Sid. Nick was really angry about it and didn't want to go. But he changed after he met you guys. He was more relaxed. He got worried about the custody thing. I really wish Rachel had let him tell you what was going on. It would have reassured him. But there's so much that she did with him, letting him stay alone when she was working, that just made me so angry. But I couldn't abandon her when she needed me. She'd been abandoned herself so many times. Anyway, I am glad I got to see him at your wedding. He was so happy. I'd never seen him so happy before, and I don't think it was just the day. It's what he said. He had a real family again, and what he didn't say was that it was a more loving one than the one he'd had."

"I see," I said quietly, feeling somewhat at a loss. "Well, I appreciate you telling me this, Marlou. Please keep us up to date on your address. I mean, I understand about not wanting the contact right now, but if that ever changes, you know we'd love to hear from you."

Marlou sniffed. "You guys are so great. Thanks. I'll have to be in touch with Sid or you in terms of the escrow, anyway."

We said goodbye, and I hung up the phone feeling both sad for Marlou and utterly peeved at her. I understood her feelings. Rachel had gotten me steamed plenty of times over the year and a half I'd known her. But I really resented Marlou wanting to drop out of Nick's life, and worse yet, expecting me or Sid to explain it to the boy.

But I did the explaining. I asked if I could tuck him in that night and he said yes, and I told him that Marlou was having a lot of trouble dealing with his mother's death and would rather not talk to him just yet. He took it better than I would have thought.

"You sure you're not feeling hurt?" I reached over and played with the wavy hair falling over his forehead.

He stood next to the top bunk of his bed and shrugged. "I don't think so. I mean, I like Marlou. But we never really had that much to say to each other. Besides, I kinda know how she feels. It's not fun talking about Mom dying."

"I can imagine it's not. But it's not good to hold those sad feelings in."

"I don't. I talk to you and Dad. That's enough."

"Okay, sweetheart. Good night."

I kissed his cheek and gave him an extra warm squeeze, then left the room so that he could get undressed and into bed on his own. Sid was reading in bed when I got upstairs. He'd already said goodnight to Nick. I got undressed and washed up, then read for a bit longer. All-in-all, it was a normal night until shortly after midnight, when we both woke up to the sound of weeping from the intercom.

"I'll get it," I said, my voice still fuzzy with sleep.

"I'll come with you."

I grabbed my robe and Sid simply followed me downstairs. I knocked on Nick's door.

"Come in," he said sadly.

"We're here, sweetheart," I said, going straight for the bunk bed. I climbed up the ladder and sat down next to him, my legs dangling over the edge. "Was it the same old dream?"

He nodded, laying on his back. "Yeah. It won't go away."

"I know how that feels. But your dad and I are here now." I played with the hair above his forehead.

"I'm not a little kid."

Sid chuckled. "You're not acting like a little kid. You're acting like somebody who's had a lot of hurt in his life."

"I don't want you guys to think I don't want to be here."

"Why would we think that?" I asked.

"I don't know." He turned his head to the wall.

Sid came over and touched Nick's arm. "Son, if you were unhappy with us, I think we would have seen it by now. You're unhappy now because you're still grieving. That's to be expected."

"And the anniversary of losing someone close to us is always hard." I gently squeezed his other arm.

"Yeah. I guess it is."

"Nick," Sid said. "We're a real family, right?"

"Yeah."

"There's nothing more important to me right now than being here with you, and I think I can safely say the same is true for your mom."

I sent Sid a mock glare. "Well, I don't normally like it when your dad speaks for me. But he is right this time. Being here with you right now is the most important thing in the world to me. I love you so much, Nick. And I am so proud of what a strong and brave young man you are. You may not feel very brave at the moment, but that doesn't mean you aren't. We all have our low spots. The one thing you can hang onto is that your first mom loved you. Whatever else happened, that much I know is true because I saw it. She loved you deeply, and if she wasn't the most perfect mom ever, well, neither am I. None of us is perfect. But love is the important thing. Okay?"

His smile was a little weak, but it was there. "Yeah." He took a deep breath. "Can I get a new bed?"

"Why?" Sid asked.

"I'm not a little kid anymore."

"No, you're not, son." Sid chuckled. "Okay. We'll get you a new bed. It may take a few days, okay?"

"Why don't you try to go to sleep now, sweetie?" I toyed with his hair, then ran my finger down his nose.

He laughed softly, but a minute later, he was asleep.

We ended up going out the next day to get the new bed, after we'd taken Esther to work and spent time with Frank on the shooting range. Frank even found a family that could use a bunk bed, and Nick grinned as the family came and picked it up.

To Breanna, 7/31/00

Today's Topic: Something I've Never Told Anyone Before (cont.)

As I've talked to Mom and Dad over the years, I don't think they ever knew that I liked being with them more than being with my first family and how guilty that made me feel. The weird thing is, they still knew what to say to me to make me feel better.

August 5, 1986

S id was not happy when he, Nick, and I got back from our run that next morning to find Josie Prosser and two of her girlfriends waiting near the end of our driveway. Kathy and Jesse had taken Frank and Esther to the gym, then Kathy would work with Frank on codes, and Jesse would get Esther to and from work.

"This is harassment," Sid grumbled as we got inside the house.

"I know." I shook my head as Nick ran ahead to his bedroom to shower and change clothes. "Even Lety's getting fed up. If those girls aren't here, they're over at her place."

"That settles it." Sid glanced at the office. "As soon as I get dressed, I'm calling Whiteman. We've tried talking to the parents. We've tried talking to the girls. Nothing has worked. I want to find out where we stand legally before I call the cops out."

The problem was, because the girls weren't on our property and weren't threatening Nick in any way, they weren't committing any crime. Worse yet, it would be hard to prove that there was any damage to us or Nick. Which, naturally, did not improve Sid's mood any. The one thing that did help was that we'd decided to take Nick with us that day.

We were going up to Running Springs to see what we could find out about Dr. John Levinsky. There were, according to Angelique, some regular FBI agents trying to infiltrate the anti-nuke group, not to mention the agents and LAPD detectives working the Woltz murder. So we weren't expecting to find much. After all, what would Levinsky tell us that he hadn't already told the other agents and the press? We weren't even sure we would talk to him. Still, there was the chance that we'd be able to check out his office in case we'd have to break in and do an evidence swap. Or perhaps a chatty local would tell us something he or she forgot to tell anyone else. We also had a slight advantage in that we knew more than most about KGB practices.

We also went as the Chapel family. It was another set of identities that we'd collected that spring when we'd had to pose as a team of FBI agents for a quick case and realized that no one was going to buy a husband-and-wife team of special agents working together. Angelique, I was willing to bet, didn't know about that set of IDs and I had no idea if she'd ever find out who Lee and Diane Chapel were, let alone their son, Michael.

I brought a new wig of long black hair but didn't put it on. Instead, I wore a pair of jeans and an over-sized t-shirt, knotted at my waist, and my beloved, dirty-gray deck shoes. Sid had on a sport shirt and jeans as well. Nick wore a pair of tan board shorts and a Giants t-shirt and complained that all his jeans were too short and some were too tight, as well.

"My Vans are getting tight, too," he sighed as we headed into the garage.

"I guess we'll be going shopping soon," Sid said. He loaded a picnic basket into the Beemer's trunk. "Didn't we just get you new clothes last month?"

"It was last June, honey," I said. "Right before the Travel Club meeting."

Nick shrugged. "Can I have a snack out of the basket, please? I'm hungry."

Sid sighed and got a couple apples out of the basket, along with some napkins, before closing the trunk lid.

Nick still seemed sad that morning.

"Did you have another nightmare last night?" I asked as we pulled onto the freeway.

"No." Nick chewed on his apple for a moment, then gulped. "I just keep thinking about her, is all."

"Have you tried thinking about happy memories?" I asked.

"Huh. No." He thought for a moment. "I could."

"Why don't you share some of them with us?" Sid glanced at him in the rear-view mirror.

"Well." He frowned, then smiled. "There was the time Mom took me to the tide pools. I was a little kid, maybe six. She told me all about them, too. It was really neat. We didn't go to the beach much, though. Mom didn't like all the sand. We mostly went to the movies. She really loved going to the movies."

"That's right. She did," said Sid softly.

Nick didn't notice. "Then there were the times she let me go to the hospital with her. That was really cool. I got to see her save lives. I mean, I couldn't be in the treatment rooms with her. But you could hear her yell when she was helping somebody, and you knew it was about making sure that person kept living. That was the most important thing in the world to her. Saving people. You know?"

Nick talked on and the few times I looked back at him, I could see that he was feeling better. The look on Sid's face was a little odd, though. I didn't get a chance to ask him about it until we got to Running Springs and stopped at a small market across the street from the clinic where Levinsky had his office. Nick ran ahead of us into the market. I held Sid back.

"You okay?" I asked.

"Why wouldn't I be?" Sid looked genuinely perplexed.

"You just looked so odd when Nick was talking about his mom."

"Oh." Sid winced. "Yeah. That. I was trying to figure out how to deal with it if he has any questions about her."

"You answer the questions, right?"

"If I know the answer." He sighed. "I really didn't know Rachel that well. Even accounting for my problems with relationships back then, Rachel was unusually focused on the sex. The six or seven times I took her out before that weekend we conceived the kid, all she wanted to do was go to a movie, then have sex. She didn't want me sleeping over, she didn't care about dinner, didn't even care about talking that much. That weekend, she didn't even care about the movie. After that weekend, I didn't see her again and didn't really think about her, either, until she brought our son to the doorstep."

I shrugged. "You know, I would be surprised if our boy hasn't figured that out. He knows what you were like, so even if he hasn't, I doubt he'd be surprised to find out you didn't know his mother very well."

"I just don't want to disappoint him."

"There's only so much either of us can do to prevent that. We've been honest with him from the start. I think the only thing that would surprise him is if we lied or pretended."

Sid smiled. "You're probably right." He looked at the gas pumps near the front of the market. "I'd better get the tank topped off while we're here."

Sid is pretty religious about keeping our gas tanks full. Given that we don't always know when we'll be chased, running out of gas at the wrong time is a big problem.

In the store, Nick had three full-sized bags of chips in his hands and looked pleadingly at his father.

"One," Sid growled.

"But I'm hungry."

"Be thankful I'm bending this far."

Nick sighed the sigh of the truly beleaguered, then chose a bag. Sid paid for it and the gas, then left to get the gas pumped. Nick followed him out.

The clerk, a heavy-set woman in a brightly colored blouse, laughed. "They eat so much at that age."

"They do." I chuckled, then noticed a stack of pamphlets next to the register. "Wow. That anti-nuclear thing must be pretty big up here."

"Not really." The clerk jerked her thumb across the street. "It's the doctor across the street. Dr. Levinsky. He leaves the pamphlets here. I humor him."

"Levinsky?" My eyebrows rose. "I think I've heard about him."

The clerk rolled her eyes. "Everybody's heard about him. He's a good doctor, but what a wuss. He's got all those crazies in that group of his and he can't keep them under control." She paused. "Don't believe everything you hear about him. He is a good doctor."

"That's nice." I smiled, then noticed Sid replacing the nozzle on the pump. "My spouse is done pumping. May I have the change, please?"

The clerk looked at me a little funny, but gave me the change from the cash Sid had given her.

"Well?" Sid asked as I settled into the front seat of the car.

I shook my head. "Nothing we haven't already heard. Levinsky's a good guy but can't control some of the bad element that's gotten into his group. She called him a wuss but said he's a good doctor."

We drove around the little town for a bit, then found a scenic overlook with a couple picnic tables. Conchetta had packed a truly awesome picnic. There were three different salads (green, chicken, and barley), a bunch of sandwiches, plenty of fruit and lots of iced tea, ice-cold water, and even a nicely chilled white wine hiding in a metal thermos. However, even I was a little shocked at how quickly Nick sucked up the lion's share of the food. I held Nick back just long enough to be sure his father had all he wanted, got a decent serving for me, then let the boy eat. And he did. Sid was still finishing his lunch when Nick realized there wasn't anything left, including the chips, then went running around the overlook.

"Maybe you should have bought that extra bag or two of chips," I said, laughing.

"Maybe." Sid's eyes rolled, but then he started. "Son! Stay away from that edge."

"It's solid," Nick called back.

"Do as I say." Sid sighed and looked at me. "How is it you can love them to distraction and still want to pound the living daylights out of them?"

"I have no idea, darling. I just know we do." Grinning, I rifled through the tan leather monster of a purse that I normally carry. "I've got some binoculars. We should be able to see the clinic from here."

Sid nodded. I got the binoculars out and went near the edge of the overlook. I could sort of see the clinic, but it looked normal. There was a large corrugated steel shed behind the place. The shed had no windows or markings, so I couldn't tell what it was or why it was there. I thought I saw something in the clinic's window and stepped forward, hoping to see more.

Only Sid's concern about the edge was more than valid. The ground gave way under my feet, and I felt myself sliding down. A small pine tree growing out of the side of the slope broke my fall. The binoculars bounced down the slope.

"Honey!" Sid hollered.

"Mom!"

"I'm okay," I hollered back. Well, my left foot was feeling pretty sore, but that wasn't that big a problem at the moment. "I'm just trying to figure out how I'm getting back up."

"We've got a rope. Son! Stay back!"

The rope dropped reasonably close and with some stretching, I could reach it.

"Got it!" I called as I tied it around my waist.

The tension on the rope tightened immediately, and I slowly began the climb back up, wincing because my left foot was bare and it hurt, too. I looked behind me to see if I could find my deck shoe, but it had disappeared below the slope. As I crested the edge, Sid gave one good solid yank on the rope, then pulled me close into an embrace so tight I could barely breathe.

"I'm okay," I said when I could.

Sid cursed. "You scared me."

"Mom, your foot's bleeding."

I looked down. Blood covered the top of my bare foot along the outside edge.

"Shavings." I tried to put my foot down and step on it. "Oh, man. It hurts, too."

Sid scooped me up and sat me down at the picnic table. He grabbed some napkins and the thermos of water and cleaned my foot.

"Well, your foot isn't swelling, and it looks like just a bad scrape." He poured a little more water over my foot and dabbed at it some more.

I winced. "Honey. I have an idea. Why don't I check out Levinsky firsthand? I've got an injury and there's that black wig in the back and I have the ID to go with it."

Sid made a face. "I was just thinking that we should get Dr. Kline to look at your foot. Alright. Let's go."

Inside the car, I double checked to be sure that I'd put the wallet with the appropriate ID in the inside pocket of my purse. I got the wig on and secured, then told Sid not to go into the doctor's office with me. After all, he would be easily recognizable, especially with Nick in tow. So, I hobbled in on my own from the parking lot.

The receptionist was a medium-weight brunette with glasses and an attitude. The nameplate plate next to her read "Danelle Parks."

"Have you seen the doctor before?" Parks glared at me.

"Uh, no." I smiled weakly. "I just fell down this slope and messed up my foot. I was hoping since this is a clinic that I could get in and get it taken care of sooner rather than later."

"You and everyone else." Parks rolled her eyes, but picked up a clipboard with several forms on it. "You'll need to fill these out. What insurance do you have?"

"We pay up front." I glanced at the window that held the symbols of several credit cards. "I've got my credit card on me."

"We'll require a five-hundred-dollar deposit and I'll have to run it now."

"Fine." I dug a card out of my wallet and gave it to her.

Sid and I do have insurance through the FBI. [Given the risks we ran for them, it was the least they could do. Which I'm sure was what they had in mind. - SEH] But since almost nobody accepts the plan we have, it's easier to just pay for any treatment up front, then work on getting reimbursed. Which says a lot about how easy it isn't to get our plan accepted.

Noting that there wasn't anybody behind me, I spared myself the hassle of limping to the chairs and back and filled out the paperwork at the window. Parks glared at me a couple times but couldn't really say anything. I snuck brief glances at her desk and didn't see anything out of place or odd. However, I did see a flyer for Stop Nukes Now taped to the window between us.

"Boy, I've seen a lot of this anti-nuke stuff around here."

Parks rolled her eyes yet again. "I'm not part of the group. I just work here."

"Oh. Sorry." I handed over the clipboard.

Parks glared at it, then handed it back to another woman behind the desk.

The woman wore a pink uniform and almost immediately went around the desk to the door leading to the treatment rooms.

"Hi, I'm Glynnis. You're Diane, right?"

"Yeah," I said, and hobbled after her into the hall.

She led me into an exam room with the standard bed/table and other stuff, including a rolling stool.

"So, you hurt your foot?"

"I slid down a slope."

Glynnis looked at my foot. "That looks nasty. Good thing you came in."

"Your receptionist doesn't think so."

"Please don't mind her." Glynnis laughed. "You'd be surprised how many people try to stiff Dr. Levinsky and she always takes it personally."

"Dr. Levinsky? You mean the guy protesting that satellite?"

"The very same." Glynnis laughed. "Not that any of us here have anything to do with that group. I don't even know who's in it. I like the idea that Dr. Levinsky is so devoted to his cause, and it's a good cause. Seriously, do we want nuclear warheads in space?"

"No, I guess we don't."

She took my temperature and cooed over how low my blood pressure was, then told me that the doctor would be in shortly and left. The room was utterly normal for an exam room. I debated looking through the cupboards, but decided that could get me in trouble if Dr. Levinsky walked in while I was doing it. It was a good thing I didn't.

The doctor knocked on the door within a couple minutes of Glynnis leaving me.

"Come in," I called.

Levinsky was on the short side of average height, with light brown hair ringing the shiny top of his head. He wore the traditional white coat over a blue dress shirt and black slacks.

"Ms. Chapel?" he asked, and I nodded. "Good to meet you. I understand you had a bit of a fall?"

"Yeah. I messed up my foot." I put the foot in question out where he could see it.

"Hmm." He gently picked my foot up and looked it over. "That's a nasty scrape, but looks like the bleeding is already stopping. I don't see any swelling, either. Can you twist it?"

I did. "Yeah. It just hurts walking on it."

"I'll bet." He pressed it softly here and there. "I'm guessing it's just a scrape, but let's get an x-ray, just in case."

He left a minute later, then the x-ray tech, a fresh young kid with brown hair and an earnest look, came in and helped me hobble to that room. We got the films made. I mentioned the anti-nuke group, and he said he didn't know much about it. I didn't get his name, unfortunately. He helped me back to the exam room, and I waited several minutes more. Dr. Levinsky knocked again, then came in when I said it was okay.

"Well," he said, slapping the x-ray onto the light box on the wall. "There's no sign of a fracture or anything. So, that's good news. We'll get this bandaged, then you stay off it for the next couple days."

"Oh. I run every morning."

Levinsky grinned. "That's a good thing, but skip it for the next week or so until the scab falls off. As long as you can walk without pain, go ahead. But no running. And call your doctor if the pain gets any worse."

"I can live with that."

"I'll have Glynnis come in and get you set up, then."

He left and Glynnis was there within seconds to clean the scrape and get it bandaged. She even gave me a pair of crutches.

"You'll only need these for a few days, but we've got some extras," she told me.

I was not surprised to see the crutches on the itemized bill that Parks handed me as I left. I signed the charge slip and left the clinic. Sid pulled up within a minute, with Nick in the back seat munching on potato chips.

"Hey, can I have some of those?" I asked.

"Sure." Nick handed me the bag.

"Well?" Sid asked.

"It's just a nasty scrape." I stuffed a couple chips into my mouth. "No breaks. I'm just using the crutches because he wants me to stay off the foot for the time being."

Sid winced, but let it go.

"And no running for a week." I handed the chip bag back to Nick.

"I'm not surprised." Sid sent me an annoyed grin. "I'll bet that's breaking your heart."

"Not really."

"Anything else?"

I shrugged. "He seems like a nice, decent guy, and a fairly good doctor. The staff has no connection to the anti-nuke group, although the nurse is sympathetic. Nothing else to say."

Sid sighed. "In short, everything we expected."

"I'm afraid so." I looked down at my bare left foot and sighed.

"What's wrong?"

"No more deck shoes."

I could see Sid biting his tongue. He hated those deck shoes and could never figure out why I was so attached to them. At least, he was decent enough to not sigh too loudly when I put the lone shoe, which had also sprouted a hole that day, back into my section of our closet after I'd gotten undressed for the night.

"We'll get you a new pair this weekend," he said, sliding his arm across my shoulder. "We've got to take Nick out to get clothes, anyway."

"Thanks." I put on a smile and nodded.

"You still seem upset."

I left the closet. "I'm not sure why, but I'm feeling a real loss."

"I'm not surprised." Sid tossed his silk boxer shorts into the hamper and followed me from the big walk-in closet into the bathroom. "You've been holding up for Nick for the past three days. It's probably getting to you."

"That's probably it." I smiled at him again and got out the toothpaste and dental floss.

August 6 – 8, 1986

The next day found me back in my blond wig as Special Agent Linda Devereaux. Kathy had taken Esther to work, but then Sid and I got paged almost before we'd finished breakfast. Sid made the pickup, and it didn't need extra processing, so I called Esther after we'd chosen a route and let her know that she'd be making her first drop during her lunch hour. Given that I'd been seen with Esther as my alter ego, Sid and I decided that it made sense for me to keep that persona up whenever we went near the defense plant.

The only problem was my foot. The scrape had scabbed over, but the whole foot was pretty tender when I tried walking on it, which meant using the crutches. I had Frank drive us. That way, he could also act as look out. After all, the last thing we needed was a tail. As Esther climbed into Frank's car right before noon, Frank kept an eye out. Sure enough, someone was following us, but Frank lost the car almost immediately.

"Amateurs," Frank laughed.

"I agree, but we don't need them," I said. "Now, Esther, you're clear on the process?"

Esther shrugged. "I drop the envelope next to the target, then go get lunch. What could go wrong?"

"Plenty." I checked the right side-mirror again. "But we're looking pretty clear."

As it turned out, it was. We stopped at a taco stand near the plant where Esther worked. The outside tables were full. Frank and I grabbed a table just as four friends left. Esther spotted the Blue line mover, code name Blue Water, wearing a Led Zeppelin concert t-shirt and a Cincinnati Reds baseball hat. She double checked to be sure he was the only one sitting alone in such a shirt and hat, then walked past him to get to the order window. The envelope fell to the ground. Blue Water picked it up. Esther got in line to order.

Frank frowned. "That guy was tailing us last month."

"He was part of the team protecting you and Esther until your adoption came through."

"I ditched him."

"I know." I shook my head. "It was a pain in the butt. On the other hand, it was a good sign."

Esther returned to the table with two bags of tacos and three sodas. Blue Water had already disappeared.

"Good job," I told her.

She shrugged. "It was easy."

"It won't always be." I sighed.

We divided up the tacos and ate. Esther and I slathered hot sauce on ours. Esther cursed as she dribbled hot sauce down her front. I sent Frank after some cold water and napkins.

"What's that for?" Esther asked me.

"So you can clean your top."

"Why?"

That's when I realized why Esther usually wore front-buttoned shirts in colorful prints. They didn't show the stains so much. Esther bent over and licked up the hot sauce from her front. When Frank got back, she shrugged and wiped down the remains with the cold water.

"The stain will come out a lot more easily when you clean it up right away," I told her.

"I use stain remover. It's fine."

My pager went off. The code in the display meant that Sid needed me at home as soon as possible.

"We've got to get you back to work," I said, pulling together taco wrappings.

We hurried back to the plant, Esther went inside, then Frank and I left.

"Do we have a tail?" I asked Frank, after checking and not seeing one myself.

"Nope. They must be watching from the parking lot."

"Which means we'd better start letting her off at different entrances."

Thanks to sitting out in the sun, my scalp was sweaty, so I pulled the wig from my head and fluffed out my hair as Frank drove us home.

At the house, Frank followed me in, and we started for the office, but then saw that Sid, Tom, and Angelique were in the living room. Tom sat next to Ange on the couch, his arms holding her. Tom is a big man, tall, broad-shoul-dered, with receding blond hair and wire-rimmed glasses. Sid sat on Ange's other side, close enough to be comforting without touching her.

I signaled Frank to hang back, then went over to the couch.

"I'm here," I said softly. "What's going on?"

Ange blinked back tears. "Lydia died this morning."

"Oh, no!" I looked at the couch next to her.

Sid slid out of the way, and I sat and put my arms around her.

"I'm so sorry," I whispered.

"It's okay," Ange said, weeping. "I mean, it's terribly sad and I'm going to really miss her. But she was in a lot of pain, and all."

"What happened?"

Ange swallowed. "She took a turn for the worse last night. At least, that's what Conrad said when he called his morning. She didn't want to go to the hospital. Said it would only prolong things. But both Conrad and Colton were there with her and Henry, and she died at home, like she wanted to."

Conrad and Colton were Henry and Lydia's two sons.

"How's Henry doing?"

"I don't know." Ange began weeping harder, then sniffed. "Conrad said he's managing, but I have no idea what the hell that means."

There was an odd undercurrent from both Sid and Tom as Ange tried to get her tears under control.

"Haven't you been to see him?" I asked.

Ange shook her head and sobbed for a moment. "No. Colton only wants family there."

"But you're family."

"No, I'm not. At least, not as far as Colton's concerned."

I heard Tom mutter something obscene.

"No, Tom!" Angelique gulped and got a hold of herself. "I mean, yeah, he's being pretty rotten, but it's for good reason. He's always hated how his parents took in every waif off the street, and he never said anything about it. Then he blew up at his dad the other night when Henry wanted me to come over. Colton always felt like he wasn't enough, and because he didn't say anything, Henry and Lydia couldn't reassure him." Ange sniffed again. "That's why he resents me and Sid, too. We were their latest adoptees."

"You poor thing," I said, squeezing her tighter.

Angelique had a difficult relationship with her own mother, and Lydia always said that Ange was the daughter she'd never had.

"You know, Ange," I said, giving her another squeeze. "This really sucks and I'm sure it hurts like crazy. But it is really, really kind of you to give Colton his space."

Ange nodded. "I'm only glad Tom's here, and that I've got Sid and you. Even my brother doesn't get how close I am to Henry and Lydia."

Sid made a point of calling Jesse and having him pick Esther up from work. Jesse took Frank with him, and I do not know what all they did. Nick had already gone over to Josh's and the two were having a sleep-over there. I don't know if Sid set that up or it just happened. [It just happened. - SEH]

We spent the afternoon talking about Lydia and Henry. Lydia's slightly wicked sense of humor that popped out at the strangest times. The way Henry had to take care of everybody within reach. We even got to talking about Sid's and Angelique's former relationship.

"I have to say the two weeks thing was probably my fault," Sid said as we finished dinner in the breakfast room.

"No, I don't think so," Ange said. "Henry used to warn me off you, and it wasn't that he didn't like you. I know that because he'd warn me off some of the guys down at the office, and it was obvious that he didn't like them. You and I just weren't a good match. We liked each other okay, but something was missing."

"I'm sure there was something missing." Tom grinned at Sid. "I remember your aunt saying that she was not surprised to see you settle down, only that it took so long. She was right. You were looking to settle down even before you got sent to Vietnam. Coming back, you seemed to want it even more."

Sid frowned. "You know that's possible. But I sure as hell didn't have the relationship skills then."

"Did any of us?" Tom laughed loudly.

"Huh," I said. "I wonder, Sid, if you were trying to make it work with Angelique. I mean, Ange, you were around more than anybody. You got Sid talking when I got engaged to George."

Ange looked at Sid. "So why couldn't we make it work?"

"You're asking me?" Sid looked befuddled, then paused. "You were too nice in a way. Lisa forced me to communicate with her."

"Well, we had to if we were going to work together," I said.

"Yeah, but I know what Sid's saying," Tom said, reaching over to take Ange's hand. "Ange, you don't let me off the hook, either. We work at our relationship."

"We never worked that hard at ours," said Sid. "I don't know how much of that was the sex."

Ange made a face. "You know, I thought that might be where we blew it." She looked sheepishly at Tom. "One of the reasons I held you off for so long."

I grinned. "Oh, so you finally did it?"

"It's been over three weeks now," said Tom.

Sid laughed. "It's been months! And you only first got it on three weeks ago?"

"Hey, it worked for you and Lisa." Ange giggled, then fondly looked over at Tom. "Let's face it. We were both seriously gun shy."

"Yeah." Tom sighed. "We both come from messed-up families. I have the whole addiction thing." He winced. "There was Beth."

"Beth." Sid's eyes rolled. Beth was Tom's ex-wife. "I never could figure out what you saw in her."

"Somebody to support my disease." Tom sighed. "And speaking of, I saw Stan a few months ago. He's still a mess. Divorced twice and working on number three."

Stan was part of the group of six friends that included Sid and Tom in high school. One of the guys had died in Vietnam and both Sid and Tom had lost track of the two others.

Sid groaned. "God, we were stupid back then."

Tom shook his head. "You were stupid. I was an addict and still am. I came by it honestly, but that's the reality."

"Your folks weren't drunks, were they?" Sid asked.

Tom laughed loudly. "Are you kidding? Mom pretty much had a buzz on constantly. Dad usually stayed sober until he got home from work, but after that, it was cocktails and beer for the rest of the night."

"Huh." Sid looked thoughtful. "I bought it that your mom was just a klutz."

"Nah. She was miserable and had no way to express it. They're both still together and still miserable." Tom sighed.

"Not unlike my parents," Angelique said. "They don't drink that much. But they hate each other. They'll never divorce. I could never figure out why Mom wanted me and my brother to get married so badly when she was so unhappy with her marriage. For some reason, she still thinks that marriage is what makes you happy."

We all shuddered at that.

Eventually, Tom took Angelique home. Frank and Esther came back to our place shortly after. They offered their sympathies on Lydia's death, then went to the guest room. Sid and I made our way upstairs.

"How are you feeling?" I asked him as we got into bed.

He made a face. "Sad. Strange." He sighed as he settled onto his pillow. "How do I say this? I've had several father figures in my life." Sid doesn't know who his father was. "Including quite a few who thought they were more important than they were. But Henry never played that game. He just was. There was something about him. I could talk to him in a way I couldn't to anybody else, except you, and still can. And Lydia was the same. I mean, I didn't talk to them the way I talk to you. Still, Lydia paved the way for you. She didn't push me to communicate, but she didn't let me off on my B.S., either. I didn't know what a gift that was until I met you. If it hadn't been for Lydia getting on my ass that week we started fighting, right before we left for DC and had that really bad fight, I wouldn't have stayed in that room and kept talking, and you would have been gone."

I pulled him close to me and held him tightly.

The next morning, both our hearts were heavy, but we went over to Henry's house. Ange and Tom were already there, for which I thanked God. Colton was still annoyed when he saw us. At the same time, there were so many other people coming by to thank Henry and Colton for

Lydia being there for them. Henry wasn't quite a mess. He was terribly, terribly sad. But he had also found some peace in being grateful for the time he'd had with his wife. I tried to imagine what I would feel like losing Sid after thirty-six years and couldn't.

Colton asked Sid to give the eulogy for Lydia at the funeral, which would be the following Monday. Sid agreed and started taking notes among the other people at the house. We spent most of the day there, which was a little awkward, given Frank and Esther's training, but it was important.

Friday, I finally got to go to lunch with my friend Leslie. My foot was a lot better, and I could abandon the crutches. I still couldn't wear anything that covered my instep or that outer edge of my foot, but I had a pair of flat sandals that had a strap over the big toe and an ankle strap that missed the scraped part quite nicely. Of course, I couldn't wear nylons, but we were coming into the hotter part of the summer, and I was perfectly happy skipping those.

I met Leslie in Burbank, near the studio where her station operated. We got settled inside the restaurant and ordered.

"Looks like you're doing really well," I said as we waited for our food to arrive. "It seems like every time I turn on the news, you're on it."

Leslie laughed. "They've been keeping me busy. I am so glad I caught that satellite story while it was still small. Now that there's a murder connected to it, I'm running with it. Oh, and thanks for connecting me to that FBI guy. He's a pain in the arse, but he likes me, so I get stuff."

"You're welcome."

We paused as the waitress brought a pastrami on toasted rye with cole slaw for me and a salad for Leslie.

"Speaking of the FBI, though," Leslie said, putting her fork through the greens on her plate. "It's kind of weird that they're investigating the murder alongside LAPD."

"That's not usually their jurisdiction." I got a hold of my sandwich and bit into it.

"I know. Merryweather hinted that there's something else connected to the murder that is their jurisdiction, but he won't say what."

I was grateful for that.

"I just wish I could get some real information on Levinsky," Leslie continued. "I went up to Running Springs on my day off last week and didn't get squat. He's not talking to the media anymore. Plus, no one knows which of the group members are the ones supposedly getting violent. You'd think they would. But all the actual threats have been made anonymously, and as far as the group members are concerned, the threats are just rumors, anyway."

"Huh."

Leslie chewed thoughtfully for a moment. "You know, this would still make a good story for you and Sid."

"It might." I shrugged. "Only we're not doing as much writing these days. We've got that editing job now, and it's pretty time consuming."

Lunch went on. Still, as I drove home, I tried to make sense of what Leslie had said about the group members.

"Sid?" I asked, limping a little as I went into the office.

He looked up from his desk. "How was lunch?"

"It was good." I slid into my chair. "Where are Frank and Nick?"

"Kathy took Frank on a pickup and drop. And Nick went skateboarding at the beach with Josh and Rob. Rob's mom is doing the driving."

"For a change." I tried not to roll my eyes.

Sid's eyebrow lifted hopefully. "Any reason you're asking?"

"It's a Need to Know issue, as in they don't." I shifted. "And you're the one who keeps saying we shouldn't be getting into any bad habits."

He sighed. "True. So, what's up?"

I told him what Leslie had said about the members of Stop Nukes Now not being able to say who the violent members were.

Sid thought it over. "So, either the entire group is bent on protecting each other, or the violent folks are not part of the group, or the violent folks are really good at covering up who they are."

"I think those latter two seem more likely." I bit my lip. "This is crazy. We've seen some real amateur behavior on this, and some truly professional behavior. What the heck is going on?"

"I have no idea. Why would the professionals be involving the amateurs? The only reason I can think of would be to cover the pros' activity."

"But anybody like us or even the FBI guys working this would be able to tell which activity is which. The amateurs might not get it, but the professionals surely would and would know that it's not much cover."

Sid shrugged. "I have no idea, and when we get right down to it, it's not necessarily our job to figure it out. Our job is to protect and train Frank and Esther."

"I suppose that's true." I drummed my fingers on my desk. "But it would be a heck of a lot easier to do that job if we had the rest of this solved."

"That's why we went up to Running Springs. Which leads me to ask how your foot is doing?"

I winced. "It's still a little sore, but I can walk on it."

"So, no running still."

"Not 'til Tuesday."

Sid grinned. "How about some other activity that does not involve you on your feet?"

I grinned back. "Bad habits?"

"Just a quick one."

I looked at him, but I couldn't resist.

August 9 – 11, 1986

That Saturday proved to be one of those days. It had started the night before when Esther's carping about her boss, Ross Sorensen, led to the conclusion that one of us should search his office just to be on the thorough side, and to the conclusion that I should be that one.

Normally, a Saturday in summer means that I've got an entire day to enjoy sewing or reading or whatever. Having to put on a wig in the heat of August, put on business wear so that I look like the aboveboard FBI agent I am not, and go break into a defense plant where all the employees are on high alert was not my idea of a nice way to spend my weekend. Nonetheless, that's how I spent my morning.

Sid drove to the plant. He, Nick, and Frank would stay in the car while Esther and I went into the plant from a back entrance. Nick was with us because we were going to go clothes shopping after the search was done. All five of us were wired. I limped a little because my foot was still a little sore and the nylons and pumps didn't help.

As Esther and I got up to the top floor, Sid's voice in my ear told me where he'd parked a couple blocks away. There was a side entrance to the building that could not be seen from the parking lot, and we decided we'd leave through there and walk back to the car, on the theory that no one would expect us to take that route. The fact that whoever didn't was probably what saved us.

It took a while to search Sorensen's office. Esther was meticulous about it, and I have to admit, I was impressed. Alas, we didn't find anything. Esther hadn't found anything in Gil Woltz's office, either.

I told Sid through the wire when we were heading out the side door. The three buildings that made up Esther's plant all fronted onto the street, with a variety of bushes and plants in between them and on either side of the two outside buildings. Esther's building was at the end of the complex. More plants and bushes filled narrow spaces in front of the buildings, and the sidewalk was broken up by trees planted every so often along the curb.

Across the street was a series of generic office buildings, and none of them were particularly secure. As Esther and I walked to the street, movement caught my eye, and I pulled Esther back just as bullets rained down on us. Esther screamed. She struggled against me and tried to run in front of the building, unfortunately, away from where the car was.

"Big Red, we're under fire," I yelped, pulling Esther into some bushes.

"Copy, Little Red. Tiny, can you see where it's coming from?"

"Yeah," said Nick's voice in my ear. "It's that building directly across from the side entrance."

Esther slid out of my grasp and started running for the front of the building. I dove after her as the gunfire started up again.

"Red Gate, you're panicking!" I hissed at her as I shoved her into the bushes. "You almost ran right into the line of fire." I pulled my Model Thirteen from my purse. "Tiny, where is the sniper?"

"On the roof."

"Tiny, stay in the car," Sid's voice said. "Red Door, we're going to stay close to the buildings and see if we can't provide some crossfire. Little Red, can you cover us?"

"Can do," I said.

I looked between the fronds of a small palm tree and fired at the top of the building across from us.

"Red Door, move. Now." Sid's voice was tight.

"Don't we have a rifle?" Frank squeaked.

"Not at the moment. Now, let's go!"

I heard two car doors slam and sent another couple rounds at the top of the building, hoping I had some extra ammo in my purse. I don't always. It's heavy and I seldom need it. Another couple minutes later, I heard gunshots across the street and saw Sid and Frank firing at the top of the roof. The sniper seemed to back off.

"Little Red, can you get Red Gate across the street?"

"How much extra ammo do you have on you?"

"Plenty. Ready?"

I got a solid grip on Esther's arm. "Ready."

"Move out firing."

I did, emptying the gun. Esther almost beat me across the street, but then I was firing and had a slightly gimpy foot. When we got to the cover of the other building, Sid nodded, and I pushed Esther ahead of me to where Sid's Beemer was. Sid let off several more rounds and kicked Frank into a run behind us. A minute later, we were all in the car and Sid pulled out as fast as he could, even before we'd all gotten our seat belts on.

Esther sobbed in the middle of the back seat, while Frank shook and gasped for air.

"Is everyone okay?" I asked.

"I think so," Frank gasped. "Man, I messed up."

Okay, he used another word for messed.

"It's your first brush with violence, Frank," Sid said. "Everyone freaks."

"I didn't freak," Nick said.

"No. You were stupid." Sid glared at him in the rear-view mirror. "Something I am very glad you've gotten past."

"What did you get us into?" Esther screamed, adding her usual vile epithet.

I turned on her. "We didn't get you into this scenario. The KGB did and your job did. And you might want to be thankful we did get you into this business. If we hadn't, you'd be dead by now."

Both Esther and Frank turned pale and swallowed.

"How's your foot?" Sid asked, whipping the car around the others on the 405 freeway.

"It hurts," I grumbled and lifted the nylon stocking away from the scab. "But there's no bleeding."

"All right." Sid glanced at me. "We'll go get some lunch and bring it home. Think we should call Kathy and Jesse?"

"Can't hurt," I said.

"What about my clothes?" Nick came perilously close to whining.

"We'll go out after church and errands tomorrow," Sid said.

"The deli okay?" I asked Sid, then looked back at Frank and Esther.

"Deli's good," said Frank, listlessly.

Fortunately, I had the number to the delicatessen I was thinking of in my purse and used the car phone to call in an order. It wasn't that far out of our way and was well worth it when we got home. I'd also called Kathy and Jesse, and they were waiting for us when we pulled up.

Both Frank and Esther were still very shaky. Bless her, Kathy had gotten Jesse to make a stop before getting to the house. Sid took one look at the bottle of bourbon they'd brought and got the water glasses from the kitchen. I sighed and went upstairs to Sid's and my closet. In the far corner is a stack of notebooks and binders filled with cipher. I got the first couple sets of wire-bound notebooks and brought them downstairs with me. The dining table was cluttered with paper wrappings, boxes of potato, macaroni, and green salad, and stacks of sandwiches. The bottle of bourbon was almost emptied. Even Nick got a small snort, which he made a face at. We let Nick have a little bit of alcohol with food, hoping that he'll learn to respect it and not see it as tempting forbidden fruit. He really likes wine, but in small doses and so far, is not enthused by spirits.

"How do you deal with it?" Esther asked, adding multiple curse words. "I've never been so scared in my life. We had to sneak out of Vietnam in the middle of the war and I wasn't as scared as I was today."

"You were fourteen, Esther," said Frank. "Even you said you felt invulnerable."

Esther let out a string of curses, both in English and Vietnamese.

"It is scary," said Kathy with her own special calm. "You should have seen me when I first got shot at. I was a basket case and scared to death that I wasn't going to be able to do this when Jesse really wanted to."

"I was just as much a mess." I plopped the notebooks in front of Frank and Esther. "You wonder about that thing I have with stiffs. Read that and you'll know why."

I blinked back the tears. I hated sharing those journals. But they'd helped Kathy and Jesse get through that first shooting episode. I had to hope the journals would help Frank and Esther.

"Being scared is part of the job," Sid said softly. "But we learn to deal with it, and in a healthy way, I hope."

Esther opened the first notebook. "R-four cipher. Oh, that's an easy one." She read the first few lines. "Woh." She looked at me. "Okay. We'll read this tonight."

"I'm sorry I got so hard on you today," I said.

Esther sighed. "You were probably right." She cocked her head. "You know. I think we can do this. I mean, it was scary today. But you guys are okay. Why not us?"

Jesse grinned. "Absolutely, why not you? You guys have something. And we all have something. This is going to be good."

We continued talking, even explaining why Nick had been so stupid the first time he'd encountered people shooting. We eventually ordered in some pizzas and spaghetti for dinner. Sid got out a couple of Angelique's better bottles of wine. As the night finally drew on, Frank and Esther went to their room and Jesse and Kathy hugged us and went home. Sid and I followed Nick into his bedroom to say goodnight.

"Was I really that stupid that first time?" The look on his face was quite pained.

"Yes, you were," I said. "We were really worried that you were not going to be able to follow a command when it was that crucial."

Sid pulled him close and hugged him. "The good news is you learned. A lot of people don't. I was proud of you today. You kept your head, and you stayed out of trouble. That made it a lot easier for me to deal with Frank. I love you, Nick."

"I love you, Dad."

They kissed each other's cheeks.

My hug was next. "I love you, my sweet guy."

"I love you, Mom."

I suddenly realized that the top of his head was really close to my cheek. Still, I kissed him good night without comment, and Sid and I went upstairs.

"You're looking awfully pensive," Sid said as we got undressed.

I made a face. "A lot going on, I guess." I gestured on my cheek. "Nick's up to here now."

"I thought he seemed a little taller." Sid shook his head.

"That's how it's supposed to work," I said, sighing. "It still feels weird."

Sid nodded. "How's your foot? Still sore?"

I looked down at it. "No, it's fine."

The only problem was that I noticed my lone deck shoe on the shelf in the closet. We got washed up and got into bed.

"So, what are you thinking about now?" Sid asked as he pulled me next to him.

"My deck shoes."

"They're just shoes, Lisa. We'll get another pair tomorrow."

I shook my head. "This pair wasn't." I sighed. "Sid, do you realize that pair of shoes was one of the few things I have from my life before you?"

"You have several stacks of books and records."

"That are now our books and records and are intermingled with yours and whatever we've acquired since then."

"What about clothes?"

"Believe it or not, I gave all those clothes away that first spring after we met. They didn't fit anymore. They were too big."

"Really?"

"Yeah." I rolled onto my back and sighed. "I had no idea what I was doing then. Between having to sell everything because I was out of work, then getting rid of the extra because I didn't need it anymore, I really don't have much of anything from before when I met you. There's that necklace with my name pendant, which I can't wear because of the side business." We didn't use monograms or anything like that lest we give someone a clue that would lead them to our real selves. "Then there are the Christmas ornaments that Mama gave me last Christmas from our old tree. But those are it. And the deck shoes, and those are gone, now, too."

"Oh, honey." He snuggled up against me and nuzzled my ear.

I blinked back tears. "It's not like things aren't better now. They are. It just feels weird losing that last bit of my life."

"I think I understand that." He brushed my cheek with his hand. "Do you want a new pair?"

"Yeah, I think I do, but they won't be the same." I shrugged. "It's kind of like seeing Nick grow. On one hand, that's what I hope will happen because he should be growing. But at the same time, I kind of miss the boy we had."

Sid's chuckle was both rueful and sad. "Yeah. I do, too."

I sighed again. "You know, the other night, after I first lost the shoe, you asked me why I was upset."

"Of course."

"It's not just the shoes. I'm missing a lot of things right now. Lydia. Our life before." I rolled over and faced him. "You know what I really miss? It just being the two of us. You and me against the world. Now, we've got a team and team members and everything." I sighed again. "It's just so much more complicated. It was so nice when it was just us."

"It was also a lot more dangerous and a lot more difficult."

"True." I smiled at him. "How do you feel about it all?"

His eyebrows rose. "The same way you do. It is better now, but there's that twinge. Nick's supposed to grow, but damn, he was cute as a kid. It's good having backup and team members, but there was something about it being just the two of us." He caressed my cheek. "If I haven't been thinking about how life was, it's because this is our life now. I'm happier now than I've ever been, and I hope you are, too."

I rolled onto my back and thought about it. "Yeah. I am. The funny thing about the past is remembering all the nice parts and forgetting the nasty bits. It's better being here with you than it ever was."

Yeah, it was one of those moments and led where you might expect. And I was glad that it had, especially the following Monday. That was the day of Lydia James' funeral.

Oh, it was sad. It wasn't the kind of sad that meant regrets and anger. It was just people feeling bad that they hadn't had more time with her.

Truth be told, I hadn't known Lydia all that well. We were friends, of course, but I hadn't had the chance to get to know her the way Sid or a lot of people at the funeral had. It was a graveside service. Lillian Ward, aka The Dragon, was there because she was a good friend of Henry's and Lydia's through our Travel Club, which, while it had civilians in it, was our primary contact within Quickline and with other agencies. So were Clint Foster and his wife, Dierdre. Clint was the CIA liaison in the club. Marian and Andrew, the driving forces behind the Travel Club, hadn't been able to get away for the funeral, but had sent a huge wreath of flowers on a stand.

Thank God, the funeral people had erected a large canopy over the chairs and the grave. The sun was murderously hot that day, and even in the canopy's shade, it was broiling. Sid and I left Nick at home. Nick barely knew who Lydia was and given how he was feeling after the anniversary of his mother's death, he was not in the mood for a funeral.

Sid's forehead glistened with sweat as he went to the podium for the eulogy. For once, he didn't seem to mind. He used his pocket color to wipe the sweat from his forehead, then shuffled his notes, and swallowed.

"When Colton asked me to give the eulogy today, he said he figured I had the best chance of not breaking down." Sid swallowed again and blinked. "I'm afraid, Colton, that may have been more optimistic than not. There are a lot of stories to share. I've heard many of them over the past few days. The time Lydia yelled at the Little League coach for not putting all his team in the game, never mind that it was the league finals. The time Lydia went after Henry's boss about the hours he was putting in and not getting paid for. Lydia's standard response to any unplanned guest for dinner, that she just put another potato in the pot." Sid chuckled. "Of course, if it was my Lisa coming for dinner, Lydia always teased her that it was more like four or five potatoes because of how much food my darling can consume in one sitting. It was never mean. Lydia simply knew Lisa and appreciated how my sweetheart loves to eat." Sid paused again and blinked. "The thing is, I would not have Lisa if not for Lydia. When I first met Lisa almost four years ago, I had nothing resembling good relation-ship skills. I have to give Lisa the credit for forcing me to communicate with her. However, if it weren't for Lydia, Lisa would not have been able to. You see, there was a fight that was sort of happening a couple months after I'd hired Lisa as my secretary. Lisa wanted to talk about it and settle it. I avoided it, as I did most such conflicts. It was easier that way. The only problem was, I really needed Lisa's skills, and letting her go would make my life infinitely more difficult. So, one night during that time, I ended up at Henry and Lydia's for dinner, and complained to Henry about how difficult some women could be. Lydia laughed at me, long and loud, then said that if this woman was such a pain in the ass, then she must be good for me and that I should listen to her. I am so grateful for that dig. Less than a week or so later, the fight between Lisa and I had escalated. Lisa delivered a body-slam for the ages, but still thought that we could work it out. I came this close to walking out. But Lydia's words came back to me, and I gave Lisa a chance." Sid looked straight at me, and I started weeping. He took a deep breath. "I cannot tell you how glad I am that I did. Lydia literally paved the way for that confrontation. If I have any regrets, it's that I never told Lydia how much she had to do with my relationship with Lisa. I sometimes think Lydia knew. She would look at the two of us and grin, and I have to wonder. The funny thing is, I don't think it mattered to her. She was who she was, loving, reaching out, finding the good in everyone she touched." He took another deep breath. "So, here is the challenge I offer to every one of us today. Lydia chose to love deeply and broadly. The broad part of it may have been a little hard for some of her family, but it has meant the world to the rest of us. If she could do it, why can't we? Let us make loving others her legacy. It is what she did. Why can't we do the same? Let us see others, especially those in need of a loving hand, as part of our families. Let us reach out in acceptance and joy, not settling for B.S., but choosing to care, to love. If Lydia could make me, who had no frame of reference for love, see how to be loving, then we all can. I will miss Lydia. I know that Henry, Conrad, Colton, their wives and kids will miss her far more than I will. But thanks to her, we can make this world a better place, and I believe that would make Lydia glad."

Several people came up after Sid to share their memories, although Angelique chose not to. Eventually, the minister presiding over the event led us through The Lord's Prayer, and the crowd slowly filtered away. There was to be a small reception back at the house, but it was for family members only. Sid offered to take Angelique and Tom to lunch, but they declined.

"Colton invited us to the reception," Ange said, swallowing. "I'll call you later this afternoon?"

"Sure," I said.

Sid and I ended up agreeing to lunch with Lillian. Clint and Dierdre paid their respects to Henry right away and left the cemetery quickly. When it was our turn to talk to the family, Colton thanked Sid for the eulogy. Henry and Sid just held each other for several minutes, then Henry held me.

"Thank you, guys," Henry whispered, then turned to Lillian, who was behind us.

We moved on, pausing only to confirm which restaurant we were going to.

It was a quiet lunch and while it was pleasant enough, Lillian said that she had to get back to DC, and Sid and I agreed we had work to do back at the house.

Ange called around four that afternoon.

"It's no big deal," she said. "But it could be a problem. Tom's not excited about the top-secret part of my job."

"Oh, no," I said. "Just when things were going so well."

"We're fine." Ange laughed a little. "Really. It's just something Tom said. He can't help wondering which of the people I'm working with are doing the top-secret stuff."

"As in, he might be wondering about us."

"Yeah. I think I put him off. I told him he doesn't want to be wondering too much or he'll be suspecting everyone and getting paranoid. At least, he knows not to ask questions."

It was small comfort, but there wasn't much to be done about it.

W hen I got back from dropping Esther off at work that morning, Sid and Frank were in the office staring at a huge piece of my tracing paper. Sid had sketched in a map, but I wasn't sure of what.

Sid looked up as I came in. "Frank, why don't you take off for a few?"

"Why?" Frank asked.

"Because I need to talk to Lisa privately."

Frank looked at Sid, then at me. "Oh. Okay."

He scuttled off elsewhere in the house. Sid double checked that the intercom was off. We hadn't told Frank or Esther how it worked, but we wouldn't have been surprised if they'd figured it out.

"So, what's up?" I asked, locking the door.

"We got a call this morning from Angelique. The agent in charge of the Levinsky case is requesting covert ops support, and Ange said that according to Henry, that means us."

"Oh, goody."

"There's a Stop Nukes Now rally happening today in Westwood. Apparently, the group is going to be lining the sidewalks, handing out flyers, and trying to get people to honk in support."

"So, why aren't the Feds handling it?"

Sid sighed. "Because the good Doctor Levinsky has become something of a political problem. It's gotten out over the past few days that he's being persecuted by the Feds because of Woltz. And the Feds haven't been able to penetrate that far into the group's inner workings because the group leaders keep things pretty well locked down. Anyway, the Feds have two different objectives. They want someone to keep an eye on Levinsky, himself, and a team on the protesters. Hopefully, we'll be able to figure out who the violent folks are."

"Sounds like fun. Who do we have in town?"

"Scott Morgan." Sid shuddered.

He really did not like Scott, whose code name was Red Light. Sid had good reason for his dislike since Scott had blown Sid's cover on a case a couple years before. Scott had gotten somewhat less cocky, but he could still be a pain in the butt. However, he was darned good at tailing people.

"Why don't I take Scott and Frank, and we'll tail Levinsky," I said. "I'll keep the blond wig on. That should keep Levinsky from recognizing me."

"I was hoping you'd say that. I'll bring Nick and keep Kathy and Jesse with me and see if the Blue hub team is available for the crowd surveillance."

"Sounds good."

I looked at the map Sid had sketched out and found at least two different places I could use as a base for the operation, then paged Scott.

Frank and I met Scott later that morning at a restaurant south of the Westwood Village on Westwood Boulevard. Frank laughed when he saw Scott's rangy figure and straw-colored hair and full mustache.

"You were tailing me," Frank chortled.

"Yeah, and you ditched me." Scott grinned. "Man, that was beautiful."

"Red Light," I said to Scott and pointed at Frank. "This is Red Door. Red Door, this is Red Light."

Frank grinned. He still wasn't used to being called Red Door, his code name, but he'd get used to it in time.

I made sure the three of us had our transmitters on the same frequency and sketched out our plan. I'd put our transmitters on a different frequency than Sid's crew to minimize the confusion. Sid would ping my transmitter once he or someone on his team had eyes on Levinsky.

Which would have been what happened, except that I saw Levinsky first from the pizza parlor where I had landed with a Complete Works of Shakespeare and a notepad. I sent Frank after Levinsky first and spotted both of them a minute later from my perch next to the window. I changed frequency just long enough to let Sid know we had the tailing operation in progress.

The protest was noisy, but seemed pretty peaceful. I took some notes on Richard II, mostly because it is not my favorite play and I wouldn't get too absorbed in it, and every so often directed Frank and Scott to switch up tailing Levinsky.

The doctor stayed on the fringes of the protest. The few times he wandered past the pizza place, he accepted congratulations from different protesters. A couple stood in awe of him, and he seemed truly kind and almost bashful. I tried not to sigh when I saw Barb DeMarais, the teen from my church, handing out flyers. I changed frequencies again and let Sid know. We'd already figured it would be possible we'd know some of the protesters. We have more than a few activists in our parish. I later saw Nick teaming up with Barb to hand out flyers, then saw the boy charming the socks off a woman who was making sure everyone had enough flyers.

I ordered some more pizza. Levinsky wandered back and forth along the sidewalks. Horns honked. People yelled. Flyers were everywhere on the sidewalks. Sometime around two, someone started shooting. We never found out who or why. Screaming erupted all over the boulevard as people dove for the sidewalks. I looked frantically around for any of Sid's crew.

Frank hissed into his transmitter that Levinsky had left the boulevard for one of the parking structures to the west.

"I'm on him!" Frank said.

"Right behind you, Red Door," came Scott's voice.

Frank yelped. "He's got a gun."

"Does he look like he's about to shoot someone?" I asked.

"I've got a clear shot at him," Frank said.

"Take it, Red Door," Scott said, laughing.

"Red Door, stand down!" I all but yelped. "Now!"

It was too late. I heard the gun go off. Frank cursed.

"I missed," he grumbled.

"It's a good thing you did," I snarled. "I told you to stand down. That means no shooting."

"But he had a clear shot," Scott protested.

"Red Light, shut up. Do not say another word." I looked out the window. People were running all over, but the street seemed to be emptying. "Where's the target?"

They had lost him. I was ready to unload on both of them, but changed frequencies and pinged Sid.

"Everyone okay?" I asked.

"Everyone's fine, but the protest seems to be over. I say we end operations."

"May as well," I grumbled.

"Uh-oh. What happened?"

"I'll explain later." I switched back to Frank and Scott. "Operation over, you two. We'll meet back at that restaurant where we started. Go. Now."

The two confirmed, and when I got to the restaurant's parking lot, I was happy to see them looking at least a little contrite. That didn't mean Scott would not attempt the strong offense.

"We could have ended this thing," Scott announced as I walked up to them in the parking lot behind the restaurant.

"You don't know that, you idiot!" I went right up to him and shoved him in the chest. "As usual, you assumed you knew, and you didn't!"

I shoved him again and Scott tried hitting me. I saw the punch coming, blocked it, blocked another, then whipped Scott around and pulled his arm behind his back and pulled his hand back. Groaning, Scott sank to his knees.

"There's a reason I'm lead." I twinged him with each point. "And if you don't understand how that works, then I will bust your backside all the way back to Langley. The Company loves idiots like you." I released the hold and shoved him to the asphalt face-first. "And your hand-to-hand skills suck. Now, get the hell out of here!"

Scott scrambled to the back of the lot where he'd parked the cab of a semi-trailer truck. His cover was as a long-haul trucker.

I turned on Frank, who backed up in fear.

"I'm not going to hit you," I told him. "But, yes, I am angry. Now, get in the truck!"

Frank swallowed as he got into the cab of my Datsun pickup.

"I... I... I didn't hear you telling me to stand down," he mumbled. "I really didn't."

"I had a feeling." I took a deep breath and started the truck. "I probably should have warned you not to listen to Red Light. But I would have thought you'd check with me first."

"I had a clear shot," Frank said, weakly.

"Was he pointing the gun at you or anyone else?" I pulled the truck out.

Frank sighed. "No."

"Then it doesn't matter. You don't know that he's the guy we're trying to catch. We don't know if he's the guy we're trying to catch. You could have killed an innocent person. Believe me, killing someone you know is guilty feels bad enough."

"Oh." Frank winced. "You sure took Red Light down fast."

"That's because Sid and I practice. We practice a lot. You might want to keep that in mind."

He looked like he was going to say something else, but the glare I shot him stopped that.

We rode home in silence. I switched my transmitter to Sid's as I drove and could hear him talking to the Blue hub team. I cut in and told Sid where I was headed, then signed out. By the time I pulled into the garage, I was utterly drained. Frank went ahead of me into the house, and straight to his room. I took my Shakespeare and notes back to the office. I still couldn't figure out what it was about the incident that had made me so mad at Frank. He really hadn't known better. I was so afraid that I'd turned a dear friend against me.

A minute later, the office phone rang. It was Esther.

"Frank just called," she said. "He's pretty upset."

"Oh, no," I groaned.

"No, Lisa. You were right. He shouldn't have shot at that guy. It's just that you don't understand." Esther sighed. "You know Frank's father was a cop, right?"

"Yeah. He was killed in the line of duty."

"His partner had a clear shot at a suspect and didn't take it. The suspect shot and killed Frank's father. Frank was twelve."

"Oh, crap."

"It's okay, Lisa. He's not mad at you. More at himself, really."

"Double crap. I'd better go talk to him. Thanks."

As I hung up, I thought I heard the garage door opener but decided that taking care of Frank was more important at that moment. I wasn't even that sure of what I was going to tell Sid.

I knocked at the door to Frank's room. "It's Lisa. Can I come in, please?"

"Sure." Frank's voice was flat.

I slid inside. "Esther just called."

"Oh." Frank sat on the edge of his bed, petting Coco and Reilly, who were, for once, quiet.

"You were right to call her." I sighed and sat down next to him. "She told me about your father and the clear shot."

Frank hung his head and squeezed his eyes shut.

I shook my head. "I'm guessing today was about getting that clear shot."

"I'm still a screwup."

"No, you're not, Frank. What you are is green. We all screw up in the beginning. I know I was angry. It was mostly at Red Light. He's been this stupid before."

"You're still pissed at me, too."

"Yeah." I sighed, then took a deep breath. "I don't know why, but it felt really bad when you were willing to listen to an idiot like Red Light, but you didn't listen to me."

"I didn't hear you at first."

"I know that now." I blinked my eyes.

"This is why I didn't want to do this spy thing." Frank swallowed and looked away. "I screwed up last weekend, too. That's all I'll ever be. Good old goofy Frank. The big screwup. Can't take care of myself, let alone anyone else."

"Is that what your brother told you?"

"All the time."

I squeezed my eyes shut. "That wasn't fair or even close to the truth."

"Except that my wife supports me and has for the past year and a half."

"You're doing really well with the choir direction. You take good care of Esther." I smiled and touched his arm. "And now you're bringing income into your household."

"Huh?"

I laughed. "You think we're doing this spy thing for free? We get paid, and pretty nicely, too."

"Oh." He sighed. "I sure didn't earn my keep today, though." He winced. "The worst of it is, you were right. We didn't know if he was the guy we're trying to get. We didn't even know if he'd shot the gun." Frank swallowed. "He could have been just trying to protect himself. I could have killed an innocent man."

"Yes, you could have." I shut my eyes. "But, Frank, you are not a screwup. You do learn from your mistakes. You didn't panic today when the shooting started. You kept with your target. I'll stake my life on you any time. I'm not going to trust Red Light to cover me."

He looked at me. "So, how do I know when to shoot?"

"When either you or somebody else is going to die if you don't." The tears started to roll down my cheeks. "I hate shooting my gun, Frank. I don't want to kill anybody. I don't even like wounding people. I do because I have to. But it's not easy." I sniffed. "I don't have your history, though. I don't have a brother who kept calling me names, and a father who might still be around except for one fatal mistake." I swallowed and wiped my eyes. "If you've got someone who's lead on an operation, the only reason not to check in first is because it would be fatal to wait that long. The reason we do things that way is the lead usually has more information about what's going on. I know Sid and I have a reputation for insubordination. But we don't ignore a team leader unless the consequences would be so dire, we have to."

"Mom!" Nick's voice hollered through the intercom. "Dad wants to talk the operation over."

"I'll be there in a few minutes."

Frank groaned. "He's going to kill me."

"You'll be fine." I couldn't help a rueful chuckle. "Red Light has a lot more to worry about. We'll tell you the story someday, but Sid really does not like him. He not only blew Sid's cover on a case once, but almost got him killed."

"Ouch." Frank winced. "I'm glad I'm not him."

"I'm glad you're not that stupid."

I pulled Sid aside to tell him what had happened and how Frank was feeling about it. Sid nodded and sometime later spent some time with Frank. Kathy and Jesse came over with Esther, so we didn't have to worry about that. Dinner that night was both comforting and tense. Tense because we still didn't know what the heck was going on with Levinsky's group and where the KGB mole was. Comforting because we'd all been in Frank's shoes at one point or another and were willing to share how we'd gotten over that.

The best part was Nick.

"They really don't know who's making the threats," Nick told us as we ate. "I talked to a bunch of people today. They told me all sorts of stuff, like how worried they were that Dr. Levinsky was going to get a really bad rep, and, and how scared they were about the satellite. But they really don't know who's making the threats. One of the ladies even said she thinks the threats are coming from outside the group."

I grinned at him. "You did a heck of a job today."

"Nobody else got as much as he did," said Sid, smiling.

"I'm so proud of you, Nick." I blinked and smiled at him.

Nick rolled his eyes, but still grinned. "Like anybody is going to suspect a kid."

"Yes, but you know how to use it to your advantage, my sweet guy," I said.

Frank looked at Nick, then me, then sighed. I suspected he had not heard anything like that from his family when he was a kid. I know Sid makes a point of praising Nick because Sid had gotten so little praise from Stella. I can't help praising Nick because, well, he is pretty awesome, and I'm happy to say so.

Wednesday proved to be quiet, even with Josie Prosser and her friends hanging around outside on the sidewalk. That afternoon, Sid and Jesse glared down at the group from the living room. I watched from the office door.

Sid shook his head. "The thing that worries me is all the people from the church that were at that anti-nuke rally yesterday. If any of them know those girls and find out that Frank and Esther are staying here, it might bring some of those crazies here, and we can't afford that."

"I know." Jesse scratched his chin. "Kathy was saying the same thing this morning. We have that guest room. It's a lot tighter space-wise there, but the building is a lot more secure."

Kathy and Jesse's condo was also larger than the one Sy and Stella were in, with a third bedroom they usually used as a TV room.

"Do you mind getting them to the gym and the dojo in the evenings?" Sid looked over at me.

"On top of getting Esther back and forth from work?" Jesse chuckled. "No problem. You two have been doing enough running."

"Thanks," Sid said with a smile. "I'll make a point of getting Esther and we'll meet you at the dojo for a workout before dinner."

"Sounds good."

But we weren't done with the girls by a long shot. Thursday morning, with my foot finally healed and no need to get to the gym before the crack of dawn, Sid dragged both Nick and me out to go running together for the first time in a while. We had Motley with us, as usual, and Nick and I had gotten to sleep in until seven-thirty, which was lovely.

By the time we got back to the house, the girls were there. Josie saw us coming first and ran up to us on the sidewalk. Her friends flanked her and the three of them blocked our path. Both Sid and Nick looked like they were about to plow through the little group, but Nick suddenly ran off the sidewalk into the street.

Tires screeched, and I looked up just in time to see the chromed front of a Mercedes Benz stop just short of Nick and Motley. The girls looked terrified and ran off. Nick hurried back onto the sidewalk, waving at the car's driver. The man behind the wheel looked seriously annoyed and shook his head as the car peeled out. I blinked and tried to swallow my heart back out of my throat.

"That's it!" Sid snapped as we went into the house. "I can't take any more of this. We've got that launch next week, too. Nick, we've got to get you out of this house. And I want to talk to those girls' parents. Not just Prosser, but the other two, as well."

"Can I eat first?" Nick asked. "I'm starving."

"We'll get dressed, then eat breakfast," Sid said. "Then I am making some phone calls."

In the shower, I remembered something Sy had talked about earlier that month. Sid was okay with the idea, but left me to propose it to Sy and Stella.

The other two girls were Eliza Ramos and Tiffany Barton. I got the phone numbers for their parents from the parents' list at school. Sid left messages for each family. Stella, when I called her, was completely sympathetic, especially after I told her about Nick almost getting hit by a car because of the girls.

"That's absolutely ridiculous," she grumbled. "We were thinking about taking off a week from tomorrow, but I believe we could speed things up and leave tomorrow instead. Would that be soon enough?"

"Are you sure?" I swallowed. "That's awfully fast to put together a camping trip."

"We've been putting it together for three weeks now. I just have to ask Sy if we can get the camper van rented right away. I don't see why not. We're paying for a premium one. And we'll need a campsite. Oh, and Nick's friend Josh. He's being harassed, too, isn't he?"

"I'm afraid so."

"We'll bring him then. We're already taking Darby. One more boy won't be that much trouble." She paused. "I don't know if we'll have room in the van for everyone to sleep, though."

"I have a tent you guys can use."

"I'll have Sy check with the rental company and call you right back."

Sid and I tried to stay focused on editing work, but the sped-up trip meant extra phone calls. Not only was Sy able to get the van, Stella got a campsite reserved in Yosemite by some miracle. Lety was thrilled to have Josh going.

"I have had it up to here with those girls," she told me on the phone. "And Ramon, he's talking lawsuit."

Ramon was Lety's husband and Josh's father.

My sister Mae wasn't as thrilled but felt she couldn't say no to letting her son Darby go.

"Those boys are going to be spoiled rotten." Mae sighed. "Is Stella even up for this?"

"Well, she raised Sid and said that after what she put up with from his friends, our boys are going to be a lark."

I spent the rest of the day coordinating lists, checking what gear I had that I could send with them (which was quite a lot). We bought an extra cooler for all the extra food the boys wanted. Darby's appetite hadn't slowed down, and Josh's had sped up. Nick was eating pretty much anything he could get his hands on.

Sy brought the van over to our house that night, and we packed. Darby and Josh spent the night with us so that they could get a good early start the next morning.

Sid was up before dawn that morning and went and got Sy and Stella from their condo. Then Sid and I waved goodbye as they all took off, the sun rising behind us. I decided there was no point in going back to bed, and Sid and I went running.

I was still pretty dopey after breakfast when Sid took a call.

"What's that all about?" I asked.

"There's a press conference scheduled for Monday morning for the satellite launch." Sid pressed his lips together. "Esther said that she'll have to be there."

"I wonder if Leslie has the press contact." I tapped my fingers on the desk. "She still wants us to do the story."

"Then let's do it." Sid frowned. "In the meantime, I say we take the weekend off."

"Sid, even if we didn't have to worry about Frank and Esther, we are so behind on the editing work."

Sid grinned. "Oh, we'll get that done. But I'm going to let Kathy and Jesse worry about Frank and Esther. Do you realize, my darling, this is the first time we've had the house to ourselves in weeks?"

I swallowed as my breath caught. "I suppose we should take advantage of it."

His chuckle left no doubt that we would. We got caught up on the editing work, too.

August 16 – 17, 1986

I must admit, I slept like the proverbial log that Friday night, which turned out to be a good thing, because Saturday morning sucked pond water.

It started around nine a.m. with a call from my mother. Her dog Murbles had died overnight. We'd gotten the huge old mutt as a puppy the spring of my junior year of high school. While he was only eleven years old, for a dog his size, that's pretty old.

I burst into tears as I hung up the phone. I don't know why it felt so awful. Sid held me but I could tell he didn't entirely get my upset.

Then the phone rang again, and it was Don Haslip. We'd just been finishing breakfast when Mama had called. Sid put Don on hold and went into the office to take the call. I got the breakfast dishes into the kitchen and the dishwasher, then wandered into the office.

"Here's Lisa now." Sid looked up at me. "Don, why don't I put you on hold so I can bring her up to speed and then I'll be able to give you an answer." Sid paused a second, then pressed the button and sighed. "Don wants us to work with him and Pat on the fundraising committee. Darlene Sutton has to bow out, which puts the anti-Casino Night people in the minority. If we jump in now, then those other ding-a-lings won't get their shot at stacking the committee with their friends. And we'll get our volunteer hours covered for the year."

"If you want to," I said with a sad shrug.

"The alternative is pushing everyone around us to buy crap wrapping paper and over-priced cookie dough."

We both shuddered over that one. We'd bought a fair amount of both over the years from Mae's kids. I didn't think Sid would be a good mix on the casino committee thanks to his tendency to lose patience with the ding-a-lings, but he was right. Without the money from the Casino Night, we would probably be stuck with the more traditional school fundraisers, which meant wrapping paper and cookie dough.

"Go for it. It's like you keep saying. This is our life now."

Sid looked at me for a moment, then got Don back on the line and told him we were in. The first committee meeting was the following Thursday and Don, who was the committee chair, was going to hold it at his house.

Sid hung up the phone and looked at me.

"It's only one more year," I said bleakly. "Then Nick goes to high school and according to the other moms, those schools don't demand parental involvement beyond writing checks."

Sid slumped back in his chair and swore. "Nick in high school. It seems like yesterday he wasn't even eleven and making me crazy that he wouldn't stop running around everywhere." Sid looked back over at me. "You okay?"

"Yeah." I shrugged, then blinked as my eyes filled. "I'm sorry. I'm not okay. I just don't know what's wrong. I don't feel like myself or something."

"I've noticed." Sid sighed and shook his head. "I'm beginning to wonder if this getting married thing wasn't a mistake after all."

I started weeping. "I thought it was the right thing to do."

"So did I."

"It did make our commitment to each other stronger."

"It did." Sadly, he got up and pulled me into his arms. "I can't say it didn't and I'm glad that it did." He squeezed me and sighed deeply. "But you're not that happy, and that worries me."

"Sid, I'm not going anywhere." My throat started closing.

"I know, Lisapet, and I trust you. The problem is, I'm happier than I've ever been, and you're not. It's got to be the whole married thing. I may not have believed in marriage, but I wasn't scared of it. You believed in marriage and were terrified by it. You're just not that happy as a married woman. Hell, you won't even call me your husband."

"I do, too!"

"No. You call me your spouse. It's like you're trying to pretend we're not really married or something."

"I'm not that unhappy." I blinked and tried to smile. "Yesterday was great, and I'm really loving our sex life." I swallowed. "I just don't recognize myself anymore. I was going to be a college professor and stay single. Now, here I am, married and with a kid. It was the last thing I wanted for my life and that's exactly where I am."

"Maybe you're going about it a little bass-ackwards, but there's no reason you can't work on the college professor thing."

"How am I going to get a PhD working the hours we do? You're having enough trouble with your master's program."

"That's not what's important." Sid held me close to him.

"You're what's important to me. Nick is what's important." I pulled back a little. "It's not marriage or whatever. It's being with you guys. That's when I feel happy. And it's not just the sex. It's being close to you, talking, goofing off."

He smiled softly. "Our sex life would not be this good if you weren't happy being with me. But you're right. It's not just sex. We have a lot of other life to deal with, and that seems to be bothering you."

I winced and pulled away from him. "I wish I knew what was going on, Sid. But I really don't. Yeah, you're right about the whole being married thing. But it's not just that. It's all the people at Nick's school who can't deal with us not having the same last names. Or me having to explain that, no, I'm not worried about your past girlfriends, or having to explain why I married you in spite of them. There's a part of me that really does not care what all those others think about me. But then, I get really tired of the questions and people obviously trying not to say something about how we live our lives, especially when I'm feeling so lost in all of it. And all the other losses. Lydia. Murbles. And, yeah, the deck shoes are just shoes, but they are one more loss on top of several others." I blinked. "Including myself."

Sid frowned and looked at me deeply. "Funny. You're not acting that lost."

I shrugged. "I have no idea at this point."

Sid chuckled. "Then why don't we spend some time to find you?"

"What?"

"I'm just thinking about something you said the other night about your old deck shoes being your connection to your life before me. Maybe we need to explore that. I probably do, too. There isn't much in this house that I owned before you came into my life, too." He sighed lightly and squeezed me again. "For me, that is a different issue, I understand. I had a lot less to lose by marrying you and everything to gain."

"Sid, I had everything to gain, too."

Perhaps I said that too earnestly. And yet, I fully believed what I'd said. Sid didn't buy it, and if I'm honest, he had good reason. It wasn't that I was trying to fool myself. [And we later learned that you weren't. - SEH] It was more that both everything to gain and everything to lose were the truth. For lack of better terms, Sid was (and is) the love of my life and the sacramental part of marriage was (and is) important to me. There was no question that having done the church thing had made our commitment to each other even stronger than it had been. Still, it was hard to see myself as the married woman I was. It was just so far from what I'd envisioned for myself.

Sid softly kissed my lips. "Let's get away for the weekend."

"We've got the house to ourselves for the first time in weeks."

"And we enjoyed that last night." He quickly kissed my forehead. "But I think we both need to get away from everything and just focus on being who we are and being in love with each other. I am taking what you've told me seriously. But maybe getting away from it all for a bit will help clarify things."

I couldn't help smiling at him. "You know. You're right. Let's do it."

Sid's chuckle was utterly lascivious. Okay, maybe my Freudian slip was showing.

Anyway, we were ready to go by ten. Sid drove us in his Beemer up to the garage in the San Fernando Valley, where his Mercedes Benz 450SL was in storage. He'd retired the car for a lot of reasons, but it was still in excellent shape, and it was fun to take it out every so often. We couldn't when Nick was around because the 450SL only had two seats.

We took the hard top off. I got a scarf on to keep my hair from whipping into my face. We drove up the coast, stopping here and there to watch the surf come in. We ate lunch at a burger shack in Carpinteria. And we talked a lot. Some of it was the usual joking around. Some of it was about Nick and how we were raising him. A lot of it was about our lives before we'd known each other.

"What did you like so much about teaching?" Sid asked me over dinner at a little place in San Luis Obispo.

I thought about it. "I liked helping people, and I liked getting to know the students. It might not seem like it's that big a deal to write, but it can make a huge difference in how you approach the rest of your schoolwork, not to mention how you work. It's like your ability to write logically. It's because you think logically. Not a lot of people do, and you need to in the working world. Learning to write correctly can help people learn how to think logically. And I really loved the students. That's why I always did Off-Campus Office Hours. Aside from not having an office that year I taught, it just made it so much easier for some of them."

Sid suddenly laughed. "Honey, do you remember a year and a half ago when I suddenly found myself with a lot of time on my hands?"

It was when Sid had given up sleeping around, which had also meant that he was no longer going out to chase women most nights of the week.

"Yeah. You almost drove me nuts."

"And you talked me into going back to school to get my music degree."

"Well, it is your passion."

"One of them." Sid smiled at me, his blue eyes glittering. "Why don't you go back to your passion? You love Shakespeare. You love Romance poets."

"Some of them." I rolled my eyes.

"You also love teaching. I saw that when we were on that case in Wisconsin. It didn't matter that you were undercover. You didn't have to work as hard as you did at the teaching part of it. You did anyway because you seemed to really like it."

I made a face. "Yeah, but how am I going to teach with our side business calling us out of town all the time? It's going to be hard to keep a job when we have to run off and do an undercover operation for two, three months. Not to mention pickups and drops and having to run to Europe at a moment's notice." I frowned. "And here's the funny thing. I do not want to give up our side business, even if I could. I know it wasn't part of my life plan, either. But in a way, it was. I always wanted to do something adventurous. When I was five, I wanted to be a fireman, and not just any fireman. I wanted to be a smoke jumper."

"Oh, honey." Sid laughed softly and reached over and stroked my hand. "We'll figure out a way to keep all the balls in the air. It's more important that you do what you love."

"What about the writing? I like that, too, and it makes a very convenient excuse when we have to go running off. Not to mention getting us interviews with suspects and at that press conference on Monday."

Sid shrugged. "We can cut back. We're not doing that much of it right now, anyway."

I shuddered. "Do you like the editing?"

"Not really." He winced.

"Neither do I." I sighed. "So, what do we tell Hattie?"

"That we're friends. We will continue to be friends. But we're cutting back because we both want to go to grad school."

"Okay." I nodded. "I don't want to say anything to Hattie yet. I'm going to need to spend some time praying about this. That's when I make my best decisions."

"You didn't pray about coming to work for me, as I recall. You just made the decision."

"I made the decision because I'd been praying about what my next step was going to be, and when that door suddenly opened, I knew I had my answer."

That made Sid laugh and shake his head. Being an atheist, he doesn't get me praying, but he respects it.

We headed south after dinner and spent the night in Shell Beach at a rickety little inn that still had lovely rooms. We spent that Sunday wandering through the Santa Ynez Valley and Solvang. Solvang was busy since it was a pretty popular tourist spot. But the rest of the valley had a lot to offer that no one really knew about, namely wineries, and some of them were pretty darned good. Sid and I got back to our house just after ten that night. The 450SL had been returned to the garage, and we'd transferred our bag and the two cases of wine into Sid's Beemer.

We were tired when we climbed into bed and the lovemaking was pretty relaxed. We fell asleep before eleven-thirty, only to be awakened less than an hour later by the beeping of the security system. As I sat up, blinking the sleep from my eyes, I saw the small red light flashing over the bedroom door.

"Intruder," Sid grumbled, getting a snub-nosed pistol out of his bedside table. He always wakes up faster than I do.

I grabbed my snub-nose as well and the two of us hurried to the bedroom door.

We could hear scraping on the other side, then the crash of a huge piece of glass breaking. Sid glanced at me and whipped the door open. I go through first because I'm the better shot.

A slight figure picked its way inside the house through the remains of the sliding glass door on the other side of our loft.

"Freeze!" I hollered, my gun trained on her.

Sid was next to me in an instant, his gun trained on the intruder as well.

The girl - and it was clearly a girl - froze in terror.

"What the hell?" muttered Sid. Okay, he did not say hell.

"Go get some clothes and some shoes on," I told him. "I've got her covered."

Sid slid back into our bedroom. The girl stayed frozen in place, as well she should have. I blinked and slowly saw that she was Josie Prosser. Sid returned a second later, clad in gym shorts and flip-flops. He pointed his snub nose at Josie, then tossed me my robe and a second pair of flip-flops.

"We've gotta call the cops on this one," Sid said.

"I know."

Sid picked up the handset to the loft phone and made the call with his gun still trained on Josie.

"Come here, young lady," I said, sliding into my robe. I tied it on with one hand because I was not going to chance her running or doing something else stupid.

Josie swallowed, blinked her eyes, and walked further into the loft.

"Why are you guys naked?" she asked, starting to weep.

"That's not important right now," I said. "Why are you breaking into our house?"

"I need to see Nick."

"He's not here," I said.

"I need to see his room. Something. Please."

Sid was talking to the dispatcher at 911. A minute later, he hung up.

"I have to call her mom," I told him, not taking my aim off Josie for one second.

Sid aimed his gun at the girl while I dialed.

"Mrs. Prosser, this is Nick Flaherty's mom." I sighed. "Your daughter is here. She just broke into our house."

"My daughter wouldn't do anything like that." Mrs. Prosser sounded awfully alert for that time of night.

"Well, she's here. She broke the glass on our sliding door and says she wants to see Nick's room." I rolled my eyes. "The police are on their way."

"Why did you call them?"

"She committed a crime."

"She just wants to see your son."

"And she broke into our house in the middle of the night." I almost wished I could have shot Josie's mom through the phone lines. "That is a criminal act."

"Well, if you're going to be unreasonable about it."

"Yeah, I am." I gave her our address. "You may want to get over here as soon as possible, since your daughter is going to be arrested."

The phone on the other end of the line slammed down. Josie wept quietly. The poor thing was utterly terrified, although there was part of me that could not understand why she hadn't thought that far ahead of herself.

The cops were decidedly annoyed that Sid and I had guns and that we'd kept Josie under cover until they'd arrived. Sid pointed to the broken sliding glass door.

"We didn't know what the kid was up to or even whether she was armed or not," Sid said. "Sorry, but any kid crazy enough to climb onto our roof and break in a sliding glass door with people inside cannot be trusted."

The two detectives rolled their eyes but agreed. They checked Sid's and my permits for the guns. Mrs. Prosser showed up around then, and started screaming that it was our fault her daughter had broken in. I'll give the detectives credit. They didn't buy that scenario for one second. They put Josie in handcuffs in spite of her mother's screams and told Mrs. Prosser that she could meet them at the police station.

August 18, 1986

Sid was seriously annoyed the next morning when another detective showed on the doorstep just after breakfast.

"I'm sorry, Mr. Flaherty," Detective Walsh said. "Mrs. Prosser has accused you of exposing yourself to her daughter, and we do have to take that seriously."

Sid glared at him. "In the first place, Detective, my name is Hackbirn. My son's name is Flaherty. In the second, my wife and I sleep au naturel. As far as I know, there is no law against that and we were in the privacy of our own home, a home that was trespassed by this kid. In the third place, our security system alerted us to an intruder. We reacted as if this intruder presented a significant danger, which most intruders do. We had no way of knowing that this intruder was, in fact, a thirteen-year-old kid. In fact, as soon as we realized who the intruder was, the first thing I did, while my wife held the girl, was go put on some gym shorts. And finally, may I point out that the girl in question has been relentlessly chasing my son for weeks now and even almost got him hit by a car last week. So, yeah, we saw her as a credible threat."

Conchetta was already upstairs, picking up and vacuuming up the broken glass. A handyman was on his way and Conchetta agreed to let him in while Sid and I were at the press conference.

Walsh swallowed. "I see. Well, thank you for your perspective. I hope you understand that we have to double check these things."

"Of course," I said quickly, before Sid could let loose. "You never know. But it was as Sid said. As soon as we saw who the intruder was, I had Sid get some clothes on and he brought me my robe."

"Okay." Walsh shrugged. "Thanks for talking to me."

The detective left, but Sid was not mollified.

"This is not something we need right now," he complained as he drove us to the hotel in Culver City where the satellite press conference was to be held.

"It never is," I said.

He sighed. "My darling, you are right, as you so frequently are. However, that does not help at the moment."

"Well, maybe we need to stay focused on getting through the press conference first."

"And you are right again." Sid grimaced. "You realize that we will be Esther's primary protection at this thing."

I shrugged. "Why would somebody attack a press conference? It's a sure way to get attention."

"Which might be exactly what this crew wants."

"I'm willing to bet they don't want to get arrested, though."

"More than likely."

Leslie had given me the contact for the conference, and Sid and I had gotten on the press list because of our connection to the magazine we're editing.

Sid and I don't do a lot of press conferences because we're freelance writers as opposed to regular journalists.

But we got sent out every now and then to cover something that would be part of a larger story we were writing. This conference had a lot more immediate interest. All seven TV stations in the area had sent cameras and a reporter, including Leslie and her cameraman. The video cameras were all set up at the back of the room in a tangle of tripods and wires. Several rows of chairs had been set up in front of the long table covered with white tablecloths. Four microphones dotted the surface of the table, and a podium and mike had been set up at the table's end. Photographers from several newspapers and a couple news magazines milled along the side of the room, the guys and two women all wearing khaki-colored vests with tons of pockets and two or three camera bags apiece. I put the name badge I'd been given on my suit coat and went to sit up near the front, next to the podium. Sid stood in the back, next to Leslie and a private investigator who had been hired as security by the defense plant. Esther also sat in the front row, several chairs down from me.

The receptionist I'd seen at Esther's office, Rhonda Swenson, walked in front of the table, putting tented name cards in front of the microphones. Ross Sorensen was one of them, as was Fred Merryweather. Jim Beacham was from NASA and Arnold Wyland was from the FBI.

The men wandered in, sat at their places, then Merryweather got up and stood at the podium. He was in his late fifties, with graying hair, glasses, and a tired look about him.

"Thank you all for coming today," Merryweather said, blinking over his notes. "In light of all the misinformation out there about this satellite project, we want to reassure the public that there are no nuclear arms on the satellite.

In fact, there are no arms of any kind. It is strictly a communications satellite. Each of my colleagues will give you a brief statement and then we will take questions."

Gun shots cracked, and people screamed. Sorensen's head landed on the table. I realized my chest had exploded in pain. I looked down at the blood seeping through my good silk blouse, then crumpled.

To Breanna, 9/8/00

Topic of the Day: The Car Breakdown

Okay. I admit it. I over-reacted. But, come on. You were three hours late. I got no phone call. Nothing. I had no idea where you were or what had happened. I can't believe it took the CHP that long to find you.

The problem is, sweetheart, when my parents don't answer their phones or don't show up, it frequently means something's gone really, really wrong. Trust me, there's nothing worse than wondering why they're not where they said they were going to be, then getting that call from the hospital. That's why I panic. I can't help it.

I respect that you don't want me buying you expensive gifts. And, okay, it probably wasn't appropriate for me to insist that you let me buy you a new car. I still wouldn't mind and, God knows, I can afford to. But you're right, that may have been too much.

On the other hand, would you please, please let me buy you a mobile phone and the plan to go with it? At least that way, if that stupid junker of yours breaks down again, you can let me know what's going on. And who knows? Maybe I can get to you faster than the fucking CHP.

(Sid's Voice)

I didn't see the shooters. I don't think anyone did, even Zack Peters. He was the private eye hired as security at the conference, and a tall man with filled out shoulders, medium brown hair, and an attitude. I spotted a Special Forces tattoo on the back of his wrist peeking out from underneath his shirt cuff. We said hello and chatted a little before Merryweather got up to the podium and started lying to us.

I heard the shots, but I think they came from another part of the room. I was too woozy to really tell, anyway, and was out a second later. Zack may have been given the knockout rag even before I was.

When I came to, I was blindfolded and cuffed with my hands in front of me in some sort of car, and I was seated between two other people. I debated working on the cuffs, but if the two people on either side of me were my guards, then popping the cuffs wouldn't help. I had no idea how long we'd been traveling, nor did I know where we were when the car stopped. The doors opened and from the moan I heard, I figured someone else had been captured with me. We were walked into some building or other, but simply left there. I heard a metal door slam.

I still had my suit jacket and tie on, along with my shoulder holster, but the holster had been emptied. With all the FBI around, I'd brought an automatic instead of the Model Thirteen and was glad I had.

I pulled the blindfold off. The room was almost completely dark. One tiny shaft of light blazed through the door I'd heard, but it didn't illuminate much.

"Where are we?" a female voice asked.

It was Leslie Bowman. Her blindfold hung around her neck. Not far from her, Zack Peters had his blindfold off and was working on his cuffs with something or other.

"I don't know," I said, swallowing.

This was going to be tricky. Peters obviously had some of my usual non-traditional skills. He had his cuffs popped in no time and whipped a penlight out of his jacket pocket. As it clicked on, I saw the tattoo on the back of his wrist again.

"Special Forces?" I asked.

"Yep." He chuckled, one war vet to another. We'd never met. But there are times when you just know who you're dealing with. "You were carrying today."

I shrugged. "Force of habit."

"I see." He came over and started working on my cuffs. "When did you get out?"

"Seventy-one." I kept my voice steady. I rarely like talking about my time in the service, but with this guy, I especially did not want to get into the usual banter about where I was stationed and what unit I was with. I had a bad feeling he'd been doing a lot of the same work I had, which was not the usual fighting or clerking. "I don't talk about it."

"Yeah. I understand." The cuffs fell off, and he glanced over at Leslie. "I hate to ask, but I gotta. You see action?"

I nodded. "Plenty."

"Will you be okay if you see some more today?"

"Um... Should be." I swallowed for the effect.

Peters walked over to Leslie. "Okay, honey, we're going to get you out of these cuffs."

"Where are we?" Leslie asked again, then she noticed me. "Sid. What's going on?"

"We were kidnapped," Peters said. "They used ether on us. I'm guessing the gun shots were supposed to be a distraction."

"But why kidnap us?" Leslie asked, as the cuffs fell off her wrists.

"That's a good question," Peters said. He flicked the penlight around the room.

It was huge and windowless, but at the end of the room were stacks of AK-47s and dynamite.

"What the hell?" Peters asked as Leslie gasped. He went over and examined one of the dynamite sticks and a gun. "Russian." He thought as he looked at the stash. "I wonder..."

"So, do we want to use any of those?" I asked.

Peters tossed me a rifle. "Why not?"

"I don't think..." Leslie gulped and shook her head.

"No problem." Peters grabbed a rifle for himself and made sure he and I both had plenty of shells.

He took the lead, first listening at the door, then slowly opening it to let us get used to the light outside.

"Shouldn't we wait until dark?" Leslie asked.

Peters nodded back at the explosives. "Do you want to risk them deciding to destroy the evidence and us along with it?"

Leslie swallowed. "What do I do?"

"Stay between us," Peters said. He glanced at me. "Can you take the rear?"

I nodded and gasped a little as if I hadn't been doing shit like this again and again since I left 'Nam.

Peters peeked out, then nodded at us. We slid out the door and stayed close to the building, which turned out to be a large corrugated-steel shed. I realized I recognized the building in front, facing the street.

"We're in Running Springs," I said softly and pointed at the clinic. "We go skiing here all the time. That's Levinsky's clinic."

Peters quickly ducked behind the shed. Leslie and I followed. Peters carefully poked his head around the edge of the shed and gazed at the clinic.

"This is too easy," he grumbled.

"I don't understand," I said, even though I knew exactly what was worrying Peters. I was worrying about the same thing.

"We don't have a guard on us. The clinic is empty. If they were going to blow up the joint, why haven't they by now? And why even take us if they were going to blow the place?"

"Maybe they wanted some hostages," said Leslie.

"Then why isn't there a guard on us? They didn't even lock the shed door." Peters set his rifle down and looked at me. "Can you cover me?"

I took a deep breath. "Sure."

But it turned out, Peters didn't need covering. He walked right up to the back door of the clinic and opened it. He listened for a moment, then waved us over.

"It's empty, alright," he told Leslie and me when we'd hurried in the door. Peters led us through the hall to Levinsky's office. "May as well do a little search or two."

"That's illegal," Leslie said.

Peters laughed as he began going through the drawers of the desk. "It's illegal if you're a cop."

"No," Leslie pressed. "They can't use evidence that would have been protected under search and seizure laws if the cops don't have a search warrant when they enter."

"But if they enter legally and a search warrant would have turned the evidence up, they can use it." Peters' grin grew even bigger. "And lookie here. A whole bunch of ID badges for that plant where Sorensen works. I'm going to put these out on the desk and give our local boys a call."

"Are they going to arrest us for breaking and entering?" I asked.

"The door was open, and we were looking for help." Peters shrugged as he picked up the phone.

I thought of something else. "I'm going to call my wife. She's probably worried."

It was getting close to two o'clock, and Lisa was probably very worried. I called our personal line, but it just rang. Then I called the business line, and the answering machine picked up.

"Shit," I grumbled.

Something seemed really wrong. I called Kathy and Jesse's place and got no answer there, either. My stomach twisted. There had been gun shots...

(Lisa's Voice)

I didn't lose consciousness, but there wasn't much I could see from the floor where I'd fallen. I wanted to get up, but it hurt too badly. Esther was right there.

"It's going nuts," she told me.

She had a couple napkins from a pitcher of ice water that had been at the side of the room. She put one on my wound, and the wet, cold fabric made me yelp. People were still screaming, but from what I could see, several were getting onto their feet.

"You hurt?" I gasped. It hurt to breathe.

"Not a scratch."

"Sorensen...?"

"He got hit, but he's still alive. They're doing first aid. Merryweather and Wyland went after the shooters." Esther looked at the napkin she had. "You're not in bad shape, I don't think."

"Hurts."

"Well, yeah."

"Anyone else?"

"Nope."

A minute later, two paramedics pushed Esther out of the way and tore open my blouse. Apparently, I'd gotten more than a scratch, but I wasn't coughing up blood or anything, which was a good sign. Esther stayed with me as they bundled me onto a gurney, then into an ambulance. Esther got into the front seat with the driver.

"Where's Sid?" I hollered to Esther as the siren wailed above us and tried not to groan.

"That's right. He was there, too." Esther sat back and thought. "I don't know."

"You and the guy at the head table were the only two who got shot," said the paramedic riding in the back with us.

"But my... my husband," I gasped.

"Your friend will find out when we get to the hospital," the paramedic said. "It was pretty chaotic back there. I could have sworn there were more casualties when I saw the gurneys coming down the hallway."

"Gurneys?"

"Three of them. But they said you and that other guy were the only victims. Must have been some other conference. Probably food poisoning. Happens all the time."

There wasn't much I could say or do. The one good thing was that it took a while for the doctor to get to me when we got to the hospital. That meant my injury was not serious, no matter how much it hurt. I was put in an exam room and helped out of my clothes by a nurse. Esther hung close by, only leaving to make a couple of phone calls. Her face was grim when she returned.

"Sid's missing," she said. "There was a security guard and a TV reporter that they can't find, either. They think they were kidnapped."

I swallowed. "Put on gurneys and hauled out of the hotel. The paramedic saw them."

"Yeah. The shooting was a distraction."

"Why?" I asked, my eyes filling both with my physical pain and my worry over Sid.

"We don't know yet. I called Frank. He's trying to find out what happened. He called your friend Henry James. Henry said to call Angelique. It's good that Sid was there as himself."

I nodded.

When the doctor appeared, a medium-sized Black woman with a tough, but calming demeanor, she looked at the wound, then tsk'd.

"Ever been shot before?" she asked.

I had to think. "No."

"Hurts, don't it?"

"Yeah."

"Looks like it just grazed you, maybe scraped your rib a little. Any trouble breathing?"

"It hurts to take a deep breath and talk."

"All over or in one spot?"

"In the wound."

"Well, we'll get an x-ray to check that rib, then we'll get you stitched up and on some of the really good drugs for that pain."

"Thanks. Oh. Wait. Barbituates make me barf."

The doctor laughed. "That's not what we're giving you."

As it turned out, my rib was fine. It took a while for the stitches, but they'd gotten me some pain medication that put me to sleep. I was barely aware of Frank coming in and getting me into his car. I wasn't sure where Esther had gone, but I'd given her my set of keys to Sid's car. The next thing I knew, I had somehow gotten on a t-shirt and gym shorts, and Kathy was tucking me into the waterbed at home.

The phone rang and I picked it up, hoping for news.

"Hi, I'm looking for Nick Flaherty's parents," said a male voice on the other end.

"This is Lisa Wycherly." I swallowed. I had no idea why I hadn't hung up on the man. "I'm Nick's mom."

"I'm Dan Prosser. Josie's dad. I need to apologize to you guys about last night."

"Huh?" I blinked. Kathy handed me a glass of water. "Oh. Break-in."

"Yeah. I appreciate you guys calling the cops. I know my ex-wife was pretty upset, but it was a good thing that you did." He paused. "I've now got custody of Josie."

"Oh?"

"Yeah. The whole chasing the boys thing? Josie was crying for help. Her mom is manic depressive. We thought she was taking her medication but turns out not. Josie told me there was a problem, but there wasn't anything we could do. Her mom had passed the court interview and everything. But getting in trouble last night, that blew everything open, and now I've got an emergency order and it looks good that I'll have custody permanently."

"Oh." I swallowed. "I'm glad. Um. Thanks for calling."

We hung up, and I blinked. Something about calling for help had me worried. It meant something, but I didn't know what and couldn't quite get through the fog in my brain.

"Time for your next pain pill," Kathy said. It was a little after four.

"No!" I yelped. My side was still a little sore, but it wasn't that bad, and I was talking without pain. "I'm feeling a lot better, and that pain pill is leaving me icky. Any aspirin or what's that other stuff? Motrin?"

"Yes." Kathy sighed. "But you'd better get some food on your stomach."

"Toast would be nice."

Kathy brought it to me.

"Where are Frank and Esther?" I asked.

"Frank's downstairs. There may be some news about Sid and the others, but they don't know what yet. They caught Levinsky, though, and he's confessed to everything."

"He's a KGB mole?" I blinked, but there was that darned fog. "He sure didn't seem like it."

I finished the toast and took one of the super-sized Motrin pills I had for when my back went out.

The phone rang again, and it was Sid.

"Oh, honey, thank God!" I gasped, trying not to sob.

"I'm fine, sweetheart. The Feds are just keeping us here at Levinsky's office for some reason." He paused. "They told me you'd gotten hurt."

"Just grazed. It hurts like the dickens, and I'm a little foggy from the stuff they gave me at the hospital, but I'm fine otherwise." I swallowed. "I can even talk and take a deep breath."

Sid's voice lowered. "They found a bunch of defense plant IDs in Levinsky's desk. The names matched that list that Esther brought us a couple weeks ago."

"Why would he have them?"

"We have no idea, but they were not secured or anything. Neither were the three of us. They just dumped us in that big corrugated shed behind the clinic and didn't even lock the door. Turns out it was loaded with Soviet guns and dynamite. It was almost as if they wanted us to find it and call the cops in."

The penny dropped. "Levinsky's not the mole."

"That makes sense. They told us he'd confessed, but that seems a little off."

"It's way off, Sid." I looked over at Kathy, whose one eyebrow had risen. "Levinsky was crying for help. The mole has gotten some sort of hold on him and the only way he could stop that person was to get himself caught."

"Then who's—" Sid stopped. "Um, honey, what's the name of that receptionist on the floor of Esther's office?"

"Rhonda Swenson. Why?"

"Because Danelle Parks, Levinsky's receptionist, is meeting Rhonda at 4 p.m. at a restaurant, I think, in Santa Monica, according to a note on her calendar."

"It's after four now. I wonder if Rhonda still has her ID."

Somebody was talking to Sid. "I'm sorry, honey, they were talking to me. Looks like they're about to take us home. We should be there in a couple, three hours."

"Can't wait to see you. I love you so much."

"I love you, too, and can't wait to see you, either."

We hung up. I looked at Kathy. "Where is Esther?"

"She went back to work. They've got that launch tomorrow."

"No! She's not safe there." I grabbed the phone and called Angelique, who said she had to make a call first.

She called back, saying that the agent in charge said there wasn't enough evidence.

"Crap!" I slammed the phone down, then wincing, got out of bed. "She's not safe there."

"Lisa! You need to stay in bed."

"I can't." I staggered to my closet and got out a dress, jacket, and my blond wig. "Sid found the mole, and she's getting her hands on a legitimate ID with access to Esther's floor even now. I can get in as Agent Devereaux. They're not going to send anyone else out with Levinsky's confession and just a note on a calendar as evidence."

It wasn't easy getting dressed, but I did it. The Motrin was kicking in by that point and it helped. Jesse stayed at the house so that someone would be there when Sid got home. Kathy insisted on driving, and I made sure Frank was armed and ready, with a t-shirt over his jeans and an automatic in a back holster. Kathy got us down to the plant as quickly as she could, but it was still well after five when we got there. She let us off at the curb in front of the usual entrance facing the parking lot.

I limped in with Frank on my heels and whipped my ID out of my jacket pocket. I'd left my purse at home.

"Special Agent Linda Devereaux," I told the security guard at the door. "I need to get to the top floor. Now. We've got a situation developing."

"This is not usual procee—" The guard put his hand to his ear and gulped. "Shots fired."

"Get us up there now!" I demanded.

The guard let Frank and me in and got us on the elevator with him.

"I don't get it," he complained. "We check for guns."

"I've been getting one in here several times this past month," I told him.

The guard glanced at Frank. "But you're an agent. You're supposed to have one."

We burst onto the floor and almost immediately ducked several shots. I sank down behind Swenson's desk.

"Who's on the floor?" I hollered, gasping. The guard looked panicked.

"Two of the guys," Esther hollered back. She cursed as a shot fired. "And Leon and me."

More shots cracked. I looked over at Frank, who was kneeling next to me. "Did you hear where she is?"

"Yeah."

I squeezed my eyes shut. My wound was aching, but there wasn't much I could do. I pulled my Model Thirteen from the holster under my arm.

"I'll cover you from here," I told Frank. "You find Leon. He's a Black guy, and the two of you flank Parks. Leon should be armed."

Another gunshot cracked.

"Almost got you, witch!" Esther laughed. She didn't say witch, however.

"I'm guessing our girl is, too," Frank muttered.

I slid to my feet and saw the receptionist from Levinsky's office, Danelle Parks, wandering among the burlap-covered partitions. Ducking, I looked at Frank, who gulped and nodded. I looked at the guard, then pointed at Parks.

"You've got to stay here and make sure she doesn't get out," I told the guard.

I slid up to the top of the receptionist's wall and let off a few rounds. Frank scrambled away and toward Ross Sorensen's office. I slipped back down and went the other direction toward the parking lot side of the floor.

Parks apparently heard me and let off a couple rounds that whizzed over my head. I slid a few cubicles further down, then looked up. Parks frowned and looked around her. She'd obviously figured out that the cavalry had arrived. I only wished I'd felt more like the cavalry.

Whispering floated out over that far corner of the floor. Parks looked straight at it. I fired a couple more rounds and realized my gun was empty. I had put a box of bullets into one of my jacket pockets and began fishing them out and re-loading. I dropped a couple shells. No surprise. I wasn't at my best, and I knew it.

"We got her, boss lady!" Desmond/Leon yelled from yet another corner.

Parks whipped around and fired. I gasped and ran toward that end of the office. A moment later, I saw Parks drawing a bead on Esther and Frank behind Parks. In the half a second that followed, I realized there were decent odds Frank would hit me or Esther. Frank's face turned to stone. He drew a breath and squeezed the trigger.

Parks fell forward, the back of her head bright red, and that was all I could take before sinking into the nearest chair and gasping, trying to keep the contents of my stomach in place.

Desmond, Frank, and Esther all ran up to me.

"You okay?" Esther asked.

I winced. "Hurting." I waved them off. "I've got to make a phone call."

I called in the code nine, which meant an arrest to be made or clean-up needed by aboveboard agents because covert ones were involved. I explained I needed to get my partner and myself out of there discreetly because there were civilians around, then hung up and looked at Desmond/Leon and Esther.

"You two, ditch your weapons and go hide. You're civilians. Let's keep that intact."

Esther hesitated as she saw Frank, who was clearly slack jawed.

"I told you going slow would work when it needed to," I gasped. I opened the button-front of my dress near where the stitches were. There wasn't any blood on the bandage, but that didn't mean there wouldn't be later.

I steadfastly kept my eyes off the corpse. Frank did the same.

The FBI team that showed was pretty decent about getting me and Frank out of there with a minimum of fuss. We waved at Kathy, who came roaring up. Frank eased me into the front seat, then mechanically got into the back. Kathy called the house from her car phone and got Sid on the line. He was home and waiting for us.

"I can't say I'm not glad I missed this one," she told us as she sped up the freeway.

Neither Frank nor I had anything to say at that point.

August 19 – September 8, 1986

I spent the next couple of days in bed. Alas, it wasn't the kind of staying in bed that resulted in all kinds of nice noise and other fun and games. It was the recuperating and "if you ever try to leave your bed when you're that hurt again, you will be pounded into oblivion" kind of staying in bed.

Okay, I understood. Not that Sid would ever be that violent with me. But, yeah, I could understand him wanting to. I would have felt the same way if he'd done what I'd done. The good news was that I didn't pull any stitches.

Nick called the next day and told us he'd called the day before and was worried that we hadn't been at home. I conceded things had gotten... Interesting. But I reassured him that it was looking like the rest of the week would be quiet. We also agreed that he'd call at the same time each day so that we could make a point of being home when he did. Stella was a little worried that he'd been so upset when he hadn't been able to reach us the day before and I blamed it on Rachel's death, which Stella bought.

The satellite got launched on time, and Esther turned everything on without trouble. The day after, she and Frank went to Chicago. Leslie made considerable hay with her dramatic re-telling of being kidnapped. Sid refused to talk on camera, and oddly enough, so did Zack Peters. In fact, Peters disappeared. No one was quite sure who had hired the P.I., which really made Sid and me wonder. Still, Leslie's first-hand account of the kidnapping got her station some major ratings, which made her bosses very happy.

Levinsky made headlines when he pled guilty to several counts of attempted murder. The espionage counts were dropped, however, since there was now one less KGB mole to worry about. That part of the whole affair got quietly swept under the proverbial rug and I was glad of it. Rhonda Swenson got transferred to another facility where there wasn't any top-secret work going on, even though it hadn't been her fault. As far as she'd known, Danelle Parks was just a nice person. Rhonda hadn't even known that Parks had worked for Levinsky.

By Thursday, I was up and around. Sort of. The really nice thing about being in bed was that I was alone during the day, which was Heaven. So, while I got back to my desk on Thursday, I was still looking for peace and quiet, and Sid obliged me. He obliged that other way, too. We still had the house to ourselves for a change and wanted to take advantage of it.

Saturday, Sy, Stella, and the boys returned from their trip, ebullient with its success. I got the Ladies' Night Out group to put off our meeting one more week. Mae and Neil brought their kids, and the rest of the Sandovals arrived at the house soon after everyone else had arrived, and we all heard the many tales of touring Yosemite and campfires. Some of the neighboring sites had heard the music from Sy and Stella's site that first night and Darby, whose skills at playing the violin were getting darned good, got talked into giving a small concert at the campground campfire on Sunday. Then he'd given a second campfire concert on Tuesday and got lazy, which got Sy and Stella all over his backside and then some. So, Darby had to do one more concert and gave it his all.

Nick was surprisingly sad to hear about Josie Prosser. He was glad that the girls wouldn't be chasing him anymore, as was Josh. But when I explained why Josie had been chasing him, he almost teared up.

"That really sucks," he said vehemently, then held me really tight.

I tried not to gasp too hard because he'd hit my stitches.

Frank and Esther showed up for dinner on Monday, both looking rather pensive.

"You guys okay?" I asked.

"We're fine," said Esther. She winced a little, though. "I mean, it's not about Frank and me. We're just trying to figure out if I need to be working at that plant. Those guys are assholes, you know."

"They are," I said.

Frank and I got to talk alone for a few minutes after dinner.

"You okay?" I asked.

"Yeah." Frank nodded, then sighed. "I am, but you were right. Killing somebody totally sucks."

"I'm guessing you went to visit your family."

"We did, but I really went to see my dad." Frank shrugged. "At his grave. Esther was there, but it was about me." His eyes seemed to fill, and he blinked it back. "I've been really angry at that partner of his ever since Dad died. Funny thing is, I think I know how that partner felt. It wasn't easy pulling that trigger last Monday. If it hadn't been about keeping Esther safe, I don't think I would have. I talked to Dad about it. I think Dad got it." Frank looked at me. "I mean, there's no real way of knowing, but it felt better after that. Does that make sense?"

"Yeah."

He blinked. "And you know what? For the first time in my life, I feel like I'm not a screwup."

I squeezed my eyes shut because they were filling up with the tears that would not go away.

Still, life settled into something that resembled a normal routine. We ended up making Kathy and Esther the Red line hub team since they weren't as mobile as Jesse and Frank were. Esther decided to keep her job at the defense plant in the short term, although she was more invested in finding some great new technology that would make tons of money in the consumer market.

The day after Labor Day was another not a good day for me. When the mail arrived, there were three different large envelopes, all with my name on them. I had requested the envelopes, but now that they'd arrived, I knew I was going to have to make a decision, and I really didn't want to. Which was probably why I came unglued that afternoon.

"Nicholas Wycherly Hackbirn Flaherty!" As in mad enough to use all four of my darling son's names.

"I'm sorry! But I need a lab."

"No, you don't!" I looked at the foaming brown mess on the breakfast room table that reeked of sulfur. "You need to be more careful. You know better than to run off and leave one of your experiments on its own. If that tabletop needs replacing, it's coming out of your allowance."

"Mom!"

"Don't 'Mom' me. Now, clean up that mess right now!"

Sid agreed, but we talked it over. That Thursday, we met with the architect and contractor and arranged to set up a sun porch on the patio outside of the rumpus room that would be protected from the elements, but still have lots and lots of ventilation and two hoses. There was no way I was going to let Nick keep a lab in his bedroom, where there was only one window and plenty of carpeting to ruin. The sun porch takes enough of a beating.

I was still holding onto the applications I'd received in those three big envelopes. Monday morning, we were up at five-thirty so that we could go running, get dressed, and still have time for Nick to go to his first day at school. Sid went to his first day of the semester at the little arts college where he's taking his master's classes in music. I finally sat down and filled out the applications for PhD programs in English Literature.

Coming Soon

The stage is set for a massive undercover case

Three students have been murdered on a university campus in Kansas. Sid Hackbirn, Lisa Wycherly, and their son Nick Flaherty are sent in as the Devereaux family to find the killer. The local police can't know that the three students were also KGB moles finishing their training to assimilate into American society.

Lisa poses as a theatre student to protect the KGB operative overseeing the student moles. Sid takes on teaching history to coordinate with the rest of their team. Between faculty politics, Sid's chauvinistic colleagues, and Lisa and Nick getting cast in a production of Shakespeare's Richard III, there are plenty of suspects and little time to check them out. With the help of their teammates, Sid and Lisa take on one of their most challenging cases yet.

Thank You for Reading

I do hope you enjoyed the book.

If you can do me one small favor, please. Can you go to one of the social media/retail profiles below and leave a short review? It doesn't need to be a lot, just honest.

a amazon.com/These-Hallowed-Halls-Operation-Qu ickline-ebook/dp/B0938CDH1H

BB bookbub.com/books/these-hallowed-halls-operatio n-quickline-book-6-by-anne-louise-bannon

g goodreads.com/book/show/59695574-these-hallow ed-halls?from_search=true&from_srp=true&qid= mtoiwM2ryT&rank=3

Other books by Anne Louise Bannon

I'm so glad you liked this book! Check out my other novels, available in print or ebook at your favorite retailer:

Old Los Angeles Series:

Death of the Zanjero

Death of the City Marshal

Death of the Chinese Field Hands

Death of an Heiress

Death of the Drunkard

Operation Quickline Series:

That Old Cloak and Dagger Routine

Stopleak

Deceptive Appearances

Fugue in a Minor Key

Sad Lisa

These Hallowed Halls

My Sweet Lisa

A Little Family Business

Just Because You're Paranoid

From This Day Forward

Silence in the Tortured Soul

Freddie and Kathy Series:

Fascinating Rhythm

Bring Into Bondage

The Last Witnesses

Blood Red

Daria Barnes:

Rage Issues

Mrs. Sperling:

A Nose for a Niedeman

Brenda Finnegan:

Tyger, Tyger

Romantic Fiction:

White House Rhapsody, Book One and Two

Fantasy and Science Fiction:

A Ring for a Second Chance

But World Enough and Time

Time Enough

And I would be honored if you left a review for this and any of my books on the below sites. It really helps.

BB bookbub.com/profile/anne-louise-bannon

g goodreads.com/author/show/513383.Anne_Louise _Bannon

f facebook.com/RobinGoodfellowEnt/

twitter.com/ALBannon

amazon.com/stores/author/B00JCRXST2?ingress
=0&visitId=bfadb491-d1ac-4575-84da-bb4f7d325a
d9&store_ref=ap_rdr&ref_=ap_rdr

Connect with Anne Louise Bannon

Thank you for sticking it out this long! Please join my newsletter. It's the best way to stay up-to-date on my upcoming projects, blog posts and even the occasional game and giveaway.

You can sign up for the Robin Goodfellow Newsletter here: http://eepurl.com/zH0Ab or by visiting my website, annelouisebannon.com

And don't forget to connect with me on your favorite social media platforms:

BB bookbub.com/profile/anne-louise-bannon

g goodreads.com/author/show/513383.Anne_Louise _Bannon

f facebook.com/RobinGoodfellowEnt/

a amazon.com/stores/author/B00JCRXST2?ingress =0&visitId=bfadb491-d1ac-4575-84da-bb4f7d325a d9&store_ref=ap_rdr&ref_=ap_rdr

P pinterest.com/AnneLouiseBannon

O instagram.com/annelouisebannon4/

About Anne Louise Bannon

Anne Louise Bannon is an author and journalist who wrote her first novel at age 15. Her journalistic work has appeared in Ladies' Home Journal, the Los Angeles Times, Wines and Vines, and in newspapers across the country. She was a TV critic for over 10 years, founded the YourFamilyViewer blog, and created the OddBallGrape.com wine education blog with her husband, Michael Holland. She is the co-author of Howdunit: Book of Poisons, with Serita Stevens, as well as author of the Freddie and Kathy mystery series, set in the 1920s, the Old Los Angeles series, set in 1870, and the Operation Quickline series, plus several stand alones. She and her husband live in Southern California with an assortment of critters.

Milton Keynes UK
Ingram Content Group UK Ltd.
UKHW050631150424
441175UK00013B/409